ISBN-13: 9798530752773

Cover design by: SHANI CLARKE

To Heidi
my wonderful
daughter-in-law, special
friend. Pearl Clarke

D1601376

PROLOGUE - 1700'S

The Campbell Castle sat on a small hill overlooking a green valley. Thick forests and rolling moors were springtime fresh. The harsh Scottish Highland winter was behind them, and mother earth was renewing herself in all of her green glory.

The doting parents watched as their four young children played in the Keeps garden. Only here, behind the Castle stone walls, could the couple steal a few minutes of private family time.

The man smiled at his youthful wife. The last few years had been good ones. Three years ago, she had bore him twin sons, Patrick and Peter, looking much like a young himself with their dark hair and eyes. And then the following year, she had given him twin girls with the green-eyes of their mother and the fiery hair of the Ramsey clan. Now the five of them were his heart. He was fast approaching forty while his love had not seen twenty and three. He had told himself that he had married her to protect her, but in truth he had loved her since the moment he saw her.

People feared what they did not understand. Second Sight was her Gift from the Creator; passed down by sacred blood through long-dead ancestors of ancients Druids and Celtic Senae priestesses. As a Seer, she was fated to know an elemental wisdom and an alternate reality that was beyond her control, or her desire to have. His destiny as Lord of the powerful Campbell clan was to lead with wisdom, and to protect all those under his banner, especially the woman who was his soul mate.

He had met her when she had saved many clan lives by Knowing of a plot to poison powerful leaders whose named historical deeds had already been written in The Book of Time. When he had asked her brother how she knew what was to come, her brother had touched the hilt of his sword, but answered, "She's fey."

A hush had fallen over the Castle hall. There was complete silence.

"Ah, Druid and Celt. A Seer." He had exclaimed softly. "A Khadil. My people say my great-great-grandmother was a Seer." For several long moments he had gazed into the depths of the girl's grass-green eyes before returning to the other Lords.

Minutes had passed as the seven leaders spoke in whispers to each other. Finally, he, as Lord Campbell, turned and stood in front of the silent girl. He had lifted his sword with his right hand upward to the heavens. Five leaders followed suit surrounding the lass until she was canopied under a circle of six swords. At a nod from him as the leader, her brother's sword had added the seventh prone in the touching swords.

"I am The Campbell," he had declared. "I invoke the ancient rite of Drvanetism, of those going before and those coming after. I owe my life and those of my clan to the lass beneath the circle of swords." He had shuddered as a spear of white light hit his body and danced upward to the tip of his sword to join the other touching swords.

"I am The McCordy," Lord McCordy had chanted. "I invoke the ancient rite of Drvanetism, of those going before and those coming after. I owe my life and those of my clan to the lass beneath the circle of swords." The white light had lit the tip of his sword that joined his own. Each ensuring Lord repeated the chant, and each time the white light had lit the end of their sword. Then all seven of the swords were bathed in the mystical white light to make a ring of shimmering fire.

Upon completion, he as leader, had raised his left hand clasped in a tight fist to the sky keeping his right sword hand raised with the others and proclaimed, "Hundreds of people's lives have been saved by this wee lass and our history remains. We invoke the spirits of the generations past, and the spirits of the generations to follow, for all time to come. Let the lass and her descendants be protected forevermore. Let the Gift of Second Sight and all other Gifts bestowed upon her progeny remain a Gift of her blood eternally. This we do as a rite of the old Magy and as part of our connected souls."

"We swear," each Laird had voiced as he raised his left hand in a fist. With his right hand, his sword firmly touched the other gleaming sword tips.

Each clan Lord had moved back to his men and knelt on one knee, his gleaming sword tip placed across his chest to cover his heart. Each soldier in the room had quickly dropped to one knee and followed suit. Servants and others in the hall had done the same, until all knelt before the slim girl.

As The Campbell, his voice had rung with power throughout the rooms. "In secrecy we swear to protect you and yours forevermore. All clans that can hear my voice will be subject to this Holy Oath. We will always be your Sword and your Shield, we swear with honor." Each lord followed suit, then each soldier, and then each person in the hall until all within had sworn their fealty to the young maiden.

"Let death be the judgment of any man or woman who speaks of this event of today. Today will forever be shrouded in secrecy as our own beginnings are shrouded." The lit swords dimmed, and the light disappeared.

CHAPTER ONE

"Doctor Ramsey, there's an emergency call for you." A young Haitian worker in a scrub suit explained, driving up in a beat-up old pickup. "Your phone is not working," he said hurriedly. "The clinic called and called."

"A call, Antonio? Did they say from whom?" asked the young doctor, sharing a worried look with her assistant, Kelly Pierce.

Kelly felt around in his backpack for his own phone. "The Council has my number and knows that I'm with you. If the call is from them, why didn't they call me?" Coming up empty handed he complained angrily, "Either I've misplaced it or someone's stolen it. The phones are sealed and encrypted so thieves can't even use it. Damn it to hell."

"They didn't say who was calling you, but its from the States," the young worker answered, glancing wryly at the doctor's huge male assistant. "You'll have to return the call from the main building. I'll take you back. They said it was an emergency."

"I'll be back as soon as I can Kelly, but maybe you'd better finish up here just in case. I'll send word to you from the clinic office as soon as I know something ..." her voice trailed off. Kelly gave a quick nod as Brenna climbed into the passenger side of the old truck.

There was little point in trying to guess what the phone call was about, so she spent the time looking out at the tents of refugees. This was her fifth mission volunteering for the medical assignment for Haiti, and she had a special love for the country and its people.

On Brenna's first assignment to the country, an old brick building had been one of the only things standing after a devastating hurricane. The International Aid Organization had taken over its use temporarily. Four years later they were still using the building. Building progress in Haiti was on a path from slow, to stall, to no-money-so-forget-about-it.

"Thanks for the ride, Antonio," Brenna told the young driver, giving him a bright smile as her mind refocused on her upcoming telephone call. No one from home called her unless it was an emergency no one else could handle. Those incidents were very few. "There's a call for me?" Brenna asked of the clerk sitting at the front desk. "Antonio said it was from the States."

"They left a number," replied the clerk holding up a sticky note. "I'm sorry Dr. Ramsey, but we couldn't reach you or Mr. Pierce."

"Not your fault. Somehow our phones are gone. Thanks a lot," Brenna said as she took the note.

"Use the front office, Doctor. You'll have a little privacy."

Brenna smiled her thanks as she followed the suggestion. The only furniture in the little front office was a beat up wooden desk, three metal folding chairs, and a black old fashioned dial phone. She dialed the number the aid clerk had given her, recognizing her sister Raina's number.

"Hello Raina? What's wrong?"

"It's Catherine," replied the other voice briskly. "She has vaginal bleeding, mostly spotting, a little backache, and some cramping. I think someone needs to check her but you know she can't leave the valley for any length of time. She's 32 weeks pregnant now. I think you should come home," Raina replied.

"Yes. You're right, of course. As fast as possible," Brenna replied chewing on her lower lip as she thought about her much loved sister, Catherine, and her late term pregnancy.

"I knew you would say that so Liam left here some time ago to pick you and Kelly up. He's in the baby Lear so he should be at Port Au Prince soon."

"Where is Dr. Richardson? Let me talk to him," Brenna demanded. "Why in the ...?"

"That's the problem, he isn't here," Raina interrupted. "He fell and broke his hip hiking the day after he arrived. Sean took

5

him to Fortuna to the hospital, but there is some kind of complication with the titanium screw and an infection. He won't be released for a couple of more weeks. Catherine wouldn't let us tell you. She said you'd be home soon anyway. And that she was feeling fine."

"Damnit. I'm going to have her head when I get there," Brenna fumed. "I did tell her to rest more. She keeps forgetting she's not invincible. And neither is that baby."

"You're going to need to stand in line. We're angry with Catherine, but also with ourselves for not seeing that she needed to slow down and rest more. Trent's worried and as we all are. All of Shadow Valley is in an uproar. Probably in a lot of other places too."

"Her husband has a right to be upset and so does everyone else. Catherine thinks she's indestructible." Brenna blew out a deep breath of air. "I'll send for Kelly to meet us at the airport. In the meantime, tell Catherine to rest and do absolutely nothing. Nothing."

Quickly reviewing alternatives in her head she added firmly, "Raina, there's a contour chair in the infirmary clinic. Put that in Catherine's and Trent's room. Set the controls at plus three, that will make her knees up. Put a small pillow or rolled towel on the back of her neck, that will give an additional tilt to her chin and make breathing easier just in case there's a problem. It will also help with her backache. Have Trent carry her to the chair. No walking."

"Done. I'm putting you on the foltron phone now so everyone in the house can listen. Anything else?"

"Let me talk to Catherine and keep the foltron phone on. Everyone in the Stone House needs to hear."

"This is Catherine. You can say I was an idiot when you get here. And I know I was. Please tell me what to do. We don't want to lose this baby."

"Absolute bed rest. And I mean absolute bed rest. Thankfully you're not the panicky kind. Spotting is not unusual during the early months of pregnancy, or in the latter part. I'll be there within hours to check how serious this is."

"Do you need to examine me with the skype electronic connections right now? I have a new screen that can give an almost perfect image with our satellite. I'll do whatever you say even if I hate the idea."

Closing her eyes, Brenna quickly reviewed in her mind's eye the last time she had run her hands over her sister's pregnant belly. She unconsciously moved her hands as if she was moving them over Catherine's stomach. She let her mind focus on the feelings that had flowed from her hands to her brain the last time she had examined Catherine. The uterus had been well within the limits of normal for a third-trimester pregnancy. The baby had been curled in a fetus position with a regular heartbeat and sleeping peacefully. No trauma and no abnormalities she could feel with her hands or mind.

"Are you in pain? Any Braxton Hicks contractions? Doing everything I said when I saw you three weeks ago?"

"What's a Braxton Hicks contraction?" interrupted Trent, Catherine's husband.

"Braxton Hicks is a painless uterine contraction that are not labor pains. Sometimes they're mistaken for the beginning of labor, but they're really false labor and don't progress," answered Brenna.

"No pain, a slight backache but I'm not having any real contractions. And yes, I've done everything you said. We want this baby," Catherine said with some fervor. "I'm so sorry. I should have rested more. And told you about Dr. Richardson."

"Brenna, Trent here again. Could she handle being moved to Fortuna or anywhere else? Sean's got the little helicopter on the pad here at the Stone House. I know she wants to have the baby at home in Shadow Valley, but the valley is so damned isolated if anything goes wrong...," he choked, leaving the rest of the sentence dangling.

"No. She can not be moved," she stated firmly. "She wouldn't be able to handle the stimuli anywhere else and would have to be moved again, which would only worsen the problem.

As you know, she becomes physically ill when she's bombarded with other people's stress and outside mental stimuli."

Brenna paused for a moment, and then said, "What you can do, Trent, is massage her feet with the lotion in the dark lavender bottle on my dresser in my bedroom. Mrs. Searle knows exactly where it is. Reflexology. It will help her relax. Don't panic when the lotion makes your hands warm. Also, above all else she must rest with no upsets. Absolute rest." Brenna emphasized again. Giving Trent something to keep him busy might alleviate some of Catherine's tension.

"Does that mean no one can say I can't have pineapple ice cream with chocolate and caramel sauce for lunch?" teased Catherine.

Knowing that Catherine was trying to relieve the anxiety of other listeners to the conversation, Brenna answered, "Sure. If it makes you happy and calm. Whatever. Pregnancy cravings are just plain weird. It's called Pica for some unknown reason. Personally it makes me shudder to visualize you putting that concoction in your mouth though. And Catherine, absolute bed rest. I do mean it. I'm already really irritated, so you better do as I say."

"She absolutely will," replied Trent in a firm voice. "I'll ensure that she doesn't move a muscle until you get here."

Brenna hung up the phone and stood in silent contemplation for a moment before she went in search of her boss at International Aid to tell him that she and Kelly had to leave immediately. Mr. Copeland was not happy but knew that family crises did occasionally occur. He asked that Kelly stay in Haiti but Brenna shook her head with a smile, knowing without asking Kelly that he would refuse.

Kelly Pierce was her unofficial, unpaid medical assistant and went where she did. There had been a kidnapping scare last year and Kelly had appointed himself as her bodyguard with the Sgnoch Council's approval. Whether it was to assist in Indonesia, Haiti, or inner-city Chicago, Kelly worked beside her. When she had objected, he had looked at her steadily with serious dark eyes as he said slowly, "That's my job. This lifetime. For now."

Brenna sent an aide to tell Kelly about Catherine's condition and the need to leave immediately. Thankfully he relayed the message back that he had already prepared for such a possibility, and would meet her at the airport. At the terminal, she hurried through the door to the back exit where Ian would have parked the little jet. Spying him, she also saw someone she disliked.

"Why are you here?" asked Brenna knowing that her tone was aggressive. Deke Paxton was the only man who annoyed the hell out of her just by walking the same earth she did.

Deke blinked but remained in his slouched position leaning against the stairway to the little Lear. Liam McKinney stood next to him, looking back and forth between Brenna and Deke.

"I take it you two know each other," Liam said cautiously, stepping forward to give Brenna a quick hug. Besides being distant cousins, they had both grown up in Shadow Valley and were close friends.

"Actually we don't know each other," Brenna retorted murmuring "thank goodness" just loud enough for both men to hear. "We only met during Catherine and Trent's wedding."

"Oh, but what good times we had," teased Deke, seeming to poke fun at her ill humor. "Best man and maid of honor duties. And you were so nice to me at Trent's the wedding," he taunted, giving back as good as he had been given.

"Someone's memory is warped," smiled Brenna insincerely. She knew that she had either coldly ignored him, or treated him as if he was a fifteen-year-old adolescent with no brains cells and an addiction to adrenaline. She only admitted to herself that he also made her skin itch. And bathed her female body parts in warmth. An awareness she would conceal at any cost.

"Where's Kelly? We need to take off as soon as possible." interrupted Liam.

"We got the message only minutes ago. Our phones were gone so someone had to first find us, and then I had to call Raina. Kelly is on his way. He'll meet us here to save time." Turning to

Deke, Brenna asked cautiously, "Is there something else wrong with Catherine? Did Trent send you?"

"No and no." Deke started to reach out to assure her, but she took a step backward. Running an agitated hand through his short dark hair he explained, "Trent called Bob at the office to inform him of the problem with Catherine's pregnancy. Bob then called me; I was in Miami on my way to Columbia. I had to refuel my little plane so I thought I would stop and check to see if there is any way I could help."

"Thanks for the thought," Liam said warmly. "I enjoyed our little jaunt to Ireland last year, and we all do appreciate your help." He stared pointedly at Brenna. "Watching you take down Gavin O'Neill was an awesome experience."

O'Neill had meant to kidnap either Catherine or Maggie; Catherine to forcibly mate or Maggie as a hostage. After seizing him, Deke, Liam and Trent Angelenos had delivered the psychotic O'Neill to his brother in Dublin, Ireland. The responsibly of deciding how to control the mentally ill O'Neill had then fallen to his family.

"Glad you don't need me," answered Deke shrugging off the praise with an uncomfortable lift to his shoulders.

"What takes you to Columbia?" asked Liam idly, his eyes on the terminal exit door.

Brenna stood silent, a combination of feeling unbalanced whenever she had any contact with Deke Paxton, and the unknown of the crisis at home with Catherine. Deke she ignored, Catherine made her heart hurt.

"An old friend needed to send some money to his parents and he was unable for a variety of reasons to go himself. I wasn't doing anything so I offered to take it to them. I was down there last year. He's a really good kid that taught me to speak Spanish years ago, so I'm doing some payback. My parents worked as kitchen helpers in Vegas sometimes, and he needed to learn English quickly to keep his job. We became friends." He shrugged carelessly.

"And you love to fly," Liam laughed understandingly, giving his full attention to another fly-lover.

"Hey, there is nothing better than that special feeling that flying in a small plane gives. Like solo soaring with nothing between you and heaven, as if you had wings."

"That's a nice poetic way to put it," agreed Liam lightly.

Deke's face reddened slightly as if he hadn't meant to put the special feeling into words, at least none that Brenna could hear. "Since you don't need me, I better get my act together and get going." Deke stuck out his hand and shook Liam's, then gave a quick nod to Brenna before striding off toward an older model Cessna 206 plane parked on the outer runway.

"What the hell was that all about, Brenna? I've never known you to be so rude and insolent to someone that was only trying to help?" Liam's arms were placed on his hips as he frowned at her.

She certainly was not going to tell Liam that Deke Paxton made her feel bothered and edgy. Instead she simply told Liam, "I think he's an idiot. I simply do not like him," defended Brenna. "He is too cocky, too sure that he's right. He irritates me. He oozes testosterone. He's too … too," she said helplessly. "He goes into countries and does all this high risk behavior. He's an adrenaline junky, going into places that will likely get him killed and he doesn't seem to care if something happens."

"But…," Liam tried to interrupt.

"I don't feel that anyone has the right to kill themselves and I believe that's what he is doing," she insisted. "He takes risks that are insane and infuriating."

"Or maybe he's just trying to help in the best way he can," said Kelly in a quiet voice behind her. "Was that Deke Paxton? I know that the nuns he rescued from the rebels in Africa will always be grateful. Adrenaline or not, their lives were saved. It's rumored that he's helped a lot of people in South America and Africa."

"You didn't meet him at the wedding?" asked Liam. "He was Trent's best man."

"Nope. I sat with a bunch of cousins from Scotland. A cousin's widow needed to talk to me." He didn't explain further as he boarded the small Lear.

CHAPTER TWO

Liam McKinney had come alone to the Port-Au-Prince airport in what was affectionately known as the baby Lear, a scaled-down, modified version of the Lear Jet. Liam and his twin, Sean, were aeronautical engineers and made Shadow Valley their primary residence. They did most of piloting for the people living in the valley, not by demand but for the sheer love of flying. They also used their flying trips to check out whatever piece of equipment they were redesigning and modifying.

Brenna was grateful. She and Kelly were both licensed pilots, but neither had the skill or knowledge of either Liam or Sean, especially on long distance flights. And landing at the mountainous Sanhicks Airport took some flight experience and skill.

She leaned back in the butter-soft leather recliner seat smiling slightly as she recalled the McKinney twin's penchant for making over aircraft, or anything else that took their interest. Clan law did not allow them to invent, but they modified everything they touched, all with the approval of Catherine, of course. This little jet had been upgraded to comfortably fit ten adults in a living room-type setting. Liam and Sean thought comfort for their loved ones was essential.

Brenna's mind kept going round and round struggling to review all she knew from her phone conversation about Catherine's possible spontaneous miscarriage in late pregnancy. A couple of times she wanted to call Catherine and ask questions. Since there was really nothing she could accomplish at the moment from the fast-flying plane it wasn't worth upsetting Catherine, or anyone else.

Nevertheless, her mind kept asking unanswerable questions. Anything that I can do from here that I haven't considered yet? Did I miss something vital when I examined her last month? She reviewed the potential problems that might be related to bleeding during late pregnancy. What was going wrong? And infection? Abrupto Placentae? Placentia Previa? Stress related?

Had Catherine developed hypertension or gestational diabetes during the last three weeks? Some abnormal problem with the fetus that she had missed? Or the normal everyday pregnancy risks of simply being on her feet too long and the body demanding rest?

"Hey," Kelly said softly as he sat down beside her, "stop beating yourself up. It's not your fault that the good doctor broke his hip while hiking, or that Catherine chose to forbid anyone from calling you. You did everything you could to prepare for this trip, even arranging for Dr. Richardson to come over from Scotland. And you know the time element when we had to be in Haiti was carved in stone. You gave your word to take that medical shift."

Brenna smiled through damp lashes. "But…," she sniffled.

"Brenna, contrary to popular opinion, you three ladies cannot control everything that happens in the valley or in the rest of the world," Kelly interrupted, referring to the three sisters, Catherine, Brenna, and Raina Ramsey.

"Catherine has the gift of Second Sight, but that does not give her any knowledge of what is going to happen in Shadow Valley. You know that her abilities are more in the line of Knowing global economies and mechanical inventions. She can't see much of human happenings, and never when she's emotionally involved."

Kelly's voice was calm and soothing. "And Raina, our young general, is there to organize and make sure that whatever needs done is done. And you know you can trust her abilities."

"I know. I know. But this is my older sister! And this is her first child. And you and I both know how important this child could be to everyone. And how loved."

"True, and we will do as we must when we get there. But not from here. Now, how many candy suckers did you promise Pierre? He said that 'the lady with the fire in her hair' wanted him to have one of each color."

Brenna chuckled softly, allowing herself to be distracted, "That rascal. You know I said one candy, and he could choose the color. Not one of each." She shook her head, "Pierre and his family are a wonder. Haiti is such a poor country but the people are warm, friendly and sociable. I could really do without all the rain and mud though," she added in afterthought.

"Again true. Its unfortunate that's there are so few natural resources down there. And that the country sits in the middle of all the hurricanes and rains. I've never seen the way it rains there. Like the rain-gods are throwing buckets of water at each other."

"I always wish and wish," she sighed, knowing that Kelly would understand that limitations placed on a person often could not be changed. And wishes were sometimes the only hope available.

Kelly was silent, gazing at Brenna with dark fathomless eyes.

Brenna in turn watched her closest male friend. Kelly Pierce was older than her by twenty-two years and was one of the stable forces in her life. In the past, he had often acted as her medical assistant whenever their paths crossed in Shadow Valley. He was usually around when she was home in the valley.

In the last year he had become her right arm, and sometimes her left. He was a dark-complexioned, Native American looking man of large proportion and in excellent physical shape. A quietly observant man at forty-nine, he stood just shy of six foot three. With black eyes and black hair pulled back and tied with a leather string, he looked like a long-ago Native American warrior.

And warrior he was. An ex-army soldier, and then a medic for a special forces team, he seemed to understand that sometimes men chose violence over negotiations. And only understood a like return. In his company, Brenna knew she was always safe.

Kelly's dark good looks and maturity had attracted many

single women in the last year when he had accompanied her on medical missions. If he did have any romantic liaisons, he had been exceedingly discreet. And silent about his activities.

"Kelly, why haven't you married?' Brenna asked, partly out of curiosity and partly to keep her wayward thoughts from dwelling on Catherine's possible late-term miscarriage. "You've certainly had the opportunity. I thought that cute Irish nurse, Coleen Ryan, was going to put you in her traveling bag," Brenna kidded.

"Who?" asked Kelly wrinkling his brow. "Ach, lassie. I donna' ken any lassie that would share me bed," he replied, mimicking the thick Scottish brogue of Shadow Valley's cantankerous handyman, Fergus. "And the lovely lassie donna' ken ye old man."

"She certainly was willing to become better acquainted," grinned Brenna. "And become a whole lot closer."

"Ach, but what would this old Native do in Ireland? Fittin' in would be a problem."

"Come on Kelly, you're so skilled you could do anything you wanted to do," Liam said joining in the teasing of the big man from the open door of the cockpit.

"Hey, why aren't you married?" Kelly asked, retaliating and putting the question to Liam. "You're young and handsome."

A telling blush stained the large redhead's cheeks. With his hair and sprinkle of freckles, the flush gave his face a reddish glow. "Well, ah, ah," he began stammering.

Brianna widened her eyes and raised one eyebrow in query. The stuttering was completely out of character for the irrepressible Liam. He could always be counted on for a quick retort said in a playful joking manner.

"All right, tell us who she is or we'll tell Raina that you're smitten with someone," Brenna taunted catching on quickly. It was more fun to harass Liam than trying to get information out of the taciturn Kelly anyway.

"Brenna, you wouldn't! Seriously, please don't. Raina would make my life miserable. I'd never ever hear the last of it. I'd be a hundred-eleventeen years old before she let up trying to find every single detail about my life. She thinks Sean and I have been placed on this earth for her to pester and boss around." Taking a deep breath, Liam asked, "Do you promise not to tell? Not anyone, at least not for awhile? Especially not Raina? We've only gone out a few times and I don't want to mess things up. She may be really special for me."

At both of their affirmative nods, he admitted, "Beth Gowan. Glenn Gowan's oldest daughter. She graduated George Washington University last year and has been working in the supply depot of their store in Fortuna."

"Is that the cute tiny blond or the redhead?" asked Brenna, thinking back to her most recent trip to the supply depot.

"Beth is blond and really pretty besides being nice," gushed Liam. "She's also smart and is working for her father until she finds out about the Masters program she's applied for. She may have to move to Idaho later, so we're taking our relationship slow for now. But I really like her."

"No wonder you've volunteered to pick up all the supplies out of Fortuna," Kelly grinned, referring to a large town where most of the household goods needed for the maintenance of the Shadow Valley were transported from.

"We won't tell anyone. We promise. Cross my heart and hope to die," she recited the age-old children's vow. "Does Sean know?" asked Brenna, referring to Liam's twin brother.

"Yep. And Beth can tell us apart," Liam beamed.

Brenna smiled at the revealing statement. Liam and Sean were identical twins and most of the people could not differentiate between the two men. Having a carbon copy of one's self was a double-edged sword. Liam and Sean had often switched identities as they shared jobs, tests, even dates. But they were two men with different needs and personalities. Individual beings with separate personal characteristics, but identical faces and bodies. It said much that the young lady knew whom she was dating.

Brenna was delighted that Liam had found someone that

could be a possible mate for him. Shadow Valley was isolated and off limits to all except members of their unique Native American-Scottish tribal clan. Add that to being different with rare abilities made finding a love interest extremely difficult.

Her thoughts flashed to Deke Paxton. She might think he was an idiot, but he was certainly an attractive one. Six feet four or so, craggy face, and the long-limbed body of a runner. And man. All male. Testosterone driven.

She shook off her wayward feelings. "Next lifetime," she thought, biting her lower lip in concentration. Envy was not for her, although she couldn't hold back a flash of regret as she listened to Liam's continuing effusive comments about his new girlfriend.

She closed her eyes to focus her thoughts back to Catherine and gave an involuntary shiver in spite of the warmth of the plane. The depth of feelings she had for her two sisters was un-equaled by anything else in her life. Even her work. Growing up with absent parents had created a strong bond between the sisters.

Catherine was the oldest by a year and Brenna's BFF, best friend forever, as her younger sister Raina would say. Catherine was eternally patient, slow to anger and slower to erupt. She could also be an exacting, no nonsense leader when necessary.

Brenna knew that the serene, calm qualities Catherine pos-sessed had completely skipped her, except when she was work-ing. She knew she was impatient and a perfectionist especially when it came to her work, but sloppy medicine annoyed the hell out of her. "Make it right the first time" had been the mantra of medical school professors. Medicine was the only area of her life where she controlled her deepest emotions and her formidable temper. Sick people didn't deserve a cranky doctor even when their own behavior was irritating.

Knowing that healing was her Destiny and written before she was born helped her to focus on what was important. A med-ical school background had given her more acceptance and al-lowed her to benefit the most people. The combination of healer and physician was who she was.

Now Brenna considered how much Catherine's duties could be modified to achieve complete bed rest during late term pregnancy if that was necessary. Undoubtedly, Raina could take over much of Catherine's duties on the Sgnoch Council as Catherine was Raina's mentor. In adulthood, Raina might be able to share some of Catherine's immense responsibilities.

A strikingly beautiful seventeen-year-old, Raina was the self-confident organizer of the three sisters. It was a truth-telling joke that she could run a third world country with little effort. The entire clan called her affectionately 'the little general" for her executive skills, her eerie ability to feel truth-telling, and her bossiness.

Brenna's own mentors had been her grandmother, Maeve Ramsey, and Grandfather Youngblood, even though neither had her Gift. They had taught her discipline, control, and about the unchangeable Destiny that was hers. Both were now deceased. Her heart and spirit ached every day with need of them. There was no one she had ever known who had her same gifts.

Except ancestors long ago dead. And thank the Creator for them, she declared silently.

"Coming up on your left. Sanhicks Airport," announced Liam in a light sing-song voice from the cockpit mimicking an airline pilot. "The scenic side of Sky Mountain and Shadow Valley, set deep in the Ozark Mountains of Arkansas".

From the sky it looked like the entire mountain range was an impenetrable green mass of trees, shrubs and bushes. Tall peaks shielded much of the green valley from view, and from weather. Shadow Valley nestled in the warmer wind currents of the banana belt at the base of the range.

From the air the valley looked like a tipped shallow bowl with tall canopied trees and green hued forests climbing to shaggy, rocky peaks. Most of the late winter snow had melted leaving snatches of white against the green forest floor. Unseen roads remained clear all year round thanks to the new chemical technology built into the brown or green-colored road base which helped liquefy the snowfall.

Sanhicks Airport was the technological wonder and brain-child of Jonathan Hicks, an eccentric ancestor, who was born and died in Brenna's great-grandmother's generation. He had served in the Second World War as a pilot of a B-17, the Flying Fortresses, and loved flying. He had carved out a dirt runway in the sloping meadow of Shadow Valley beneath Sky Mountain to make a landing strip for his small private airplane after he returned home. Gradually, he had added other planes, better facilities, and taught other people how to fly.

Having the availability of air travel made Shadow Valley more assessable to needed services and easier to live within the remote, isolated valley. It had also allowed the valley and its air strip to be more visible from the sky, and possible detection from other aircraft as air travel became more accessible for everyone everywhere.

Grandmother Ramsey, with her wide range of technological resources, had solved the problem temporally by cutting deeper into the side of the mountain. Some Scottish engineers had used Mother Nature's trees and forests for camouflage. Catherine, with her penchant for electronic gadgetry added her unique share.

Then the McKinney twins' mathematical genius for modifying machinery, along with some help from their far-flung engineering friends, solved the problem.

"It's always a thrill to watch," Brenna commented to Liam, raising her voice to be heard in the cockpit. "I know I'm home when technology picks up our DNA in the plane. I'm always amazed when it happens."

"Yeah," Liam agreed with a wide quirky grin. "I never get tired of it no matter how many times I see it. Our friends did an excellent job of camouflage even if they did think we were designing mechanisms for a theme park for the Disney Corporation."

"You and Sean were a large part of that excellent job," commented Kelly.

What had minutes before been a rock-strewn meadow with gigantic oak, pine, and spruce trees began to move toward the edges of the meadow. The large man-made stones slid back alongside them like silent centurions readying for battle. Trees and rocks sat side by side with several bush-like trees of sassafras growing on the meadows edges. The multitude of varying shades of green trees were straight out of Disneyland. In fact, one of the landscape designers of Sanhicks had helped build some of the fantasy world.

The meadow was now transformed into hundreds of feet of green, grassy-looking asphalt of modern airport tarmac. Liam and Sean insisted the entire setup was nothing more than fancy conveyor belts using electronic sensors, communicational physics interfaced with computer vision tied to an electronic satellite system. Catherine understood the technological machinery which the twins loved, but few others did. Brenna didn't care as long as Shadow Valley was safe from discovery and remain unchanged.

From the air it was impossible to differentiate the hundreds-old trees from their manufactured fakes. Guessing which trees were real and which were authentic imitations remained a favorite sport for the Shadow Mountain residents. Only on landing were green Quonset-type airplane hangers seen carved into the mountain and covered on three sides by Ozark dirt and bushes.

Set high in the Ozark Mountains of Arkansas, the area that been carefully chosen by a long-ago ancestor with Second Sight. With a land grant from the French King before the Louisiana Purchase, thousands of acres of mountain land was held under the tribal clan banner. Shadow Valley was a smaller section of those thousands of acres, all electronically fenced and visually controlled by satellite.

Here the diversity of the Native American tribes had mixed with the Scottish clans to form a unique tribal clan, each honing the best of what their clans had been. Here the tribal clan with its philanthropic goals could live in peace and fulfill their

Destiny. After two hundred fifty years, the valley still remained isolated, private and protected. A fortress home of the Ramsey tribal clan and its associates.

CHAPTER THREE

"Now, let's see what is," announced Brenna striding into Catherine's and Trent's room, keeping her eyes on her sister as she gave her a quick hug.

Catherine was a petite woman with long black curly hair and dark eyes set in a heart-shaped face. Her stomach was a large mound protruding in front of her, visibly portraying that she was in her last stage of pregnancy. She held one hand protectively over her rounded belly as if to hold it up.

Her other hand was clasped tightly by her husband, Trent Angelenos. He and Catherine had met in New York the year before and he had fallen instantly in love with the tiny gypsy-looking clan leader. Thank goodness he was on one of his increasingly lengthy visits to the valley at the moment.

Catherine had initially been attracted to the businessman, but he had captured her heart with his pursuit and willingness to adjust their lifestyles. Both had career responsibilities they loved but lived in different parts of the country. Catherine was unable to travel to areas of the country with a great deal of stimuli, as the bombardment of so many other people's emotions literally made her deathly ill. After a turbulent courtship, they had compromised with Trent living part time in New York, and part-time in Shadow Valley. The arrangement allowed them both to continue with their duties and responsibilities, and still have a married life. It seemed to work for them.

Catherine and Trent's large bedroom was filled with people. Besides Catherine and Trent, there were her sister Raina, a cousin Kamon, Mrs. Searles the housekeeper, and several other staff members. Kelly Pierce stood silently by the door, waiting to see if Brenna would need his assistance.

Several people started to talk at once, but Brenna quieted them by putting her finger firmly over to her lips. "I need to speak with Catherine first." Brenna leaned down to ask in a whisper, "Have you had anymore spotting in the last several hours?"

Catherine gazed back with a blank look, and then blinked as if confused.

Sighing, Brenna grinned. Catherine was wonderful in most areas, especially at keeping her clan responsibilities running smoothly. Unfortunately thinking about herself in any situation was not her strong suit.

"Okay, I need to see Catherine in private." When Trent started to object, Brenna added, "Just for a few minutes, Trent, and then you can come back."

Smiling at the rest of the group she teased, "Hi. Remember me? Brenna Ramsey? Yes, it's good to be home. Thank you all for asking," she grinned. "Now scat, all of you. Catherine needs some privacy." The entire group scattered, mumbling hello, sorry, and giving worried sighs.

Turning toward the door, she added, "Thanks Kelly, I think we're okay but would you mind staying around the house for awhile just in case?" Kelly gave a quick nod, and left.

Trent and her younger sister, Raina, left with more obvious reluctance. Each of them moved slowly to the door, then had to be reassured that Brenna would call them back into the room when she finished the exam.

"I'll be right outside the door, just in case you need me." Trent grumbled.

"And I'll keep him company," affirmed Raina immediately.

"Raina, instead of waiting in the hall, would you please have Kelly check to see if my large blue medical bag is downstairs. I may need it. I absolutely promise I'll call you as soon as I can," Brenna vowed, shutting the door firmly behind them.

Smiling at her older sister Brenna asked, "Okay little momma, have you had any headaches? Nausea or vomiting? Dizziness?"

At Catherine's continued negative shake of her head,

Brenna continued, "Can you pee?"

"Yes, often and then more often," answered Catherine, laughing slightly. "In fact, that's the thing I do best and most," she grinned.

"Your hands and feet are not overly swollen, your color is good," Brenna murmured as she continued to examine Catherine's body, lifting her skirt. "No undue pain or cramps?" she asked as she removed the soiled vaginal padding. "All this spotting is from several hours ago. I'm putting in new pads to check but the bleeding seems to have stopped voluntarily."

Taking out a state-of-the art portable ultrasound device from her personal medical satchel, she said, "Now let's see what the little one is doing." Placing the instrument on Catherine's swollen belly Brenna listened intently, moving the probe from one part of the stomach to another, checking first the baby and then the uterus and placenta.

"Your little one is doing great," she announced with a grin. "Heart beat is strong and within the normal limits. He or she is very active and vital."

Catherine burst into tears. "Thank you, thank you! I'm so sorry I asked you to come home for nothing," she blubbered, "but I wanted you to check me. I knew you would tell me the truth."

"You know it was not for nothing," Brenna chided. "I would have been upset if you had worried and not called me. And my job as your year-younger sister is to always tell you the truth. Part of that pact we made so many years ago."

"Now, I think you need your husband in here before he has a heart attack," she grinned.

Opening the door, she spotted Trent leaning against the wall just outside the room. "Everything is okay," Brenna assured him before he began to question her.

"Sweetheart, why the tears?" he asked in an anxious voice moving to Catherine's side. "What's wrong?" he demanded of Brenna as if somehow he could fix it.

"These are happy tears," Catherine laughed aloud. "Really

happy tears. The baby is fine and so am I."

"That's wonderful, darling. What happened, Brenna? What caused her to bleed? Everything seemed to be normal until this morning. Is there anything I need to know? Is there anything I can do? How can I help?"

"Of course you need more information," Brenna joked playfully, relieved to be able to tell him good news. It was a standing family joke that Trent was so detail-oriented that he 'worried a subject to death' as her Scottish grandmother would have said.

To lessen Trent's anxious frown, Brenna reviewed her earlier findings.

"Catherine has none of the warning symptoms of abnormalities. No headaches, no bleeding, no cramps, no contractions. There are no internal problems," Brenna closed her eyes to focus, keeping her hands on Catherine's stomach. "No placenta separation, no internal bleeding, no abnormalities of the uterus," she announced slowly. "Nothing abnormal but we will take no chances."

She continued, "There's no family history of congenital anomalies. No problems in the area of family genetics or chromosome abnormalities to worry about. There were no negative indications in the last full ultrasound Catherine and no indication that another is needed at the moment."

Moving her hand gently over Catherine's swollen stomach, she added, "The baby is in great shape, healthy, strong, and wondering what all the fuss was about."

"That's my little girl," Trent said proudly gently patting the side of Catherine's swollen stomach. "I know this baby is a she, not a he," he declared.

"You both chose not to be told what gender this baby is," Brenna reminded them. "Remember?"

"I know she's a she," stated Trent in a stubborn tone.

"Okay, daddy," laughed his wife. "As my doctor, what do I do now?"

"Nothing. Absolutely nothing. You are hereby confined to bed rest for the next three days then we'll reevaluate. Bed to recliner to chair with feet up. No work. No stress. Tell Raina what has to be done and let her do it. It'll be good practice for her since she's home from school for awhile."

"Please tell me it's okay to use my bathroom and not a bedpan?" begged Catherine grimacing. "I promise to follow all other orders but I absolutely hate peeing in a pan."

"Bedpan for the rest of this day. But tomorrow if there is no bleeding, it's okay to go to the bathroom, but I want someone to stay close by. Trent and I can share duties. Kelly and Raina too if they're needed."

"You all may come and go whenever you need, Brenna, but I'm staying put," declared Trent, running his hands through his thick dark hair. "Catherine is the most important thing in my life. What business I have to do I can do from that desk over there in the corner. Bob and Mrs. Grant can handle all other business things indefinitely. Period."

"Would you ask Raina to come back now?" Catherine asked. At Brenna's raised eyebrow, she added, "I want to instruct her in the things that need finishing immediately and those that can wait. Oh, and would you personally tell the members of the Sgnoch Council that I will be unavailable for any business for an indefinite time? They can visit me, can't they?"

"Sure, but I will inform them that for now you are out of the loop for business. No business meetings here in your room. Resting is more important. And I'll send Raina up *after* your nap," she laughed as her older sister yawned.

"I'll be right here," promised Trent, placing a kiss on the back of Catherine's hand. "Go to sleep, sweetheart. I'll be at the corner desk if you need me."

"I need to change and take a long hot shower," sighed Brenna, indicating her untidy braid and the mussed scrubs she had started the day with. "I must be getting old. Besides my family, hot water showers are the one thing I miss the most in other countries. Oh, and hot salsa is the other thing," she smiled.

Giving her sister a quick hug, Brenna left to give the happy news that Catherine was fine to the other clan members and to suggest that Raina wait for an hour or so before she visited Catherine.

Over the next several days, Brenna and Trent shared 'Catherine observation duties' but so many people dropped in to chat, that neither of them was really necessary. It seemed that the entire valley had to assure themselves that their leader was truly fine. And the best assurance was to see for themselves.

There was no more vaginal bleeding. Catherine apologized several times for asking Brenna to come home when it hadn't been necessary.

Finally, Brenna had told her sharply that for her own peace of mind it had been necessary. She also threatened that if she hid any other medical problems from her doctor-sister that her next babysitter would be the dour Scottish handyman, Fergus. Since Fergus had a reputation for a cantankerous personality and a dislike for most of mankind in general, Catherine had acquiesced.

After the three days were up and there were no further medical problems, Brenna declared that Catherine could resume some of her duties.

"Light duties. No Sgnoch Council meetings yet. You know that Raina is capable and that it's good training for her. I promise that if we need your input I will come and ask you."

Brenna held up her fingers in the Girl Scout sign, something the two of them had initiated for truth-telling as children. Neither had been Girl Scouts, there had been no opportunity living in the isolated areas where their childhoods were spent. They had seen the signing for the Girl Scouts on satellite television and had adopted it for their own use. As they had many other things growing up.

Being born a year apart had made them closer than most siblings and had bonded them together in a unique way. When they had been younger they had seldom been apart, sharing their childhood only with Diane and later with Kamon, their cousins, both born the same year as Catherine. The four of them had managed to have a play group, sharing thoughts, tutors, and peanut butter sandwiches.

A slight noise at the door brought Brenna back to the present. She smiled at the two small faces peeking around the door frame.

"Are you sick?" asked the young boy in a hushed voice, his dark, slant eyes staring solemnly at Catherine.

"I tol' you and tol' you she's not sick. She has a baby girl inside her tummy," declared the young girl, her blond curls dancing. Wide green eyes gazed intently at Catherine's distended stomach.

The twins were now almost five years old, and it was taking the entire Shadow Valley inhabitants to keep Maggie and Douglas out of trouble. Even the multitude of adults were hard pressed to keep the effervescent pair of orphans safe.

"Who's supposed to be watching you?" asked Brenna in resignation. As Brenna knew well from personal experience, all you had to do was blink and the young twins disappeared. They weren't deliberately mischievous but they attracted trouble like a magnet.

Maggie heaved a huge sigh. "Mrs. Searle said we could play in the side backyard cause it's fenced and we couldn't get out." She stopped and just looked at Brenna.

"Did you get out?" asked Trent laying down his pen and getting up from the desk where he was working.

"Nope. We played there for a long time, 'til we found the snake."

"Good grief. What kind of snake? It didn't bite you did it? Did you tell someone?" asked Brenna frowning.

"Nope, we didn't tell anyone," admitted Douglas. "We knew the snake was a green grass snake and wouldn't bite us if we didn't hurt it. Besides it was just a baby."

"What did you do with it?" asked Trent kneeling in front of Douglas, and casually brushing some of the soil off the front of Douglas's shirt.

Trent had developed a deep rapport with the young boy, acting as his father figure. The Sgnoch Council had declared that

Catherine and Trent were the orphan twin's official guardians.

"I wanted to keep it for a pet," Maggie answered, "but Doug said it needed to be free so we tied it up and came to ask you if we could keep it. Can we?" asked Maggie directing the question to Catherine.

Catherine frowned at Trent and Brenna who were both fighting grins. "No, I think Douglas is right. Snakes need to be left alone, even baby snakes."

"Okay," replied Maggie agreeably. "The baby snake was trying to get out of the rope anyway. Doug said the snake didn't like to be tied with a rope."

"You tied the baby snake up with a rope?" asked Trent, his eyes alight with laughter.

Brenna giggled.

"And it wasn't easy," admitted Maggie giving Brenna a glare. "We had to hold him really tight cause he kept moving and it was a thick rope. He's all slippery and his skin moves. Can I play with your baby girl when she gets out of your belly?"

"Of course," answered Catherine.

"The baby will be your cousin and you two will need to teach the baby all kinds of things," Brenna told the twins, deliberating avoiding any gender terms. Rapidly changing subjects was par for Maggie whose mind seemed to work on a different level than the norm.

"How do you know the baby inside the tummy is a girl?" asked Trent.

"I sawed her just before I woked up. I already tol' Doug about her. Huh, Doug?"

Douglas nodded his head, his straight black hair moving with the effort. "Yep, she did."

Maggie narrowed her eyes at Trent. "You believed I sawed her? 'Cause I told Bobby Anderson and he didn't believe me and told me I wasn't Superman. He made me really mad cause I don't lie." Cocking her head to one side, she asked Trent, "What's a cartoon character like Superman got's to do with it anyways?"

While Trent was explaining the intricacies of Superman's

x-ray vision to the twins, Catherine motioned Brenna to come closer.

"Brenna, Trent is going to drive me crazy! He hovers, asking me every fifteen minutes if I feel different. He follows me from room to room. I'm tethered," she declared. "If I'm in the bathroom longer than normal, he waits outside the door," she grumbled.

"It'll be better now that you can work a little," Brenna soothed, not sure if she believed that.

"Trent's right. There are not enough things right now for him to do here. His mind needs something to occupy it. Besides me," Catherine said pointedly. "I love him beyond reason but he's driving me crazy. Could you convince him that I'm really all right and he can safely leave for a few days?"

"I can try," Brenna said doubtfully, "but he seems set on staying at the moment."

"Then change the moment," Catherine snapped.

Catherine's irritated tone was completely out of character for the usually tranquil sister and made Brenna chuckle aloud.

"Brenna, Douglas and Maggie want me to go see their snake. You'll stay here until I get back?" he asked Brenna. At Brenna's nod, he followed the twins from the room.

"See," Catherine sighed. "I haven't drawn a single breath that was not shared in days. I'm not sure I won't be a babbling idiot in six weeks!"

"Maybe only four more, maybe even less. This baby appears to be almost ready to take its place in our world," Brenna said idly, running a gentle hand over Catherine's swollen stomach.

"Good. I'm ready," Catherine declared fervently. "In fact, I'm more than ready. I keep wondering if my feet are dirty since I can't see them."

"No, they're not."

"Well I can no longer see them so how do I know? I'm so short! Brenna I feel like I'm carrying around a very large soccer ball in front of me that moves continuously. And the soccer team is playing in the finals!"

"Remember back when we were seven or eight? You would hide all your broccoli and brussel sprouts under your bread. I told you then that you needed to eat them or you wouldn't be tall. Tol'ja," Brenna teased.

Catherine stuck her tongue out at Brenna. "You didn't eat them either and you're five inches taller than me."

"Six inches. I did eat the broccoli. Grandmother made me. Now, lean back and close your eyes while I use your bathroom to wash this goop from my hands. I smell like a perfume factory."

Brenna washed up in Catherine and Trent's newly renovated bathroom. They had arranged for a hot tub with multi-level massage spouts, music, and heat, then had it custom made to fit two people. Catherine had upgraded the wall-of-glass shower for walk-in convenience, revising the shower heads for a pulsating water and music experience.

Brenna took her time as she admired the new room with its decorations of purple and pale lavender. The effect was one of serene beauty and suited each of their unique personalities.

"No. No," moaned Catherine, her eyes tightly closed.

Brenna rushed to her sister's side, placing her hands on Catherine's stomach. Nothing. No contractions or signs of fetal distress. Both Catherine and the baby were fine. Catherine's moans were from something else.

Brenna could only watch as Catherine viewed something that only she could see with closed eyes. Whatever was happening in some far away place was causing Catherine a great deal of stress and that was unacceptable at this stage of her pregnancy. Stress was an enemy for the moment.

"Catherine, open your eyes. You have to tell me what you are seeing. You need to come out of it," Brenna urged.

When Catherine did not comply immediately, Brenna pulled out the big gun. "It is not good for the baby to be under this kind of tension. Open your eyes. Now!" she snapped.

Catherine immediately lifted her wet lashes. "Get Trent. Deke Paxton is hurt badly. He's in Colombia, South America and Brenna, it doesn't look like he can live. His injuries are massive."

"Catherine, take several deep breaths to bring a tranquil state to your body. Slowly. Good. Again. A deep breath. Slowly. Remember I said stress is unacceptable at this stage."

"You're sure about the baby?" Catherine questioned then answered her own question. "Of course you're sure. You wouldn't lie to me. Call Trent. I've got to tell him what's happening."

Brenna immediately pushed a button activating the house phone system. "Code three. Mrs. Searles, would you send Trent up to his room. No, nothing's wrong with Catherine or the baby. She needs to talk to him about something else, some new information."

The new voice activated system required a code that activated certain rooms so that some amount of privacy could be obtained in the large manor. Not much, but some.

Trent and Catherine were in the process of designing their own separate house with Kamon's help. Kamon had designed and built a cedar and glass house for himself that both Catherine and Trent loved.

Trent said he needed "to walk around in my underwear in my own house." Needless to say, everyone except the twin's dog, Rex, had comments and opinions. Most of them had been about getting on a waiting list to visit and view Trent's potential lack of clothing.

Privacy was not even remotely possible in the large Stone House where generations had built rooms onto the original manor to meet their particular needs.

The sprawling Stone House served as living quarters, offices, library, and communication centers for Catherine and the Sgnoch Council which directed tribal clan business activities. Often rooms were refitted for other people's particular need as the generations changed and technology progressed.

Trent came rushing in the door in spite of Mrs. Searle's positive directive. "What's wrong? Are you bleeding? Is it the baby?"

"Trent, honestly, if you don't calm down, I'm going to give

you a tranquilizer," Brenna sighed. "You know damn well that I would have summoned you back differently if something was wrong. Nothing is wrong with either of your little family. Catherine asked you to come as she has had a Sighting concerning Deke Paxton."

Catherine took over the story. "Deke is in the country of Colombia, South America between the cities of Palmira and Cali. He had stopped there to refuel his airplane."

Keeping her eyes closed, she continued in a calm voice, "A group of men from one of the drug cartels, the Cali Gentlemen as they are called in English, were expecting a rival cartel member. They thought it was Deke and that he had come into Cali to take out cocaine for distribution to Mexico for transportation to the United States. Simple mistaken identity. He was in the wrong place at the wrong time. He didn't have a chance. Four men beat him so badly that they dumped him in a ditch to die."

She paused a moment. "A young couple will find him tonight and take him to their shack. The couple is not altruistic - they think that if they can patch him up they can either ransom him, or that he will be monetarily grateful to them. If they can't and he dies, they've lost nothing. Either way they think they win."

Brenna asked, "So the beating has already taken place but the couple will find him tonight? Is that right?"

"Yes. I don't know why the Sighting's are immediate and then future, it may have to do with Deke's strong connection to Trent and thus to me. You know it rarely happens that way. I usually see only glimpses of future possibilities or happenings, and almost never do they involve any people."

"How badly is he hurt? Is he dying?" asked Trent blinking rapidly.

"He's extremely hurt. He's been left for dead." Turning to Trent with tears in her eyes Catherine said, "I don't know if he can live with his injuries even if you could get him out of the country. His injuries are extensive. Absolutely massive."

"Oh, I'll get him out," stated Trent. "He and Bob are my

brothers underneath the skin," he reminded them. "I need to figure out the best way of doing it."

"Brenna?" questioned Catherine. "Will you …?"

Brenna thought for a moment. Her duty - no, her life's work was healing those who needed her. If that included Deke Paxton in this unusual situation, then she would do it.

"Trent, if you can get him out of the country still alive, and if you can get the Sgnoch Council to agree, I will treat him here in the valley."

"You could go with them to a nearby city," Catherine started to say.

"No" exclaimed Brenna and Trent in unison.

"Absolutely not," said Brenna. "My first responsibility is to you, my sister. And to the unborn. I may need to be here. That's my first priority."

"Agreed," said Trent emphatically. "Catherine, you are my world, Deke is my chosen brother. Brenna is here for you. I trust her to take care of you and our little one. I want to go get Deke, or his body, out of Colombia."

Addressing Brenna, he asked solemnly, "Would you gather the Sgnoch Council together ASAP? Oh, and ask if Liam or Sean can be present, please." His eyes were sad as he said, "No matter what, I need to get him out of Columbia. He would do the same for either me or Bob. Blood brothers by choice."

Catherine looked at her sister as she wiped her own wet checks. "Light up the tree to the Council, Brenna." By 'lighting up the tree', Catherine was declaring an immediate emergency. One person responsible for calling another in an ever widening circle so that all the Council currently in the valley would be available within minutes. The maneuver was seldom used which meant that when it was, it was a true emergency.

"I wanted Trent to be busy. But not like this," Catherine lamented. "Deke is so important in his life as is Bob. As you and I both know, growing up for years and years with someone makes them extra special."

All Brenna could do was to lay soothing hands on hers.

She knew that Catherine's gift from the Creator was sometimes enormously stressful. Her ability to See glimpses of future happenings was a pressure with implications beyond imaging. And the power of the matriarch was also hers as clan chief in their matrilineal society, where property as well as other things were passed down through generations of the female line.

Electing female leaders in clan societies was not new to Native Americans as some tribes had practiced it. The Scots had also chosen female clan chiefs throughout history. In the twentieth century, many countries had chosen female Presidents to lead.

Brenna had heard Grandfather Youngblood tell a friend, "The best of each of us, might be the different kind of intelligence and empathy of the female."

She had done a thumbs up in her mind.

CHAPTER FOUR

Brenna led as she and Trent walked swiftly down the hall toward the front of the Stone House, the huge manor house built in the 1800's for a multitude of purposes. Crossing the entryway, Brenna barely glanced at the slate floors graced with thick antique Persian rugs faded to muted jewel-tones. A massive circular chandelier of iron hung from the two-storied entryway. Twin mahogany staircases on opposite walls of the huge room led to the upper rooms of the Stone House. Banners depicting ancient Scottish battles hung on the stone walls with priceless artifacts intermingling with warrior relics. A collection of Native American artifacts sat alongside priceless European ones on carved side tables.

They entered a tall mahogany door on one side of the entryway leading to a downward-leading slate stairway. The staircase walls were constructed of smooth river rock from the valley's river and had been hauled in by hand from long ago ancestors. At the bottom of the stairs was another huge wooden door, heavier and older than seen in the entrance. Hand-wrought hinges held the massive doors upright.

Both she and Trent entered the room without knocking. Brenna looked around, trying to see the room and its people as Trent must. She had been told that he had been asked to the room during a kidnapping attempt of Catherine and Maggie last year. She herself had been with a medical aid organization in Indonesia dealing with the aftermath of a hurricane.

Nothing had been changed in the underground chamber in generations. The outside heavy wooden doors matched the massive beams overhead engraved with ancient symbols. The walls were of river-rock, the floors of grey slate. A long massive table with huge intricately carved chairs sitting around it were the only items in the room. Another set of closed doors ran along the back wall.

Eight of the nine chairs were occupied. The nine-member Sgnoch Council was made up of nine chosen elders from their individual clans as clan councils had been chosen for generations. Associate clans could give their proxies to a serving member. The duties of the Sgnoch Council were to make decisions and to advise their leader. With the exception of Mr. MacPherson and Kamon Youngblood, all the Council members now serving either lived in the Stone House, or in nearby cottages. With Catherine's communication center, they could have lived on the isle near Skye off the coast of Scotland or anywhere else in the world. Instead they chose the isolation of Shadow Valley, in the most remote section of the Ozark Mountains of Arkansas.

Catherine, and now Raina, discussed all issues brought forth before the Council with their associates over the interfaced, international satellite system in operation. Communication and thus decision making had been made much easier with the advent of a dedicated satellite communication system.

Seventeen-year-old Raina was seated at the head of the table and was in charge of the Sgnoch Council until Catherine could resume her duties. Raina had been a strikingly beautiful child with her stick-straight fall of platinum hair and clear blue eyes. She was fast developing into a drop-dead gorgeous, confident woman. Their grandmother had always professed that Raina had been born bossy with an old soul that knew what needed doing.

On Raina's right was their cousin, Kamon. The entire valley knew that Raina had been "stuck" on Kamon for years. Her crush had lasted well beyond expectations. Whether it was permanent or not was anyone's guess. Their usual role was pursuer and pursued, with Raina the aggressor. Kamon did his best to ignore her whenever he could.

Six-foot-tallish with dark hair and black eyes, Kamon represented the Youngblood clan, the Campbell clan, and all their people. His Native American blood showed in the high cheek bones, chiseled facial structure, and light caramel-colored skin.

Two thin white scars ran across his left eyebrow and down to his cheek. He was twenty-eight years old, the same age as Catherine. He had come to live with Grandfather Youngblood in the valley as a very young child.

And he was born a throw-back from a long ago time, a Native American Mind Walker.

The chair to Kamon's right had been Grandfather Youngblood's; now the seat was Raina's as the newest member of the Sgnoch Council. Today it was empty as she would have the authority of Catherine, and thus had temporally abdicated her own role.

Brenna seated herself next to the empty chair. Grandfather Youngblood had passed into Great Beyond during the last year. His wisdom and sharp humor was missed greatly, especially by Brenna. She ran her hand down the arms of the chair, remembering all the times he had done the same as she held back the tears which threatened. She prayed each day that she could be a worthy disciple of his teachings. Brenna had been asked by two associate clans to vote as their proxies. She would vote exactly as they had discussed.

Kelly Pierce sat on Brenna's right and held the proxies of several clans. As always, his quiet presence steadied her. He gave her a slight smile as she sat down.

Aunt Ulla sat at the other end of the table from Catherine's chair. She had returned from Paris and private business several months before and indicated that she would be a more-or-less permanent fixture at Shadow Valley. She had resumed her duties assessing students and assigning mentors for them. Today she had dressed in a bright blue silk print with matching turban. Her ebony face was smooth and her make-up flawless. Her Parisian sense of style was apparent in her haute couture silk dress and turban. Aunt Ulla was always dressed as if for tea with the Queen of England.

Aunt Ulla continually made Brenna feel unkempt and disheveled. Since that was usually true, Brenna smiled at her own observation. The only time Brenna made a real effort to dress up was during hospital visits, or hospital rounds. Patients were more comfortable with doctors who they thought looked like a doctor, especially older patients, so she conformed. Most of the other times she didn't have the patience to shop or find matching outfits, so she wore scrubs or jeans. Her long bright auburn hair was usually braided in a single plait down her back and tied with a rawhide thong. Makeup was not part of her daily ritual either. Only on special occasions did she deem to use anything except lip gloss and heavy-duty sunscreen lotion.

Duncan Frasier and his cousin, John MacDougal, occupied the next two seats. Both men were in their seventies but still vigorous and quick thinking. They were also opposites in personality. Duncan Frasier was a dour, introverted individual skilled as a communications and electrical engineer. John MacDougal was an extrovert, quick to laugh and tease. He was also an innovative technological scientist.

Mary O'Riley occupied the chair next to John MacDougal. Mary was often absent on assignments representing Catherine in different parts of the world. Catherine seldom ventured into the world outside the tribal clan holdings as the increased stimuli of crowds made her physically ill. Mary O'Riley was a worthy liaison to other places and groups Catherine needed to do business with.

Lachlan MacPherson, Mr. MacPherson to all, was seated in the last chair, on the left hand of the clan leader. He was a tall, elegant-appearing man in his late fifties with a neatly trimmed van dyke beard. He was smart, business-like and was touted to be as ruthless as was necessary.

Trent stood beside Raina's seat at the head of the table which was normally Catherine's chair. He gave a grave smile to all the Council members. At a nod from Raina he began, "I have something to ask, and if I must, beg for your help. I don't know how much you already know about the situation with Deke Paxton, so I may repeat familiar information. Deke Paxton and I grew up together in Las Vegas, Nevada. He has been my security chief since I started our business in New York City. His background is law enforcement with a multitude of initialed agencies, both federal and state. For the last several years he has helped people in other countries. People no one could or would help."

"Last year, you, the Sgnoch Council, gave me permission to involve Deke to capture Gavin O'Neill after O'Neill attempted to kidnap Catherine, Maggie or someone else from the valley. Deke was the one who physically confronted Gavin O'Neill, and detained him. He also flew with Liam and me when we delivered O'Neill to O'Neill's brother in Ireland."

Trent paused, then added, "Catherine says that Deke's been beaten and left for dead by a Columbian drug cartel. A case of mistaken identity, the cartel thought he was a member of a rival group involved in drug smuggling. Catherine says he was dumped in a ditch outside Palmira near Cali, Colombia, but will be picked up by a couple and taken to their shack this evening. She has the general location area. Catherine also says that he may not be able to live with the injuries he has received."

He paused to take a shaky breath. "I need your permission to bring him here to Shadow Valley so that Brenna can treat him if he is living. Or I need to bring his body back." He stopped and blinked back unshed tears. "If I can successfully get him out of Columbia alive, Brenna has agreed to help him if she can. Deke is already aware of some of the facts regarding the valley. Many of you met him when Catherine and I married a year and a half ago when he served as my best man. I would stake my life that he would never divulge any of the secrets of the valley or Council."

"I also need permission for Liam to fly me to the nearest large airport so that I can get some sort of transportation to go into Colombia to bring Deke out. Whatever his condition, I need to bring him home. Even if it's in a body bag," he choked.

The group all turned toward Kamon. As Catherine's ceann-cath, the chosen tribal clan commander when physical strength was needed, he would be a major factor in what they decided. Historically, some Scottish and Native American clans chose either young male or female heirs as leaders, both in the past and in the present, so a war chief was needed. Catherine had chosen her cousin, Kamon Youngblood, as her second in command. Her ceann-cath, the War Leader.

Kamon's dark eyes watched Trent intently. "Time is of the essence. A vote. Include your proxies," he instructed the group.

"Brenna?" he asked rapidly.

"Yes."

"Kelly?"

"Yes."

"Aunt Ulla?"

"Yes."

"Duncan Frasier?"

   "Yes."

"John MacDougal?

"Yes."

"Mary?

"Yes, most definitely."

"Mr. MacPherson."

"Yes."

Brenna wasn't surprised at the vote. Kamon did not ask Raina for a vote as a clan chief did not have a vote. In her temporary capacity as leader, Raina did not either. Now he turned to Raina and asked "Acceptable?"

"Yes," was the quick reply.

Brenna knew that as clan chief, Catherine, and now Raina, had total veto power. The clan chief did not make the decisions for the Sgnoch Council, but a veto from the clan leader was absolute. All the Council together could not overturn a clan chief's veto. If a veto occurred the Council tried a different route until they could obtain a positive response from their leader. It had been thus for hundreds of years for both Scots and many Native American tribes.

"Trent, because of the overwhelming emotions you are emitting, I am picking up your thoughts without meaning to. As you all know, I am forbidden to use telepathic abilities here without permission from this Council. May I share your thoughts with the others?" asked Kamon.

"Please do. I'm feeling overwhelmed and damn near close to tears," admitted Trent swallowing. "I would appreciate any help or advice you can give me."

"Don't be too quick to say that," advised Mr. MacPherson. "We all have a tendency to take over and talk all at once. Bunch of strong personalities."

"We don't even need Raina for that truth-telling," quipped John MacDougal.

Kamon gave a slight smile as he informed Trent, "We have had an opportunity to think through several scenarios since Raina told us of the meeting. You know that as the ceann-cath of this tribal clan my duties include the planning and executing of problems that arise which affects all clan functioning?"

At Trent's nod, Kamon continued, "I hope that you approve of some of our ideas but we can modify them as you feel necessary."

Again a nod from Trent.

"Oh, you haven't met one of the Council members. Mary O'Riley. Trent Angelenos."

Trent greeted the older woman cordially. Mary O'Riley looked like a typical middle-aged woman except better dressed in her crisp navy suit with white piping. Blond hair laced lightly with gray was pulled back in a smooth chignon. Her bright blue eyes were calm and observant.

"Mary, you are familiar with that part of the country. Could you give all of us a brief rundown of about what we are facing?" Kamon asked.

In an aside to Trent, Kamon explained, "Mary is an international financier whose strength is in corporate accounting. Her law degree is from Harvard where she was a law professor for several years. Now she is Catherine's emissary among other things."

"Harvard was too tame for our Mary," teased John MacDougal.

Mary smiled at the elderly man. "A history lesson in brief.

43

Colombia is a magnificent country. It has pristine coastlines, thick jungles, and rugged mountain terrain. Located at the top of South American, it borders Panama, Argentina, Brazil, Peru and Ecuador."

"Since 2011, Colombia is the largest cocaine producer in the world. The drug cartel whose territory is out of the city of Cali is usually less violent than most of the others. The Cali Gentlemen as they are called, have a non-confrontational strategy and invest in legitimate businesses. Most law enforcement agencies pretty much leave them alone."

She took a deep breath, "Deke Paxton's beating really was a case of mistaken identity. The Cali group does their best to stay under the radar and not draw attention to themselves. Now, to practicalities. The airport, called the Alfonso Bonilla Aragon International Airport is near the city of Palmira. It's also called the Palmaseca International Airport. It operates twenty-four hours a day and is 12 miles outside the city of Cali."

"Probably the best way to do this is when you arrive, just tell the airport control tower that you are picking up files from the Banco de Americanos, and that you will spend the night on board your airplane. Use my name if you have the need. That should give you time for your retrieval."

"Sean?"

Brenna had been so involved in Mary's recitation that she hadn't noticed Sean quietly entering the room to stand at Raina's side.

"Liam has gone out to Sanhicks to prepare the plane we should use." Sean referred to some papers he held in his hands. "We've decided to use the Citation XLS. It had a range of about 2100 miles and can carry about fourteen passengers including crew. It's commonly used by most private jet owners in South America, probably because of the elevation of the Andes." He gave a quick grin, "Of course we've modified it by using a G550 engine manufactured by Gulfstream Aerospace so its new range is about 6600 miles."

"Of course you did," murmured Kamon.

"I've got the little helo cranked up so we can go out to the airport whenever you're ready," he continued, referring to a small helicopter that was often used at the Stone House for quick hops to the airport at Sanhicks Mountain. "Do you want to know about runways, or elevations or things like that?" he asked.

"Anything that you or Liam can't handle?"

Before he could answer, Raina said, "I'm sorry Sean but I need either you or Liam to stay here. I know you both want to go, but if there's an emergency involving anyone from the valley, we'll need your skills. None of us are as good as either of you," she said seriously.

Brenna knew that Sean could not voice his obvious displeasure at Raina in her role as surrogate leader, so she interrupted, "Sean, Liam can fly the Citation by himself if needed. If I need something for the very pregnant Catherine, or any equipment for someone else, you are the best person we have."

"Damn and hell, Brenna." The outburst surprised most of the people at the table. "I'm sorry," he apologized immediately. "It's just that Liam is having more fun with his planes than I am with my copters." Heaving an exaggerated sigh, he said, "You're right, Raina, but this is the first time."

The young beauty smiled back at him.

Kamon picked up the conversation, "That takes care of air transportation. Now for ground transportation. We'll need to buy, steal, or whatever, some car to use to bring Deke back to the airport."

"Stop," Trent begged. "My head is spinning. Liam is willing to fly me to Colombia, right?"

"Right," Kamon agreed. "Oh, I'm going with you. You may need another pilot, I'm Spanish speaking and...," he hesitated for a long moment, "and my background is in clandestine military operations."

"I too am going," said Kelly Pierce immediately. "My army medic training may be able to keep Deke Paxton alive until we can get him here to Brenna. I too served." He didn't elaborate on his military stints.

Brenna watched as her brother-in-law fought back the emotions that were threatening to overwhelm him.

Kelly Pierce spoke beside Brenna. "Anything different I need to know?" he asked quietly.

"No, if he's still alive you know the routine, clear airways with an oral or endotracheal tube, move him carefully, splint if possible. There's IV equipment and all the rest of the medical kit in each airplane. Give me an update as soon as you can."

"Will do," he returned softly.

Trent spoke to the group in an emotionally laden voice. "I don't have the words to say thank you, to all of you. Kamon and Kelly, it would be my honor to serve under either of you. You both know much more about any rescue operation than I'll ever know." He ran a hand in an agitated gesture through his hair. "You tell me what to do and I'll do it."

"There's also the matter of Deke's airplane. He was there to get it refueled. I doubt that the men who were contracted to beat him up could pilot an aircraft," mused Kamon.

Before anyone else could speak, Mary O'Riley inserted, "The bank has several private hangars. If the plane is still there, it can be discreetly moved inside. Also Kamon, when you get to the Cali airport I can arrange a car. No, better make that an old taxi to pick up Deke. The older models are station wagon types, there shouldn't be a problem hauling whatever equipment you need and the four of you."

"Let's see," she continued thinking aloud. "Kamon, just leave the taxi at the airport. I'll arrange for it to be picked up and torched."

"Torched?" asked Trent blinking at the grandmotherly-looking lady.

"Deke will most probably be bleeding and you won't be able to clean up the car's interior. You don't want any questions asked by the local authorities if they find a taxi with bloody seats. Its best to just burn the taxi and let the locals think it was some car-tel problem."

"You can arrange this from here?" asked Mr. MacPherson quietly.

"We have a...," she hesitated, "a colleague for want of a better word, who can easily arrange purchasing of an older taxi, delivering it to the airport, picking it up later, and burning it. Also it will be no problem for him to whisk Deke's plane inside the bank's hangar. Really, it will be little trouble for him. And of course, he will ask no questions regarding what needs to be done."

"You have an undercover agent, right?" asked John Mac-Dougal reaching over to affectionately pat Mary O'Riley's hand.

Smiling fondly at the elderly man, she chided, "Now John, you know I'd never give up that kind of information. Let's just say he's bound by the same oath that we are."

Raina stood, "Anything else can be handled by the Communication Center at the Stone House. Good luck," she told the three men who towered over her.

As Kamon strode out she whispered, "Take care, darling." Then grinned at the dark scowl he returned.

Brenna shook her head at her sister while she shared a laughing glance and head shake with Aunt Ulla and Mary.

"Ach, lassie. You are a minx," Mr. MacPherson asserted. "Reminds me of my Alma," the elegant gentleman smiled.

Brenna walked quietly back to her room at the house, her mind on her sister, Raina. She had come close to laughing aloud at Mr. MacPherson's assertions. Mr. MacPherson's Alma was a red-head with faded freckles. She was also kind, deeply intuitive, and a born homemaker, bringing mothering to the level of an art form. Well, Raina was kind. And bossy. And organized. And drop-dead beautiful. And was doing an excellent job in filling in as clan chief. She hadn't even begged to go as a co-pilot which would have happened normally. Raina loved to fly almost as much as Liam and Sean.

For herself, piloting was a fast mode of transportation. She neither loved it nor hated it but couldn't deny it was a useful skill. One she used when necessary but did not seek out for fun.

Keeping current with the licensing board was a necessary task, as was keeping track of the modifications Liam and Sean built into their airplane's systems.

Catherine had followed in their grandmother's footsteps and had chosen not to learn to fly. With Catherine's affinity with machines it had come as a surprise to many clan members. With all Catherine's other duties, Brenna could understand her choosing not to add anything else to her repertoire. And she did not have the need.

She finally let her mind go to the present.

Deke. Deke Paxton. He and Trent had been best friends, along with Bob Calhoun, since they were in elementary school. Deke was a silent partner in Trent's firm, working only when needed for a particular job. He seemed to go to the most dangerous places, looking for who knew what. He certainly found it this time, she mused silently.

My reason for being on this earth is to heal. Not to question the Creator's usage of me, but to give healing to those I can. I'll do as I must. Destiny.

CHAPTER FIVE

"Well, first item down," commented Liam as he landed the Citation on the paved Cali airport runway. The one main runway was 9,842 feet in length with an elevation of 3,164 feet. The airport was surrounded by mountains up to 14,000 feet, an easy lift for the modified Citation.

Liam had told the tower he was on an overnight stay to pick up some files for the Banco de Americanos and would not be refueling. The tower had ordered him to turn into an air park area as another plane was in the flight pattern. Liam had thanked the man, and taxied as close to a non-lighted area as possible.

"Let's review," Kamon suggested. "Liam stays with the plane in case there's a problem, he deals with any locals that show up." Turning to Liam, he continued, "I recommend that you imply that your Spanish language skills are limited, etc. The 'I'm just the hired pilot' routine, even though I know your Spanish fluency is excellent."

"Trent, you speak only pidgin Spanglish, so I think it would be best if you say nothing during the retrieval. You also have the lightest colored skin so I also suggest you pull up your coat collar as much as you can, and pull down that old cap. Keep as low a profile as possible."

"Kelly and I can pass as Hispanics, and we're both fluent speakers."

Glancing from one man to the other two, he added, "Remember, the basic plan is to pass ourselves off as members of another drug cartel come to claim the body of our cohort. We are not friendly, but will do the couple with Deke no harm if they follow orders. Understood?" At the positive nods he said, "Then let's go see if we can find the taxi or van Mary promised us."

"I've scanned the area," Liam reported. "There's an old beat up Ford van near that second light pole. She chose a van rather than a station wagon as it would be easier to transport Deke. It has Taxi written on the sides and doors at the back. According to Mary's last message, the keys should be under the passenger seat. You're to drive along the south fence to the nearest gate. The guard there will shake your hand as you give him a hundred-dollar bill, American money. The same when you return."

Trent lifted an eyebrow in question.

Kamon shrugged slightly, "It's the way much business is done in Latin America. For cash. Preferably American cash."

Trent had borrowed an older black jacket and cap from one of the mechanics before they left Shadow Valley. Kelly and Kamon were dressed in non-descriptive dark-colored clothes that would draw no one's attention. With their rough clothes, dark coloring and large bodies they could easily pass as South American thugs.

"Remember one of the first rules of entry. Look as if you have a purpose for being wherever you are. Walk rapidly to the taxi as if this was the sixth time you've done this today. Don't look around but be aware," Kelly instructed Trent softly.

"Thanks," Trent murmured, knowing he was completely out of his depth.

The three men walked rapidly to the old van. Kelly chose the back seat where he placed a duffel bag he carried besides him. There were two back doors directly behind him.

They drove down the perimeter of the airport fence following the fence line to the nearest gate. Kamon spoke rapid fire Spanish to the guard, who shook his moneyed hand and waved him through.

Catherine had told Trent that the outside of the old house where Deke had been taken had a broken down sofa on the tiny front porch, and the house seemed to be set back a little way from the road. The house was not visible on satellite but the satellite GPS had confirmed that a dry trench was on the same side as the road. The men had concluded that the house must be also on the same side if the couple had seen Deke lying in the ditch.

It was dusk and the sun would be setting shortly which

could make locating the shack harder. At least they were lucky in that the irrigation ditch was on the right hand side of the road and there was no water in it.

Kamon drove as slowly as possible without drawing attention to the old taxi. The beat up van had sagging seats, rusted fenders, but a first class engine.

About two miles from the airport Trent said in a loud whisper "There. On the right. I think that's it."

The structure was little more than a one room shed with a tiny covered entrance. An old sofa and a wooden chair took up most of the space under the small overhang. Made of rough old wooden planks, the shack looked as if a strong wind would blow it down. Dim light showed from a window.

Kamon cut the van's lights and motor to let the van crawl to a stop as close to the shack as possible. He slid out of the taxi, being careful to jam all the switches to prevent the doors from lighting as they exited. He walked silently to one of the windows, standing in the shadows to look inside.

Trent opened the back doors of the taxi leaving it ajar as they had discussed. Kelly and Trent followed Kamon's lead and moved silently toward the only door to the little shack, Kelly carrying a duffle bag.

"There's a man probably in his thirties and an older woman sitting at the table talking. They look like druggies. Deke's here. He's on an old wooden cot built into a corner of the room. He's not moving." Kamon's voice was a breathy whisper.

"We want to be in an out in less than three minutes," he continued in a murmur. "Just like we planned."

Kamon opened the unlocked door and stepped inside moving to the left of the door and letting the occupants see the large gun stuck into his waistband.

The man was dark, short and stocky with the ingrained grimy skin of the habitual meth user. The woman looked older with her missing front teeth and squat figure. The man knocked over his chair as Kamon entered, looking around wildly for a place to hide. The woman sat stone-faced not moving or making a sound.

Kamon spoke to them in his rapid-fire Spanish. Ignoring the two Columbians, Kelly and Trent hurried to the cot where Deke lay unmoving.

Trent soundlessly sucked air between his teeth when he saw Deke's bloody body. The only sound in the room was Kamon's harsh-sounding speech.

Kelly checked Deke's carotid artery neck pulse first, "Very slow and faint, but he's still alive," Kelly murmured too softly to be overheard. He then noted Deke's eye pupils and made sure his airways were clear. Kelly swiftly unzipped the duffle bag and turned it inside out to create a zipped canvas stretcher with handles at each end and small rollers on the bottom. He and Trent carefully slid the canvas under Deke, placing him inside and zipping it up as much as possible.

"Ahhh, he's big," muttered Kelly under his breath.

Kamon watched the room's inhabitants as Kelly and Trent carried Deke outside in the portable gurney. By the time they reached the taxi Kamon had sprinted ahead to start the old van. They carefully loaded Deke into the back, sliding the gurney forward and shutting the doors.

"There's no point in trying to help Deke right now, I could do him more harm than good," Kelly told Trent. "He's as stable as he's going to get for now. My equipment is on board the plane. Let's just get out of here."

"Damn, I hate meth users," Kamon said to Trent, putting the van in gear. "Those two were higher than a kite. The woman was literally stoned out of her mind."

"I would never have guessed," Trent admitted. "They just seemed terrified."

"That too. The biggest problem with meth users is the violence that can erupt unexpectedly. The man's facial sores showed that he was a long time user. Oh, and the woman's bad teeth."

Changing the subject he noted with satisfaction, "That was a really good job. We were in and out in less than three minutes."

When they returned to the south airport entrance, the guard at the gate held up his hand, then recognizing the taxi, he put out his hand. Kamon silently shook his hand palming a folded bill off to him. He waved them through with a disinterested glance, not bothering to check passengers.

Kamon drove as close as possible to the plane's stairway, trying to maneuver the taxi so that the back of the old van faced the airplane stairs. Trent and Kelly quickly pulled the canvas carrier free and carried Deke aboard the plane. Kamon drove the van back to its original position to leave it just out of the airport floodlights. He walked swiftly back to the plane, pulled up the steps and closed the door.

Liam had started contact with the tower, stating a change of plans and asked for a runway clearance for departure. The voice from the tower complied and Liam quickly put the Citation in the air, Kamon acting as co-pilot.

Kelly and Trent had collapsed the temporary carrier and strapped Deke onto a padded table. As he cleaned Deke's face and head, Kelly explained to Trent, "Head injuries cause more deaths and disabilities than any other neurological cause." He frowned as he murmured, "He doesn't seem to have any obvious skull fractures but that laceration on the right side of his head may be a problem. There's no leakage from the nose or ears, so no sign of cerebrospinal fluid leakage. But his breathing is irregular, both pupils are fixated to light, and there's motor flaccidity. He's in a deep enough coma that none of our movement has affected him."

"He's alive," murmured Trent gratefully.

"Let's take a look at the rest of him. Damn, he's big. Lean but big."

They carefully cut away his clothes, trying to move him as little as possible. Deke was a mass of swollen and bloody wounds starting to turn a dark purple. Cuts and still-bleeding lacerations covered most of his upper torso and dried blood covered everything. Swelling made the deep gashes more prominent, especially on his shoulders and arms. His injuries were so extensive that he was unrecognizable.

Kelly ran his hands carefully over Deke's ribs, sighing when he finished.

At Trent's questioning looking, he said, "No sign of broken ribs which could have meant problems with breathing, he may still have cracked ribs or a hair-line fracture but no protruding rib bones. He seems to have protected his ribs with his right arm, it may be broken."

Kelly looked at Trent to ask, "Are you able to wash the blood off so we can get a better indication of other injuries we may be dealing with? I need to call Brenna."

"Yes," Trent replied in a husky voice. "I can do whatever it takes. At least he's still alive."

Using the airplane phone connected to the valley's satellite system, Kelly called Brenna. "We have him on the plane and we're in the air. Should be there in a few hours."

"What's his condition?" Brenna asked. "How bad?"

"Severe and Critical," answered Kelly. "He's in a protracted coma, has a head injury, and shows some signs of a primary brainstem injury. No protruding fractures although there's a deep laceration on his right arm and it may be broken. His pulse is slow and faint, blood pressure irregular. Surface bleeding is almost under control."

"Don't bother to splint the arm, that's going to be the least of his worries. It might cause more trauma for his compromised system. Secure the airways and stem the severe lesions with butterflies temporarily. He's comatose?" Brenna asked.

"Yes," came the quick reply.

Brenna heaved a deep sigh, "Then give him a 5% dextrose normal saline IV for shock and keep him warm. There's little that can be done right now. And Kelly? .... As the Creator wills," Brenna reminded him, knowing that her brother-in-law was listening to the poor prognosis of his best friend.

Kelly repeated the litany, "As the Creator wills, yes, but we're going to do everything humanly, and maybe inhumanly possible to keep him alive." He carefully pulled the sheet over

Deke's torso and added a couple of blankets for warmth.

To distract an agitated Trent, Kelly asked Kamon, "What did you tell that couple back at the shack? They looked terrified."

"As well they should," Kamon answered. "I told them we would come back to kill them if they told anyone about Jose."

Trent looked stunned.

"I also gave them five hundred dollars for taking care of him. I promised them that the Medellin Cartel had long memories. It wasn't a lie, they probably do. Anyway, they're so glad to still be alive I doubt that they'll tell their own mothers where they got the money. Probably buy more drugs."

"How's Deke doing?" asked Liam from the cockpit.

"Iffy. We've stabilized him as much as possible until we get to the Valley," answered Kelly.

"We'll have to move him again at the Sanhicks Mountain Airport? Damn, I hope we don't do any more harm," said Trent shaking his head.

"This gurney is portable. See the sides? And all the little wheels?" Kelly questioned. "It literally snaps apart, we used similar ones in a war that wasn't. Of course, Liam and Sean modified the gurney for use at Shadow Valley and in the other clan holdings. Added the unique side wheels and made it easier to handle."

Several hours later Liam landed at the Sanhicks Mountain airport and the portable gurney was transported to the waiting helicopter with Sean at the controls. A few minutes after, they landed on the pad in back of the stone manor. A small green meadow surrounded the green-surfaced helicopter pad which masked it from the air. The kidney shaped pad mimicked the dips and curves of the nearby bush strewn field.

Trent, Kamon, Liam and Kelly quickly carried the gurney to a small building at the rear of the Stone House. The clinic building was sheltered under a large old oak tree with huge overhanging branches screening its rooftop.

"This way," directed Brenna coming out of the building. "Put him in the surgical room. It has the longest examining table. Through the door and to the left."

"Move on three," directed Kelly. "One, two, three." The four men carried the portable stretcher into the clinic, and then placed the canvas carrier with the unconscious man directly onto the leather table covered with a heavy white plastic sheet.

Kelly Pierce moved to the other side of the table to assist if needed. His dark eyes followed each of Brenna's movements as if trying to anticipate her needs. As Sean joined them, the other men moved to stand beside the other wall.

Brenna placed both hands over Deke's chest, barely touching the damaged skin. "Still alive, thank the Creator," she murmured softly. Closing her eyes, she put one hand over the rib cages, then moved downward to the spleen area.

"Awww." Addressing Kelly with her eyes still closed, she explained, "Badly bruised spleen. Must have been kicked several times there." She continued examining each organ without sight. "Arm is deeply bruised and some ligaments are torn but nothing is broken. Lower extremities cuts and bruises. Lacerations on right hip are particularly deep. No permanent damage to the liver or kidney. Nothing here that is causing the coma. Chest area mainly intact."

She placed a hand on each side of Deke's head, cupping the skull. "Oh, Oh," she took a deep breath. She moved her hands slowly over Deke's bloody skull for several minutes, moving from the back to the front.

When she opened her eyes, there were unshed tears. "There's TBI with brain swelling and a frontal lobe hematoma. The bleeding is seeping into the corpus collosum and into other parts of the brain. Would you all mind stepping into the other room. I need some privacy."

As Kamon and Trent started toward the door, Trent asked Kamon "What's TBI?"

"A Traumatic Brain Injury," murmured Kamon as they left.

"I'm staying," announced Kelly. "It's my job, this lifetime, for now" he reminded her. "I wish you wouldn't, Brenna, but I know you will. I'll be here to monitor."

"And you know that it's necessary if he's going to have a chance."

"And I don't have to like what it does to you though," Kelly quietly murmured in reply.

Brenna nodded her thanks to Kelly and replaced her hands on Deke's head. She let the tears flow as she started the process of 'bonding'.

Taking a deep, cleansing breath, she blocked the present and entered into a world of connecting with the past. In this ancient spiritual place, she could feel what she touched as well as sense injuries in her mind's eye. Here she was bonded with the wounded. Here universal knowledge floated within her grasp. Here she had help from all the others like her who had gone before. Here she was an Empathic Healer gifted by the Creator and connected to the ancients.

The intensity of Deke's pain came at her in waves and made her brace herself to keep from falling. She focused only on alleviating the pain before her as she allowed some of his pain to transfer to her body.

She concentrated first on the worst injuries, the ones that would cause the most permanent damage. "First, the frontal lobe where the brain's executive functions are located," she murmured to herself. "Damage to this part of the brain often means that there is no volitional goal-directed activity. No higher level cognitive activity. No working memory, or verbal fluency." She shifted her mind, working slowly to help the body reduce the bleeding and clots.

Brenna didn't have to explain her verbalizing the problem aloud to Kelly. She knew he would remain silent, not interrupting her need for talking aloud for focus. "Now the temporal lobe which has been the most injured from the beating."

She could see in her mind's eye the epidural hematoma in the middle meningeal artery of the temporal lobe. Ever so slowly and with a great deal of shared pain, she reduced the edema that was developing, allowing Deke's body to begin to absorb the fluid. The minutes elongated into hours.

"Enough for now," Kelly said removing her hands from Deke's head. "You've been working for almost two hours and your body can't stand much more. It's time to stop for now."

Brenna stood upright as the nausea hit her. Rushing to the sink she vomited into a container placed there.

"Are you okay? You have no facial color," Kelly said handing her a damp towel. "That was too long a session."

"Just a little off my pins, as Fergus would say," she smiled wanly at her assistant as she wiped her face with the damp towel he gave her. "I still have no reality of time when I'm in that zone. I've tried and tried to figure out a way to control the time myself, but so far I haven't a clue. I do thank you, Kelly."

"No thanks necessary. Thank the Creator, and your Grandmother, that you went to medical school. It gives you a better idea of anatomy and how the body and brain works, giving you more tools than just your gift. You almost never need to 'connect' that deeply with an injured person. Otherwise you would be like this most of the time. Neither of us would be able to take it," he smiled softly at wan-looking woman.

"Deke will live, though, and that's what we do," she said fighting back the wave of fatigue. Combined with the nausea, it was making her light headed.

"He will also need more assistance from us to survive,' she said slowly. "The bleeding will build again in about six hours and have to be reduced again so his body can absorb it. The next time will be easier though. I remind myself that each time is easier."

"I had Kamon bring over the cot and put it in the alcove there." He indicated the small bed with a wave of his hand. "It's time for you to sleep. You need to restore your energy level or you can't be of further help. I'll have Mrs. Searle send over some sandwiches and soup for you later. Oh, and some juice. You won't be able to do anyone any good if you don't rest for awhile."

"You're right," she sighed wearily. Brenna felt so tired as to be physically ill. She let Kelly help her onto the cot. "You'll wake me if there's any change?" she yawned in slurred speech. She knew that their mutual reliance was sustained by the trust between them. She trusted him completely and knew that he would never do anything to break that bond. Her eyes closed as she fell into the deep sleep of the exhausted.

"Yes, I will," Kelly promised, covering her with a light blanket.

Kelly opened the door to the little office waiting room, now crowded with Trent and Kamon plus Liam and Sean. He stood in the doorway which gave him a view of the motionless Deke and the sleeping form of Brenna.

"He's going to live," he told them without preamble.

"He's going to be in intense pain for several days. It will take weeks for him to recover fully but he will eventually be okay. He must be in great physical condition to survive a beating like that one must have been and still survive," he continued.

"Brenna?" asked Kamon.

"Sleeping. She's exhausted. I'll wake her if anything changes but she was joined for a couple of hours and was becoming fatigued beyond level four."

"You stopped her?" Sean asked quietly. "She's okay?"

"Yes. It was necessary. She'll probably be pissed as soon as she's recovered though," Kelly grinned. "Her patience and her temper are about equal, and both are lethal."

Trent looked from one man to the others. "I've missed something here. I know that Brenna is a healer besides being a physician. She told me herself that she has a Gift from the Creator that allows her to channel healing through her hands. She told me she uses a special sweet-smelling lotion so that her patients think the warmth is lotion-induced. I used it on Catherine's feet and it smelled like jasmine."

The three other men looked at Kamon and remained silent.

"I also just saw her examine Deke with her eyes closed. By feel. Including his brain."

Finally, Kamon spoke, "Trent, you've become one of us, but this secret is not ours to tell. You know the rule. We can only talk about ourselves, not other people. Brenna has an extra Gift that she seldom uses as it's risky for her. Very, very risky."

He held up his hand to stop Liam's interruption. "We'll leave telling of the details to Brenna," he instructed glancing at the other men, "or to Catherine if she so chooses."

"How's Catherine?" asked Kelly deliberately changing the subject. "Any more problems?"

"None," Trent smiled broadly. Mentioning his wife's name always brought a smile to his face. "Raina is with her now. Dr. Richardson will be arriving in the next week or so. He says his new hip is as good as gold. Not a particularly funny joke but we'll all be glad when he's here. Especially with Deke requiring Brenna's attention. Catherine might need something. I want him here yesterday."

"Dr. Richardson, plus Brenna, should be enough physicians for even you," teased Liam, trying to seek a lighter mood. "I heard that you tried to get Catherine to call in the entire OB department of Mayo Clinic when she had premature labor. Raina refers to you as the hover mother."

"And she's right," laughed Trent. "I can't seem to help it. I know I'm driving Catherine nuts but ...," he shrugged.

"Just you wait until you fall in love with someone," Liam taunted Sean. "You're going to be worse than Trent, like Dad is about Mom."

"Good grief I hope not," Sean said fervently.

All the men in the room laughed. They all knew that Liam and Sean's father was as besotted with his wife as Trent was with Catherine. The couple lived in Munich, Germany where the twin's dad was in the Diplomatic Corp.

"Have you worked out a schedule in your mind for Deke's immediate care? Two hours or four hours?" Sean asked Kelly.

"I think four hours round the clock for the next couple of days; we'll revise as needed." Kelly was silent for a minute. "For now, I'll sleep when Brenna does. It's not that I don't trust her, but sometimes her abilities overrule her common sense and physical strength. And I don't trust her to take care of herself. You three," he indicated Kamon, Sean and Liam, "have Emergency Medical Training so I'd like you to take the shifts for the next twelve hours which will be critical."

Trent interrupted "I want...."

Kelly continued over the interruption. "After Deke becomes more stabilized we can change the schedule. We can train Trent what to look for, and he can take a shift in between driving Catherine crazy. Sean, can you take the first shift? It's been a long couple of days. I'd like to grab a nap before Brenna wakes."

"Kamon, you and Liam can work our who's next," Kelly said.

Both men nodded.

"Sure, I'm rested. I'll wake you if Deke so much as twitches."

"I wish. But as the Creator wills." murmured Kelly.

CHAPTER SIX

Deke fought through the dark cloudiness toward the flickering of the light. The darkness was dense and thick, pulling him down into a deep void. The empty space had been neither scary nor welcoming; it was more of a not-being. A nothingness in free-fall. He strained to open his eyelids. The slight effort drew him back into the black oblivion.

When he gained some awareness again, he felt warmth on his face but remained still, not wanting to fall again into the deep recesses of darkness. Hands. Someone was touching his head with warm hands. He could feel the movement on his face and across his forehead. It felt like heaven. Soothing and peaceful.

He moved his head trying for closer contact with the comforting caress. Pain stabbed like a knife through his head, moving in a searing fire from the back of his neck to lodge behind his eyeballs. The blackness reclaimed him even as he fought the dark enveloping fog to stay conscious.

The next time he awoke he kept his eyes closed, not wanting to repeat his last painful experience.

"Damnit, you've got to back off a little. You can't take much more."

"Just a couple more minutes. The pain is less for me than for him. The transference between us makes the pain lose some of its power."

"Enough now. Damnit!"

"Okay. Shh, shh. You're okay," said a woman's voice in a soft murmur. "Lie still now. Don't try to move your head."

Obeying the soft voice was easy. Deke tried to do as the quiet female voice commanded, knowing instinctively that she was trying to help him. He relaxed the muscles in his shoulders and arms. Again there was pain, but not as intense as it had been in his head. He was able to see foggy movement from one of his eyes, not focused movement, but movement nonetheless.

"You're in the United States," a woman's voice explained. "Your friend, Trent Angelenous, brought you here. You're going to be okay," repeated the soothing voice.

Trent. He knew Trent. Was his best friend. United States. Don't move head.

Deke tried to lick his lips but they felt puffy and swollen. "Hurt," he tried to speak but knew he hadn't made a recognizable sound.

"We know you hurt everywhere. Don't try to think right now, it will make sense later. Rest," the voice added in a whisper. "Rest."

Deke tried to speak anyway, ignoring the well-meaning suggestion of silence. After a moments struggle to form a sentence, he mumbled, "Who?"

A male voice replied, "Columbian drug cartel gangsters. A case of mistaken identity. You were thought to be someone else. Sleep if you can, it will help you heal faster."

Heal faster. Yes, want to heal faster. Tired. So tired, he thought as he followed the advice, and closed his eyes waiting for sleep to claim him.

Deke felt a warm hand on the side of his neck checking his pulse and heard the woman's voice tell someone, "He's sleeping now. The worst is over." The worst over? His body was a mass of hurt. And this was better? Slowly he felt himself slide into sleepy oblivion.

Some unknown time later, Deke opened his eyes slowly. He could see clearly from his left eye but his right one was swollen almost shut. There were pale green walls with pictures of anatomy diagrams. He couldn't read the lettering. Moving his head very slowly he tried to scan the room with his one good eye. A stainless steel cart with a stethoscope and a number of bottles was in his direct line of vision. Along one wall he could see cabinets painted white but with bright green knobs. Strange, he thought. Why would someone put green knobs on white cabinets? He slowly maneuvered his head in the other direction. There was stiffness but minimal pain.

In an upholstered recliner sat a large red-headed man idly flipping through a magazine. Liam? Liam Something. The pilot he had met when they went somewhere. Focusing on pulling up the memory, he recalled putting a handcuffed man in an airplane.

"You're awake," the man announced loudly. "I'll get Brenna."

Deke winced at the loud sound. At least thoughts were beginning to make sense. Brenna. Nasty tempered. Opinionated. Gorgeous. Trent must have brought him to her to be treated. Wherever she was. Or maybe he was in a hospital somewhere.

Deke recognized the very pretty face with the large green eyes and bright auburn hair as she came into focus. Brenna. Dr. Brenna Ramsey. Trent's sister-in-law.

"Good afternoon," said Brenna in a quiet voice. "Head still throbbing?"

"It aches but not too badly," Deke replied through cracked lips. "Where am I? What happened? I don't remember."

"What do you remember?"

"Very little." Deke closed his eyes to concentrate. "I ... I remember making the decision to refuel at the Palmaseca International Airport near Cali, Colombia. I was coming from Ecuador." He searched his memory for more facts, and then added, "I'm sorry, there's nothing else until I woke a little while ago. There were a couple of times ..., but my mind is hazy. Sorry," he yawned.

"Yesterday. You woke up the last time yesterday," corrected Brenna. "You were brought here nine days ago. You came to a little yesterday, but you're better today."

"Nine days? I've been here for nine days?"

"Yes. You've had brief moments of lucidity but yesterday was your red-letter day."

Deke started to shake his head and then thought better of

it asking instead, "Red-letter what? I don't understand. In fact, I understand very little or very slowly right now. Like mush."

Brenna gave a soft chuckle. "Yesterday was the day we all knew for the first time that you were going to make it with all your facilities intact. And its normal for both verbal expressive and verbal fluency to have glitches after a severe head trauma. Those areas took a major beating."

"Will it get better?" Deke asked, hearing the concern in his own voice.

"Most definitely. Your injuries are no longer life-threatening. It will take a week or so for your cognitive functions to return to normal but they will return," Brenna assured him.

Trying another tactic Deke asked, "Do you know what happened to me?"

"Actually, I do know but I'll leave the telling to Trent. He has first hand knowledge while mine is strictly what I was told. He's on the way over from the Stone House now."

"A stone house? Where are we? I'm not in the hospital?"

"No. I couldn't leave Catherine to go to Colombia with the others. Catherine's pregnancy is full term and she could deliver their baby at any time. The decision was made to bring you to Shadow Valley for treatment and care. The Stone House is our main residence."

"Don't know where the Shadow Valley is. Am I supposed to know?" Deke asked worriedly, blinking in concentration.

"No, you've never known," Brenna assured him. "It's not uncommon to have retrograde amnesia after a head injury. Honestly, you may never remember all the details of what happened. That's normal when there is head trauma."

"Head trauma. Head hurt," he repeated.

"Hello, Trent," Brenna turned her head, greeting the large, handsome man entering the room. "Deke wants to know how he got here. I decided that you could do the honors of telling him while I check Mrs. Pierson's stitches. She cut herself accidentally yesterday."

"Glad to," responded Trent.

65

"Yell if you need me. But not too loudly," she grinned. "Deke has a major headache."

"Will do. Hey, Deke. You seemed to have found yourself some trouble," Trent smiled, his voice softening. "No, don't talk yet. Save your energy for your questions. You most likely will have a slew of them."

Deke gazed at the man who had been his best friend for most of his life. They had met in the early elementary school in Las Vegas on a rag-tag soccer field. Big for their ages and equally aggressive they could have been rivals or close friends. Thank God they had recognized a like brother, and had chosen the friendship route.

"Well, from what we can piece together, about ten or eleven days ago you flew into the Alfonso Bonilla Aragon International Airport in Cali, Columbia to refuel your little plane. We have no idea where you were going, but I suspect you were coming from Ecuador."

"Anyway," he continued, "the Cali drug cartel thought you were working for a rival cartel, probably the Medellin cartel. They did their best to kill you by beating you to death. According to our sources, it was a case of mistaken identity. They dumped you in a ditch to bleed to death. Understand so far?"

Deke narrowed his eyes, "Yes, I was coming from Ecuador and stopped to refuel the plane in Columbia. But how did I get here? My mind is working slow and is muddled."

Trent took a deep breath. "Here's where we leave Kansas," he explained, referring to Dorothy in The Wizard of Oz.

"Here is what is called Shadow Valley, deep in the Ozark Mountains of Arkansas. I've told you, Mrs. Grant, Bob and Sarah before Catherine and I married that Catherine can only leave isolated places for a short period of time. She can't handle the stimuli or stress of groups of people. I also told you that she was from a long ancestral line where a few have had the Gift of Second Sight. Precognition. Still with me?"

Deke nodded slightly.

"Eleven days ago Catherine had a Sighting of a scene in

66

which you had been beaten and left for dead. She also Saw that you were going to be taken to a shack by a couple of people for either a monetary reward or ransom."

Trent paused, "I asked, and received permission from the tribal clan council to bring you here after we went to Colombia to get you. Or your body."

"So Catherine had previous knowledge of this? Of what was going to happen to me?"

"No. The beating had already occurred when she Saw you. She did know that a couple would pick you up and take you to their shack." Not shading the truth Trent said honestly. "We didn't know if you would live even if we could get you out of Columbia. Catherine only knew that your injuries were extensive and critical."

Deke blinked hard. "That bad?" he questioned.

"Worse. Even I wouldn't have recognized you. Your body was a mass of swollen purple flesh with a multitude of bleeding cuts and internal injuries. Kamon, the cousin who gave away Catherine at our wedding, organized the trip. Remember him?'

"Yeah, he and a lot of others watched while I dressed in a kilt for your wedding. Something that I still feel is above best friend's duties," Deke tried for humor, grimacing at the pain the effort cost him.

"Well, Kamon Youngblood, Kelly Pierce, an ex-army medic, and I were flown into Colombia by Liam McKinney. Remember him? A red-headed giant who's an airplane genius."

"I just remembered that I met him when we flew to Ireland last year. He was here a little while ago."

"Yes, you did. But the person you just saw was Sean, Liam's twin brother. We've been taking four hour shifts so that someone is with you all the time. Just in case."

"We?"

"Kamon, Kelly, Liam, and Sean. Brenna pretty much stays here all the time except for the infrequent patient she sees in her clinic, and to check Catherine. Brenna doesn't allow me to leave Catherine for very long right now. Our baby is due at any time," he explained.

"Pinkie Truth, Trent," Deke insisted falling back on one of their childhood rituals. "I need to know the truth. How bad am I? Can I recover? Will I regain all my skills again?"

"Pinkie truth. Yes, you will," Brenna answered briskly, striding back into the room. "I've already told you that you will regain all your facilities. You'll live to fly off and do whatever the hell you do in another month or so. You'll be able to risk your neck again. Don't worry."

"Thank God," murmured Deke, ignoring Brenna's irritated tone.

"Trent, can you come back in a couple of hours to finish your talk? Deke is struggling to keep his eyes open. Oh, yeah. Dr. Richardson came up on the supply flight from Fortuna with Liam. Catherine wants you to meet him."

"About time. I'll talk to you later, Deke. Dr. Richardson is supposed to deliver the baby. Unfortunately, he fell and broke a hip, then had complications. That man has a lot to answer for, and I have lots of questions for him," announced Trent hurrying though the door.

"I'll bet you do at that," grinned Brenna, watching the retreating figure. "Poor Dr. Richardson."

Deke stared at Brenna. Lord, she was a striking beauty. All that auburn hair in a long, lone braid down her back and big grass-green eyes. Her two-piece cotton blue scrubs did not detract from her lithe figure. She was about five foot six or seven with a lean athletic build. Womanly with no excess poundage. She might have an attitude straight from hell but she looked like an angel. Ignoring his wayward thoughts, he asked, "If I ask something, will you tell me the truth?"

"If I can without … if I can," Brenna answered in an equally serious tone.

"Did you save my life?"

Brenna blinked, then answered with a simple, "Yes."

"I remember bits and pieces. Your hands were really warm, almost hot. You must have had some heated liniment or something on them. And there was a man's voice talking to you. Then someone else I think." Deke frowned trying to concentrate on pulling details out of the dark recesses of his mind. The darkness was so vast that only tiny pieces floated to the surface.

"The first voice was probably Kelly's, Kelly Pierce. You didn't meet him when you were in Haiti, he was packing our supplies. He's my assistant, right hand, and sometimes body-guard," Brenna smiled. "He's a former Army medic among other things. He was one of the people who went to Colombia to get you out, and his medical knowledge kept you alive until they could get you here. The other voice was probably my cousin Kamon's."

Deke felt a pang of annoyance toward the unknown Kelly in spite of trying to be grateful. He could hear the deep affection for her assistant in her voice. Brenna and this Kelly seem to have a special bond.

"Have you married since Trent and Catherine's wedding?" he blurted out, inwardly wincing at the demanding tone.

"Nope. Not ever going there," smiled Brenna, emphasizing the ever. "I'm going to leave all that to Catherine and Raina. Do you remember Raina, my youngest sister?"

"A teenager with platinum hair? Extremely pretty?"

"She's now seventeen going on thirty-seven," Brenna laughed. "Some people are born old. Raina is one of those. Grand-mother used to say her soul was old and fully developed when she was born. And her bossiness was also fully developed at birth, with the intellect to back it up. That girl could organize the country easily. And talk everyone into gladly helping her do it."

"I knew someone like that," Deke mused aloud, and then yawned. "Sorry," he apologized, and then yawned again.

"Sleep time for you. No, don't pull at the tubes, I'm moni-toring electrolyte imbalances. That one is going into a vein for intravenous feeding. Deke, are you awake enough to under-stand?"

"Yes. Sorry, I didn't know what they were. I felt a tugging on my arm. I'll be careful with them," he promised sleepily.

69

"I'm going over to the Stone House to talk to Dr. Richardson, the obstetrician who will deliver Catherine's baby, but Sean or Liam will be here if you need anything. Also Dr. Richardson is a good friend of mine, and I may need to provide some protection for him from Trent's interrogation," she said half -jokingly.

Deke woke some time later to hear children's voices whispering. He knew that he had slept for awhile although daytime or nighttime did not seem to have any meaning at the moment. The slightest exertion put him back into sleep mode.

"Sh-h, Liam's gonna' hear us," cautioned the little girl voice.

"You're making more noise than me," whispered the little boy voice. "I'm the one being quiet," the boy voice insisted.

Deke opened one eye to peer at the two faces level with his head. The little girl was a curly haired blond with grass-green eyes like Brenna. The little boy had straight black hair and eyes that definitely had an Asian slant.

"Are you awake, mister?" the little boy asked in a stage whisper.

"Of course he's awake, silly. He's got one eye open, the other one is all swolled and purpled up."

"Hi, mister. I'm Douglas. This is my twin sister, Maggie."

"Hey," murmured Deke. "What are you two doing here?"

"We don't have anything else to do," shrugged Maggie. "Liam is supposed to be watching us, but he's talking on the phone to a girl."

"Everybody is all excited cause Catherine is in labor. That's what everyone says, in labor. Do you know what exactly that means?" asked Douglas.

"I told you it means the baby girl in Catherine's tummy is gonna come out." Maggie placed both elbows on the bed and stared intently into Deke's good eye. "Do you know exactly how she gets out of there?"

The twins were so serious Deke tried hard not to laugh out loud. "I'm not sure how she gets out of there," he lied. There was no way in hell he was going to have that conversation.

"See, I told you he wouldn't know either," Maggie told

Douglas with disgust in her voice. "None of the men we've asked know, and Mrs. Searle won't tell."

"Maybe she doesn't know either," said Douglas in a solemn tone.

"What's your name, mister? Are you the same guy who was in the wedding with us?"

Deke nodded slightly, his head beginning to ache at the twin's rapid-fire speech.

"Then your name is Deke Paxton. We never heard the name Deke before. You don't look much like that guy in the wedding," announced Maggie, her eyes narrowed almost closed for a better look.

"That's because he was beat up by some bad guys called thugs. I heard Sean and Liam talking. They brought him back from Colombia. In South America."

"I know where Colombia is, Doug. Remember Raina showed us on the map when we were looking up stuff for school. Do thugs look different from real people?" asked Maggie, her elbows still propped on Deke's pillow. "I've never seen a thug."

Before Deke could answer, a large red-haired man strode into the room. "Okay, you two. I've been looking everywhere for you."

"We weren't hiding. We're not supposed to hide. We were here all the time," stated Douglas firmly.

"And here is not where you're supposed to be." Touching Deke's shoulder, Liam said, "Glad to see you getting better. Remember me? Liam McKinney. We piloted together for our trip to Ireland last year. You've met my twin brother, Sean."

"Identical, absolutely identical," Deke said softly. He felt his eyes start to close in exhaustion. "Sorry, so tired," he admitted sleepily.

CHAPTER SEVEN

"Trent is now the father of a beautiful baby girl," announced Brenna joyfully. "Catherine is doing fantastic. The baby's tiny but gorgeous, with a mass of dark hair. Her eyes are the hazy blue of all babies but they're light. Trent insists she will have golden eyes like him."

Deke blinked, barely awake. The sheer elation in Brenna's voice was heart-warming. Trent had said before that the three sisters were exceptionally close. Deke could believe that as he heard the deep affection for her sister in her voice.

"Trent is over the moon," declared Brenna with a wide smile. "We thought he was a pain when he was besotted with Catherine, now he has two females to fuss over. When I left them, he was cooing, holding the baby and telling both of his ladies the depth of his love for them. I had to leave, getting all misty-eyed and gooey," she admitted.

"I've never seen Trent like that," Deke confessed. "He's the pragmatic, consummate businessman. Very driven and very focused. Of course I've only seen him a couple of times in New York since he married."

"He is a fuss-budget here," Brenna said, turning her back on Deke to put away some equipment. "When Catherine began to have Braxton Hicks contractions, Trent wanted the entire medical staff of Mayo Clinic's OB Department flown here to check her. He had a difficult time believing the contractions were false labor pains, even after I explained the difference between them. Raina calls him hover mother even to his face."

"Brave of Raina," Deke said softly.

"We don't know if Raina is brave or is just a walking force of nature. No one has had the nerve to challenge her most of her life, except for Kamon of course. Everyone calls her the little general," Brenna grinned. "Oh yeah, you've had a multitude of visitors while you've slept for the last several days. Kamon, Raina, Liam, Sean, Mrs. Searle, most of the members of the Sgnoch Council, even the young twins, Maggie and Douglas have been here."

"I've been dead to the world, no pun intended. I think I remember who everyone is except Mrs. Searle. I know vaguely of the Sgnoch Council from last year's fracas with Gavin O'Neill."

"Mrs. Searle is the housekeeper and looks out for Catherine. The Sgnoch Council is a group of leaders who run all the clan business. Something like a tribal council or a Board of Directors."

"I remember Trent saying he had to gain permission from the clan council for our little interlude with O'Neill. The rest? You know I'm lost, don't you?" Deke offered, lifting an eyebrow in amusement. "Trent says we're not in Kansas anymore."

"Too true," Brenna admitted. "Trent told us a little of you, Bob and himself growing up in Las Vegas. How much freedom you three little boys had, doing whatever your fertile imaginations could conceive. If you can imagine the absolute complete opposite in every aspect, you have the childhood of kids raised here in Shadow Valley. The only thing in common is that there is lots of freedom to explore."

"Truth to tell, I can't imagine living within a normal family, or what I always thought of as a normal family. We grew up making choices I shudder to think about now. We had a fun childhood. Trent had the only parent that gave the three of us any supervision, and his mom was young and single." Changing the subject, Deke commented, "Trent said this was a close community with little overindulgences. The last four or five years I've tried to outrun most of my excesses," Deke said wryly.

"Truth be told, I think that's why I took such an instant dislike to you last year," commented Brenna. "I work with an International Medical Aid Society who's guiding tenant is that any life is a precious gift. You seemed to be the antithesis of everything I striven for. You didn't seem to care about your own life, as if it held little value to you. And nothing could've make me angrier."

"Its pretty much true - that's the way I felt, although this knock on the head has made me reevaluate some of my priorities."

Frowning, Brenna interrupted, "Deke, I spend my life, all my life, trying to heal people. It seemed to me that you were wasting yours and quite frankly, it just infuriated me to the point that I couldn't even be nice to you."

"You judged me without any facts whatsoever," Deke said with unexpected anger. "You have no idea of who or what I am. Or of any of my past which has affected my decisions."

"To me, excuses are excuses are excuses. I have no patience with what I consider a lack of moral judgement. Out of us sisters, the Creator gave Catherine all my patience and I have little to none, especially with people who are idiots. And who continue to be idiots, not bothering to learn from life's lessons. I think people are responsible for themselves and their families. Period. End of story."

"That's a damn narrow viewpoint," Deke said hotly, wincing a bit as he lifted his head to better meet her eyes. "And face it, you live in a fantasy world. You have no idea what real life is like. You've been shielded from reality growing up here with a loving family."

"Bull! I'm twenty-eight years old and have been a physician with International Aid in the third world since I was in my early twenties. That means I've seen maimed children that will die of untreatable injuries. Bloody wars where no one wins and the horrific injuries are permanent. The aftermath of hurricanes and tsunamis that destroy everything in its path leaving people homeless and loved ones missing. And widespread gnawing hunger that haunts your very soul. So don't give me that crap," Brenna retorted furiously.

"Whoa, whoa," chided a large, dark-complexioned man as he entered the room. "We've gone to an awful lot of trouble to bring Deke here for you to kill our patient now," he told Brenna with dark dancing eyes.

Putting out a hand for Deke to clasp, he introduced himself.

"Kelly Pierce. You certainly look better today. Brenna has a tendency to fight first and listen later," he smiled. "She did not learn the lessons of tolerance and serenity that Grandfather Youngblood tried to teach her. All other lessons she could master, but that one completely eluded her," he teased, lightening up the tense atmosphere.

"You're right," Brenna apologized again. "Grandfather would be most unhappy with me." Turning to Deke she said, "Sorry, I'll get off my soapbox. I do lean toward brawl first and express regrets later. And yes, it's true that you're getting better. I'd never argue with you this much otherwise."

Deke frowned at Kelly. "It's okay, at least I felt alive. That's something I'm deeply grateful for."

He had seen Kelly Pierce at a distance at the wedding the year before. Now he took his time to study him as he had done so many times when he had worked for law-enforcement. Kelly Pierce must be in his mid to late forties, about six foot three or four, large frame with no lack of muscle, in great physical shape. Long black hair pulled back and tied with a leather thong at his nap. Dark complexioned, but part of that might be from the sun. Black eyes and the high cheek-bones of the Native American. Deke didn't recognize any particular aspects of a given tribe. Good looking if you liked the very masculine outdoor type.

Kelly asked quietly as Deke studied him. "DEA or FBI?"

Chuckling, Deke said, "Both. After the sheriff's office. I kept moving. How did you know?"

"You went through the same maneuvers of all of us who have been there. Welcome back to the living, by the way."

"Thanks. I remember little of Colombia and whatever happened. I hope you will fill me in further. Trent has told me what happened."

"Kamon will be over later to do that in detail."

"Well, I'm forever in your debt. I hear I have you and some others to thank. I remember almost nothing about Columbia, so I hope someone will give me some prompts of all the people's names. I need to express my gratitude."

"Actually, you have mostly Brenna to thank. You wouldn't have made it otherwise," Kelly said honestly. "We got you out which was rather exciting, but she kept you from dying."

"Okay, okay. I'm wonderful but your medical assistance was a major help," Brenna laughed uncomfortably. "Oh, Kelly, have you seen the baby? They're naming her Alexandra Ramsey. Isn't that pretty?" she gushed.

"I'm sure it will be shortened to Alex or Alexa in no time," Kelly replied with a slight smile. "And yes, I peeked in to see her, me and twenty others."

"Maggie is so disappointed. She thought the baby would be able to play with her and Douglas. She says and I quote "She just lays there doin' nothing 'cept eat and she sumtimes smells bad. It doesn't look like she's going to be much fun," Brenna mimicked the annoyance in Maggie's voice. "None of us realized that the twins have never seen a tiny newborn before."

"No babies here right now," murmured Kelly.

Turning to Deke, Brenna said lightly, "You've met the twins, I've heard. They told me you didn't know the intricacies of childbirth either. They seem to have asked all the people who didn't know 'how that baby got out of Catherine's tummy.' I sincerely wish you had told them something, because it fell to me to explain. Chicken?"

"Absolutely. How old are those kids? I felt like I had been tossed headfirst into a whirlwind," Deke grinned in remembrance. "The little curly-headed blonde changed subjects with each rapid breath she took.'

"They're almost five," Brenna answered. "They wear everyone out. Maggie's energy level is phenomenal, and Douglas keeps up with her. The only good thing is that they're not triplets!"

Changing her tone, she said, "Let's see if we can get you up today. I know we've sat you up several times with help but today maybe you can stand on your own."

Deke pushed himself up to a setting position all the time expecting head pain. There was none, just some neck stiffness. His face lit up with pleasure, "My head doesn't hurt."

Brenna and Kelly exchanged pleased glances. Kelly touched Brenna lightly on the shoulder.

"Then you're ready," said Brenna. "Swing your feet slowly around until you're sitting on the edge of the bed. Slowly. Good. Now Kelly and I will be on each side of you to see if you can stand. Take it slow and easy."

Deke stood up gradually and straightened to his full height, which made him a little taller than Kelly. He was secretly delighted by that fact. He took a tentative step forward and felt his knees start to buckle.

"Whoa, big guy," Brenna cautioned. "Too fast, too soon. I promise that there will be someone to help you walk several times a day. We do not want to set your recovery time back however," she said as she and Kelly eased Deke back into bed. "Re-injures could set your progress back by weeks."

Deke nodded in agreement. Truthfully he was delighted to wait a few more days before falling on his ass in front of Brenna and Kelly.

"Goodbye Deke," Kelly Pierce said quietly, putting out his hand to shake. "You're on the mend now, so I've been asked by International Medical Aid to return to Haiti. Brenna needs to stay here for now, both for Catherine and you. Liam's flying me out to finish our medical stint. They're always short-handed and we made a commitment. I'm looking forward to seeing you in about four weeks or so."

Placing a casual hand on Brenna's arm, he said firmly, "I know you love filling in for Dr. Farrison as a locum tenens, even for a very short time. You'll be close to Kamon and Shadow Valley if you require anything, otherwise I wouldn't go. Remember though that you have promised you will take extra care of yourself at Spring Creek."

"You know I never break my word, Kelly. I'll be fine. I've spent quite a bit of time there so the people know me. You take care. See you when you get back," she smiled as she turned away.

If Deke hadn't been focusing on Kelly, and wasn't a trained observer, he would have missed the fleeting sad smile as Kelly turned and left the room. Sad to return to Haiti, sad to relinquish his bodyguard duties, or sad to return without Brenna?

"If you're up to it, you have a visitor from the Sgnoch Council," Brenna told Deke breaking into his thoughts. "You know that the Sgnoch Council had to give Trent permission for you to be here."

"I know and am grateful. I'd like to meet them."

"Just him. The Council has sent Mr. MacPherson to talk with you as its representative." She went to the doorway and said, "Mr. MacPherson, Deke would like to meet you."

Deke could hear a cultured Scottish voice reply, "Ach, lassie. I hear that you've done another outstanding job, but you be careful, you hear? Sometime Shadow Work must be done, but we don't want to lose you. You know how we all feel about you."

"You're a sweetheart and I will," Brenna grinned, her dimple deepening. "Mr. MacPherson, Deke Paxton."

Mr. MacPherson was a tall, slim, partially grey haired gentleman sporting a neat van dyke beard. He was dressed in casual but expensive slacks, and a light blue cashmere pullover.

"How do you do, sir," Deke greeted the older man.

"Very well and I do thank you for asking," replied the older gentlemen formally.

"How do I rightly thank you for your assistance, sir, for saving my life? By sending your people, airplane, and then by bringing me here for Dr. Ramsey to treat?"

Mr. MacPherson waved away the thanks with a graceful gesture. "We were glad to be of service to one who has also helped us. Your valuable assistance last year in disbursing O'Neill was much appreciated. On to another subject. Your friend Trent told you that before you came here the Sgnoch Council had to give their approval. How much do you know about the Council?"

"Next to nothing," Deke admitted. "My only information is in bits and pieces and so far none of it makes much sense."

Brenna chimed in, "It will make less sense to you after you know."

Instead of frowning at Brenna as Deke had expected, Mr. MacPherson gave a hint of a smile. "You know that Catherine is from a long line of hereditary clan women with Second Sight. She is also the chosen leader of this matrilineal matriarchal clan." He stopped to allow Deke to absorb the information.

"I knew that she had the gift of precognition. I'm not sure I know the difference between matrilineal and matriarchal."

"The simple answer is that matriarchal is like a family or tribe led by a female, while matrilineal is how property is passed down through the female line rather than the male line."

"Some of the Native American and South American tribes I know of are matrilineal, I believe," Deke said, attempting to follow. "The female owns the land and it goes to her oldest daughter when she dies."

"Yes. It works a little differently here as we are a mix of Scottish and Native American mostly, with some Celt mixed in along with a touch of Druid, and other nationalities. Scots have always chosen their clan leaders. Sometimes those leaders were female. The people of this clan can choose either a male or female clan leader, but the lineage is through the female line."

"It's really two completely separate issues, clan leadership and hereditary lineage. Probably it is more confusing in that Catherine is also a Seer. People with Second Sight are very rare indeed. The Sgnoch Council are the elected advisors to the clan leader representing different alliances and aspects of the clans."

Brenna jumped in, "Good grief, Mr. MacPherson. The way you explained it doesn't even make sense to me and I've lived it. Deke is here with permission of the Council. We all knew that he would learn who and what we are. Trent swore him to secrecy before he married Catherine. We must trust him still. Agreed?"

"Yes, although as Sean says I don't like to admit I can be obtuse," he smiled, stroking his well-trimmed goatee.

"Duly noted," she replied with affection in her voice. "Simply put, Catherine is the chosen leader but decisions are made by the Sgnoch Council. Nine people are elected and sit as commissioners, but each clan with allegiance owed to this clan chooses their own representative. Recently some of us have held proxies of other commissioners. Is that clearer?"

"Not much," admitted Deke. "May I ask questions?"

"Yes, we will answer if at all possible," Mr. MacPherson responded.

"Then Alexa Angelenos will not be the clan leader unless she is chosen."

"Right, although her legal name is Alexandra Ramsey as the Ramsey women do not legally take their husband's last names. Female children always remain Ramsey's. Male children take their father's name."

"Wow. Just the Ramsey line or everyone who lives here?"

"Thank goodness it's just the Ramsey's line," smiled Mr. MacPherson. "It's hard enough to keep clan associations straight. The Council would have more confusion than it does now."

"Do you two sit on the council? Do I know any council members?"

Brenna answered. "Mr. MacPherson is a valuable member on the Council. Kelly is also a commissioner who holds the proxies of several associate clans. As do I. Raina is a recent addition after the passing on of our beloved Grandfather Youngblood. Have I left out anyone Deke has met?" she asked Mr. MacPherson.

"Kamon Youngblood. He gave Catherine away at her wedding in lieu of your grandfather. Kamon is Catherine's ceann-cath. All the way back in time Scots have sometimes chosen females or young people as their leaders for a multitude of reasons."

"Because we're smart," stage whispered Brenna, grinning impishly. "And mean."

Mr. MacPherson gave her a mock frown. "When a female was chosen or there was succession by blood of a young person, it often meant that the newly chosen clan chief would not necessarily be physically able to lead the clan into battle. Thus a warrior was chosen as second in command, a ceann-cath. Kamon is Catherine's ceann-cath, like a commander or war leader. He planned and executed your retrieval, for want of a better word, from South America."

"And the hereditary part?" queried Deke.

"Ownership is passed through the female. During times of war and times of peace, men are more likely to die. Passing ownership through the female line assures the clan of continuation and continuity. Women bear children which add to the clan, and the prolongation of the line. It makes sense in a very pragmatic way."

"I've known several women that are unbelievably strong in spirit," admitted Deke. "Stronger than their male counterparts."

"Females seem to have a special depth," agreed Mr. MacPherson. "My Alma is exceptional."

Deke thought a moment then asked. "How do I thank all these people? Especially the Sgnoch Council? Trent told me that without their permission it would have been difficult, if not impossible, for him to rescue me."

"They'll be around to see you now that you are awake. We are delighted to have been able to do you service," Mr. MacPherson said formally.

"May I ask another question?" Deke asked, putting his fist over a sudden yawn.

"Tomorrow," promised Brenna.

"But...,"

"Tomorrow. You're making sense, but you still have a long way to go for complete recovery. And your speech is beginning to slur. Time to nap," she advised as she and Mr. MacPherson left the room giving him no choice.

CHAPTER EIGHT

The next time Deke woke up, it was dark in the room except for a small night-light over the desk. The silhouette of a man sat in the corner recliner.

Deke studied him for a moment before the man looked up. Tall, although not as tall as Kelly Pierce or he was. Slim, late twenties and dark good looks. Two thin white scars slashed an eyebrow and ran down to his cheek. Kamon Youngblood.

"You okay?" asked Kamon in a deep-voiced whisper. "Feel up to talking for awhile?"

"Yeah, I've slept so much that I feel numb. Sort of out of it. My body is better but I admit my mind is woozy."

"Brenna insisted that you sleep as much as possible to help you heal. If your body is better, that's great. I'm Kamon Young-blood, in case you don't remember."

"Deke Paxton. A very grateful Deke Paxton. I have no memory of my landing in Colombia and whatever else took place afterward. Brenna says I may never remember much of the details. That's mostly normal with head injuries she says. Thanks for your help in getting me out of there."

"No thanks needed. We were all glad to be able to return the favor. Your help in taking out Gavin O'Neill makes us all still in your debt."

"That was totally enjoyable. He was pond scum, as a friend's young daughter says."

"Pond scum. I like that," Kamon grinned.

"I wanted to ask before I forget, is the Maggie who visited me the Maggie that O'Neill wanted to kidnap?"

"Yes. Maggie is O'Neill's biological daughter. He killed his wife, our cousin Diane, in a fit of rage. He convinced the county jury that it was accidental and served only three years in prison.

He wanted to kidnap either Maggie or Catherine, although any member of the Sgnoch Council would have sufficed."

"Maggie is unique," smiled Deke. "She visited me and has turned my perception of young kids upside down."

Kamon laughed. "She does that to us every day. Douglas keeps her on track part of the time."

"Douglas told me they were twins."

"They were born on the same day, near the same time, to two different sets of parents. You know about Maggie's mother and father. Douglas was sent here by his parents after his first birthday. They died as martyrs in a war where to flee would have been worse for their countrymen than death. They are heroes in their country, but they knew that Douglas was special, so they sent him here before their war collapsed around them."

Deke mulled over the twin's background then said, "No wonder they're so special. I had an another visitor today, at least I think it was today. Mr. MacPherson. He told me that you are the war leader of this clan."

"Among other things. The Council has decided that you need to be told of our beginnings, otherwise nothing else is going to make sense to you. We know that Trent has told you some of our background. I hope to fill in some blanks and I may repeat things you've already been told."

"I'd appreciate that. I do feel much like Trent said once, that I've fallen down Alice in Wonderland's rabbit hole."

"That sounds like Trent. The Sgnoch Council gave him a bad time when he first came here. We had to make sure that he could handle information that has been secret for two hundred fifty plus years."

Deke didn't know what to say so he remained silent.

"Another good choice," murmured Kamon. "I'll make the story as brief as possible. Long ago, a young woman with Second Sight saved a group of Scottish Highland clan leaders whose Unchangeable Destiny was written in the Tablet of Time. In gratitude for preserving their history and preventing chaos, they invoked ancient vows. Those vows were of the spirits of our mystical ancestors to give her and her progeny the Gifts the Creator had bestowed on them, forevermore. They also swore to protect her and her blood as her Swords and Shields. And to keep those vows made secret going forward through time. Death is the fate of betrayal."

Deke felt a shiver run up his spine at Kamon's matter-of-fact words.

Kamon paused for several moments then continued, "The young girl-woman Saw that it was only a matter of time, a few short years in fact, before another war with England would change the Highlands, the clans, and all things Scottish. Before the battle of Culloden, a contingency of people was selected to emigrate to the New World. They chose to travel to the port of New Orleans, and then trekked up the Mississippi River through its tributaries to the Ozark Mountains, and then to what is now Shadow Valley."

"Culloden was the Jacobite uprising in the mid 1700's? Right?"

"Yes, I'm surprised you know that."

"I took classes in history, thinking I wanted to go into Law, but changed to law enforcement," Deke explained. "Then … if they traveled to the Ozark Mountains at that time, it must have been very difficult."

"Their journals say it was a challenge, but they needed the isolation to protect the clan members. And they came up from New Orleans using mostly the Mississippi River and its tributaries, making the trek a safer journey than the alternative. Then on to Sky Mountain to create a very private community here in Shadow Valley.

"Then all of Shadow Valley is secret? Why here?"

"As to why, many reasons. These mountains are similar to the Highlands of Scotland. The land here can be harsh, brutally cold in winter and hot in the summer. The craggy peaks and little valleys, the dense forests and rocky cliffs are much like that of the home of our ancestors. Wildlife and fish were plentiful here. Shadow Valley is a vast tract of thousands of acres of land with a shallow valley on the side of a mountain range. Mild winds run along the base of the mountain making the valley warmer than is normal, almost a banana belt. Even at the present time, this part of the Ozark Mountains is sparsely populated. And all of this valley is now designated a Wild Life Preserve which keeps people out."

"I'm speechless. I'm not sure what questions to ask. In my travels I've had the opportunity to see things and experience more things that I always thought impossible. I'm in awe that this enclave has remained a secret for so long," Deke admitted. "How has the valley not been discovered?"

"For the first hundred years or so, isolation and intermarriage with the locals was the key. Scots have always married into the local inhabitants. In this case, Woodland Native American tribes, and later Choctaws and Cherokees with other tribes mixed in. Few roads and even fewer inhabitants from the outside world came to this area. Almost no Europeans."

"The majority of people who emigrated from Europe came into the eastern coast of the United States. The Scots came into New Orleans, Louisiana, the southern part of what is now the United States. It was a small harbor with tributaries leading up the Mississippi River so most of the trip was river-based. France owned it at that time. France gave the Scots a land grant that was later ratified with the Louisiana Purchase."

Kamon grinned. "The Scots are a hardy people and some of the first survivalists. When the new country started to open up to trappers and hunters, the main routes of travel did not come across this part of the Ozarks. The difficulty of travel in the densely wooded areas and hilly terrain played a large part in keeping Shadow Valley undiscovered. Even during eighteen hundreds into the nineteen hundreds, the Ozarks were pretty remote and the journey difficult. Electricity did not come to all parts of the Ozarks until the Second World War, in the 1940's and 50's. With air travel, staying hidden became a problem. It was solved with our own airport and some very fancy technology."

"No local cities? Or people?"

"A few people and small villages, now small towns." Kamon paused for a moment. "It helps that most of the people who live in the neighboring towns are Scot-Irish-Native Americans. Hill people. A large number of local residents have long-ago family ties to the clans. They are cliquish people with a hearty distrust of outsiders. They have often been the subject of rude, ignorant, disparaging remarks made by outsiders. So they now have a well-deserved reputation of being inhospitable and suspicious of strangers, as Trent found out when he first came here. Getting personal and private information from a local is damn near impossible."

Kamon gave a heartfelt sigh. "Once you can accept that the Creator can, and does, bestow Gifts and talents on a few people for whatever reason, it makes a little more sense. Not equitable, but true nonetheless."

"Life is not fair, I know that also from experience," Deke acknowledged. "One of my favorite individuals died of colon cancer last year after a four-year battle. He was one of the nicest, most giving individuals I've ever known."

"Yeah," agreed Kamon. "Being born a certain way, poor, or handicapped, or with abusive parents, or any of the reasons that make life hard or painful is unfair. Grandfather always said that whoever thought life was fair was an idiot."

Deke remained silent, thinking of his own abusive alcoholic parents. "I spent many a night on either Trent's or Bob's couch during my own childhood," he admitted.

"My early background was similar. Deke, there are many Gifts that the Creator grants people. Some have more intelligence, others beauty, or being able to get along with people, or common sense, or a love for children or animals, and a host of other special abilities. People take those gifts for granted. This particular group is unique in that some of us were raised to accept and become disciplined in whatever rare or unique gift we were lucky enough to receive. We do Shadow Work. However, we did not choose to be as we are. The Creator chose. We did not."

Both men let the minutes tick off in silence. Finally, Deke asked, "Do all the people that live here have special abilities, like Catherine?"

"No, only a handful. Very, very few. As I mentioned the valley here is called Shadow Valley. Here, along with a few other places in the world, is a haven for clan people who, for whatever reason, need to be protected. Some, like Catherine, need it as a permanent base while others may need a respite for a short time. Whoever needs to be protected is protected here."

"Does that include witches and warlocks? I met some people in Africa who do downright spooky things with dolls and such."

"No, black magic can only be practiced using the back door for Spirit entrance. The original Sgnoch Council set down some fundamental rules for this particular clan to live by. The rules that were set must be followed in order to continue a pure line like the Ramsey's. I would rather not go into those. If there is ever a need, you will be told."

Kamon paused to make sure Deke was still following his history lesson then continued, "The Scots who came here inter-married with the Native Americans who were here, and who also had a clan system at least as old as the Scots and Celts. There was an intermingling of the two groups so that this clan is different in many aspects than those in other places. Not a Scottish clan, not a Native American clan, but a Scottish-Native American tribal clan."

"Trent said that Catherine can only leave for a short time as there's too much stimuli for her in other places," Deke related.

"Catherine needs serenity and harmony. She's a direct descendant of the first girl-woman with Second Sight. Apart from that she is the chosen clan leader."

Deke thought for a moment and then asked, "Brenna and Raina are her sisters which means they also must be direct descendants. I know that Brenna leaves here for extended lengths of time. She doesn't have Second Sight?"

"No, Brenna is not a Seer. And that's all I will tell you about her. Each of us is only allowed to talk about our own Gift from the Creator. Discussing another person's special gifts or a lack of gifts is forbidden."

"And you? Are you a Seer? Do you have special gifts, as you call it?" asked Deke not expecting an answer from the taciturn man.

An amused smile animated Kamon's face. "No, I do not have Second Sight." He paused for a moment. "Are you familiar with thought transference?"

"I'm not sure. I think it's reading of the mind, right? Or something close to that."

"Essentially. I have been blessed, and plagued with my gift. I was born with the ability to walk around in people's minds." He held up his hand to block any interruptions. "Grandfather Youngblood trained me and disciplined me how, and when, to use it. I do not enter into minds without permission anymore than I would enter into your private home. And I must have the Council's permission to use my gift here in Shadow Valley."

"I'm having a difficult time absorbing all of this," Deke admitted shaking his head. "I'm positive I don't want to know what other people are thinking. Or planning."

"As in most things, there are positives and negatives. It was a tremendous help for undercover strategic intelligence in government work. It does get uncomfortable sometimes, however."

"I can understand how that would be helpful in intelligence gathering," Deke grinned. "I've often wondered what my criminal opponent was thinking. Although sometimes it was probably so bad I wouldn't have wanted to know."

"That's certainly true. But you are born with what you are born with. I know that there have been Mind Walkers throughout Native American history and in other societies, even Jung and Freud understood that they existed. Being a Mind Walker has deficits," Kamon related with a shrug. "Lately, one of the two most difficult times for me was with your friend Trent. For us, a mate for Catherine is essential for the survival and lineage of the clan. We needed someone of equal strength as they would bond with each other. We knew Trent had the strength of mind and will, but we had to make sure he would be able to live with a mate so different from the ordinary. And one so tied to Shadow Valley."

"And you found what his lifelong friends already knew - that Trent is a unique individual."

"Yes, he is the other half of Catherine. As time has passed, we've all come to realize that he completes her, fills in the undeveloped side of her personality. They're both strong personalities but in very different ways."

"The other time?" Deke asked wanting to know more about the tough-appearing man he was beginning to admire.

"That's an ongoing problem with Raina. She is going to drive me completely insane by the time I'm thirty!" Giving a shake to his head as if to clear it, Kamon continued, "When I was much younger and somewhere else, I caused a great deal of trouble by speaking of what was in other people's heads. Grandfather Youngblood became my mentor and spent hours, days, and months teaching me the ethics and morals of the Native American Mind-Walker."

Kamon smiled slightly, "He was also all three sister's teacher to learn ethics, patience and living in harmony. Catherine learned the lessons well and lives within those boundaries. Brenna learned the ethics parts too well and skipped the other lessons entirely. She learned next to nothing about being mild-tempered and remaining unruffled as I think you've already discovered. And Raina! Well, Raina is so head-strong that she does as she damn well pleases, whenever she damn well pleases. And with Grandfather gone, refuses to listen to me."

Deke was taken back by the intense emotion in Kamon's voice when he talked of Raina.

Kamon abruptly stood, as if the conversation was pushing him to physically move. "Do you have pressing questions now, or can everything else wait until another time? You're free to ask me anything you want as long as it doesn't infringe on others. Okay?"

"Yes, thank you for coming. You've given me much to think about. These new truths in my mind is going in circles. Oh, may I ask one more thing before you go?"

"Of course."

"I'm still struggling to understand how this valley has remained secret. I think that's harder to understand than that a few of its people having special gifts. People have had special abilities throughout history. Even the Bible speaks of it, but a secret valley? Surely someone told someone else. Or no?"

"I can only speak for this generation and the last. And this is a repeat of what I said before. There are probably a few local rumors about Shadow Valley, but these are pragmatic hill people with a great deal of common sense. I'm sure that some of them have decided that its best to mind their own business, which hill people are famous for. If it doesn't directly affect them, they pretty much ignore it. Many people know that an old bunch of Scots and Native Americans live here, and the area is a wildlife sanctuary. None are aware that a pure line still exists. Those locals who have any knowledge of the valley understand some of our history. And all of *those* know how utterly ruthless a Scot can truly be when it comes to protecting what's theirs."

Touching Deke on the shoulder Kamon said, "Liam is sleeping in the back part of the clinic if you have a problem. I talked Brenna into going to sleep in her own room tonight. Oh, and Deke, please ask someone to assist you when you walk at night."

"Thought you said you don't walk around in people's minds without permission," Deke said irritably.

"I normally don't but…, I don't know how to explain this. Your brain right now is open to me, probably because of all the intense work Brenna has been doing. I do apologize and will try to block you out from now on."

Deke nodded in acknowledgment of the apology. "What do you mean about the intense work Brenna has been doing? Oh, and do you know what happened to my airplane?"

Kamon thought for a moment. "Brenna's work is not mine to tell, and your airplane is in a hangar safe in Colombia. Anything essential you need from it?"

Deke nodded. "There's a laptop computer and some flash drives. A duffle bag of clothes and some shoes. Later maybe you could send them to me."

"Not a problem. I'll see to that."

CHAPTER NINE

The next week passed quickly for Deke. Liam had made a special trip to Fortuna to get Deke some clothes since he was taller and slimmer even than Kelly. He also bought shoes and toiletry articles. Sean and Brenna had ragged on Liam about wanting to go to Fortuna three times a day since he had a lady of interest there. Deke was both amused and envious of the lighthearted comradery between them. With the exception of Trent and Bob, there was no one whom he had a close relationship with.

There had been a slew of visitors to the clinic to talk with Deke. Everyone wanted to ask about his stints in South America, or to just while away the time and keep him company. He had spent quite a lot of time talking to Liam and Sean, mostly about flying, and found them to be technologically astute beyond his understanding. They had modified all their airplanes, but then had branched out to include anything electronic that Catherine had thought of. Their vast knowledge about airplanes and mathematical modifications was both stimulating and intimidating. He admitted to himself that even if he didn't fully understand all their mathematical formulas and how they had derived certain answers, it was exciting to know about the modifications they were involved with.

Even Catherine visited, trailed by Trent carrying the tiny newborn baby cuddled to his chest. Deke lied and told Trent how beautiful Alexandra was when in truth he agreed with the young Maggie, she was red, wrinkled, and sleeping. The new parents beamed though, which was the exact point of the lie.

And he spent hours talking with Brenna.

Sometimes the talk was about his injuries, but most of the

time it was about everyday happenings of Shadow Valley and their own backgrounds. Deke was intrigued by the self-sufficiency and ingenuity of the people living in the remote valley. He hoped he would be able to visit the community stores she had talked about and the outlying farms before he left.

Deke had first used a wheelchair, but now he moved slowly on a metal walker. It wasn't a pain-free experience, but he could feel his body's increased energy level rise each day. 'No pain, no gain' was what the old high school football coach had said. True or not, Deke felt better as he pushed himself to do a little more exercise each day.

He stood slowly, shaking his head at John that he didn't need assistance. John Summerton was a large seventeen-year-old who had been drafted by his great-uncle, John McDougal, to help Brenna with Deke's recovery. The young man had fallen head over shoe-tops for Brenna and therefore couldn't do enough to help her with Deke. He also stuttered whenever Raina came within viewing distance, so his smitten behavior could also be a symptom of teenage hormones.

Deke couldn't decide if the entire matter was funny or pitiful. After multiple scenes where the young man's face had become red, his tongue tied in knots, and he stumbled over his own feet, Deke had decided pitiful described it best.

He had to admit the young man had good taste in women though. Brenna with her lithe figure, fiery hair, and quick temper contrasted sharply with Raina's platinum hair, perfect features, and poised self confident beauty. Neither woman seemed to be aware of their looks nor did they try to enhance their appearance with facial make-up or showy clothes.

Brenna almost danced into the room with a huge smile on her face, "We're going to Spring Creek! Hurray! We've finally made all the arrangements for me to take Dr. Farrison's practice for a few weeks."

"We?" asked Deke, raising an eyebrow in question.

"Yep, we. As in us," she pointed a finger at John, Deke and herself. She smiled broadly at John, "That is if I can persuade

John to go with us for an overnight jaunt. It will be for only one night. Raina will pick you up in the little helicopter the next morning," she told John. "Deke, you will stay with me at Spring Creek until you are well enough to go wherever you want."

"Yes," John finally answered, stammering. "For however long you need me. And Raina. I'll be glad to. Yes."

"Thank you so much, John. I really appreciate it. It will just be overnight for me to get settled, and to transition Deke onto crutches or a cane. Kelly will be back soon. He's never gone long."

As Deke scowled at her, she said, "Seriously, Deke, the only way I feel comfortable about your care is if I treat you for the next week or so. After that, you will be pretty much on your own to do whatever you wish."

"Excuse me, Brenna, but when do we leave?" asked John, interrupting. "I'll need to go home and pack some clean clothes."

"Tomorrow morning. Sean's going to take us down in the little copter. Spring Creek is just a hop and jump over the mountains. And so far it's planned that Raina will pick you up and fly you back."

"You're going to work for someone?" asked Deke. "As a physician? Where is Spring Creek? How far?"

"Yep. Spring Creek is the nearest town, just down the valley from us. I fill in for Dr. Farrison whenever I can. He's a specialist in Family Practice and is a great guy. This time he's taking his grandson to see medical schools where the young man may apply. Dr. Farrison's so proud that his grandson wants to apply in the United States and follow in his footsteps," she beamed at the two men. "I think you might especially understand why I'm so excited, Deke. I see your eyes light up when you talk of flying. It's the same for me with medicine. It gets under your skin and there's a large part of who I am that's tied to my craft."

Deke felt as stunned as John looked. Damn, she was awesome. Smart, funny, and stunning. Her heart was so big. Wanting to help. A do-gooder, he reminded himself, willing his heartbeat to return to normal. That's all I would need, even if I could talk her into being interested in an old has-been, he lamented to himself. Been there, done that!

"Is it possible for me to see more of Shadow Valley today before I leave, Brenna? I may never have this chance again. I'm grateful for all you all have done and I'd like to understand more about this place you live in," asked Deke.

Brenna thought for a moment. "Let me check something," she said as she left the room.

She returned a few moments later. "Catherine has given you permission to see the Stone House, but I suggested that you wait until another time to visit the community stores. Trent says that he would like to be your tour guide. He says he wants for you to see the house in the way he did, whatever that means. You'll have time to explore before you completely wipe yourself out," she grinned. "I figure that pushing you around in a wheelchair will make you and Trent both cranky. Sorry the motorized one isn't here but someone borrowed it and it hasn't been returned to the valley yet. I should remember to order another one to have on hand."

"Do you want me to meet you here or at the airport in the morning?" asked John, glancing from Deke to Brenna, then down to his feet.

"Sean says here at the Stone House will be easiest," answered Brenna, ignoring John's blush. "Say about nine o'clock?"

"I'll be here. I won't be late. I promise." John assured Brenna. "I promise."

Brenna gave him a bright smile which brought another flush to the young man's face.

Deke shook his head in mute understanding. It had been forever since he had been that young and that self-conscious. If he ever had been.

"Ready?" asked Trent with a wide grin, entering the clinic. "Remember when I told you we weren't in Kansas anymore? Now I'm going to prove it."

Trent pushed the wheelchair around the side of the stone manor toward the front of the house. From the slate sidewalk, Deke could see a half dozen or so different size buildings seeming to form a half circle around the huge stone house. They were mostly rectangular in shape and made of river rocks, thick wooden green planks or a combination of both.

"Those buildings to your right are community stores," Trent said following the direction of Deke's gaze. "We can't go there today. Okay, now close your eyes. I want you to see the entire front of the house all at once like I did."

"You do know this is silly. don't you Trent? We're adults now, remember?" commented Deke, still dutifully shutting his eyes tightly as Trent pushed him forward. He could feel the wheelchair movements as it was turned around and stopped.

"Okay, open your eyes."

"Holy shit," Deke said aloud. "Holy, holy shit," he repeated, hearing Trent's laughter in the background.

Before him was a huge structure built of stone and spanning what looked like more than a city block. The three story house was built of rough stones and looked similar to a castle or a large manor house in the countryside of the United Kingdom. Except this structure was more rugged and chiseled. Wide grey slate steps led up to tall double doors made of thick timber with iron hinges.

Trent was still laughing. "I did tell you we weren't in Kansas anymore."

Deke was still staring at the massive stone house. "What in the hell is this house doing in the middle of nowhere? It's obviously old, probably more than two hundred years old." Turning back to Trent he asked, "Okay, now you have to tell me who built this and why."

"I can't tell you everything simply because I don't know some of it. I was told the Stone House, as it's called, was built in the early 1800's by ancestors of the people who live here now. This tribal clan, I mean. I can guess as to why. Probably for protection. And its size is probably because a lot of people lived inside it over the years. Catherine said that each generation changed some of the things to suit their various needs."

"Okay, there's no ramp on this side of the house so I'll pull you up backwards." Trent said as he slowly pulled the wheelchair up the wide steps. "Damn, you're heavy," he complained, "but I do want to take you on a tour of inside."

"Sorry, I'm heavy," grinned Deke. "The truth is I've lost a few pounds."

Trent opened the unlocked door and pushed Deke over the threshold. "Do not repeat your 'Holy shit' because you're going to be saying it every five minutes," warned Trent with a chuckle.

Deke stared at the huge entryway. The room was two stories high with exposed wooden beams. A massive wrought iron chandelier hung from the middle of the ceiling. Dual stairways of polished mahogany flanked the sides leading upward to unseen floors. Large silk banners, embroidered with ancient heraldic scenes of Scottish warriors hung on two walls. The other two walls were interspersed with long rifles, antique swords, and ancient pikes with assorted straight and curved blades.

The slate floors were covered in antique Persian rugs in muted jewel colors. Ornately carved side tables held artifacts ranging from a small silvered shield to what looked like priceless Chinese vases sitting alongside intricately woven Native American baskets and pottery. Massive mahogany double doors were set into each side of the highly polished wooden door casings.

"Ok, Trent. I won't say it, but I am thinking it," admitted Deke shaking his head.

"We're first going to take a quick tour of this floor all the way to the back where there's an elevator. I wanted you to see it like I did, so I did it the hard way," Trent grinned. "If a door is closed here, the rule is you can't enter. Everything else we can explore."

As Trent pushed Deke down the hallway, Deke noted that the hallway walls were of smooth river rock, although the floors continued to be smooth slate. They stopped at an open door and looked into a room with a small fireplace and several comfortable looking chairs. A closed door led to a side room. "Probably some guest apartment," Trent explained. "There's a lot of people who need to come here for a short time."

Deke had a hundred questions with the biggest one being who were these people? Why would anyone need to visit? Not want but need? Knowing that this was not an appropriate time to ask, he silently stored all his questions to ask someone later.

They peeked into a room with several musical instruments. A piano, a set of drums and several horn instruments set on stands. A golden harp with angel adornments was placed in the corner of the room. Most of the other open doors accessing the hall were of sitting rooms or offices. Each was decorated differently but with upscale antique furniture. Several hallways ran off from the central one.

Deke shared a long look with Trent but remained silent.

The hall had become wider and the walls were of some sort of wallpaper, but the floors were still of slate. Trent pointed to a closed door near the back of the house. "That's Catherine's old sitting room. Our apartment is on the second floor now until Kamon can finish our new house. The kitchen is to the right and the small dining room adjoins it. There's a larger formal dining room across the hall. I'll show you," he said pushing the wheel chair on to a side alcove.

Deke blinked but didn't say aloud the exclamation he was thinking. The dining room held a long antique table that could have easily seated thirty people. High-back cushioned chairs covered in petit point were clustered around the table. A buffet table with backset glassed cabinets rose to the ceiling. Inside the cabinets were sets of dishes and a plethora of different size stemware. The other side of the room held a long ornate library-type table with a heavy silver tea set and pullout drawers built almost to the floor.

"Good grief." Deke explained. "This place is better than any museum I've ever been in."

"Yep. And you haven't seen the best yet," warned Trent.

They briefly viewed the large kitchen where Mrs. Searle introduced Mrs. Sims as her helper. Here everything was very modern except for an eight burner black wood stove. Noting Deke's interest Mrs. Searle explained with a twinkle in her eye that she couldn't give it up because it cooked haggis well. Deke laughed along with everyone else, knowing that the savory Scottish dish made of the liver, heart, and lungs of sheep, and cooked with other ingredients was not a delicacy for most people.

Deke and Trent explored the other rooms near the kitchen. The 'little' dining room, as Trent called it, seated probably twelve people. It was only slightly less formal with silver chafing dishes for self service on the side tables. Most of the other doors were closed.

The elevator could easily be a duplicate of New York elevators in public buildings, large, modern, and smooth.

The first few rooms off the second floor hallway were closed. "That's Catherine's office and the communication center," Trent pointed to a closed door. "Unless there's a national emergency in which blood, or impending death occurs, she is not to be disturbed when she is working there."

Deke lifted an eyebrow in question to his friend, meaning Trent could explain his disgruntled statement or not as he chose.

"I'm still adjusting to Catherine's schedule," he explained with a wry frown. "She's only working for a couple of hours or so a day now because of the pregnancy. Brenna says it's good for her to be involved in work now, but I need to see her. To check to be sure she's all right."

Deke chose not to answer or comment. Trent and Catherine's past included a difficult time as they both compromised on living together part time.

"Now, the piece de resistance," smiled Trent. "This always makes me happy. Ta-da," he said with a flourish as he flung open wide double doors.

Deke couldn't contain his small gasp of surprise. A huge library with shelves of books two stories high. Here was a library that could easily have been in a well-endowed small university. The lower level held floor to ceiling bookcases. An upper level ringed the lower one and could be viewed from the lower level. Mahogany shelves on the lower level housed everything from small paperbacks to heavy dictionaries. Children's books took up an entire section, along with what looked like a multitude of text books. Bright covers seemed to be books from present day best-sellers. The center of the room was dominated with a collection of tables and chairs. Antique Persian rugs in jewel tones covered the highly polished wooden floors. Beveled window panes sat over window seats, half hidden by heavy drapes.

A circular stairway of wooden steps led to the upper level of the library. The second level was featured a mahogany-railed catwalk encircling the entire upper floor. Sliding ladders were visible along with wooden chairs and small tables. The floor to ceiling shelves held books that were mostly leather bound, massive and old-appearing. In the center bookcase was a leaded glass case with several small faded bound books.

"No way," exclaimed Deke. "What the hell, Trent? Who are these people? I could *live* in this library. Just bring me food and water. I won't even ask for a blanket." He let his eyes travel the room. "This is so unbelievable, that for me, it's hard to take in. Like something from a dream, Trent. Do you know why or even how this was built? In the middle of what must have been thousands of miles of wilderness back in the day?"

"I'll give you the same answer that was given me. The why is for protection. The how I have no idea. And I have little to no details on either one."

"There's nothing like this that I've ever seen. And I love libraries and museums."

"Bob and I can certainly attest to that. You dragged us to every museum or library in every city we have ever been in. Bob and I wanted to go bar-hopping to see if we could pick up girls and you wanted to go museum-hopping," Trent grinned. "And that ends our tour. There's more to see. There's a communication center that would blow your mind, and a craft center where I'm not sure what anything is. But my watch keeps vibrating which means its time for us to head back to the clinic. Brenna isn't the most even-tempered doctor I've ever known," he grinned, pushing Deke back toward the elevator.

Deke took a last lingering look at the library. Books were his addiction and had been ever since third grade when he discovered that libraries were free. With his folk's uncertain temperament after boozing it all day, libraries were safe havens. And the one here in what they called Shadow Valley was the best of the best.

Sean showed up the next morning to take them to Spring Creek in a small helicopter, landing on a green pad just beyond the clinic. Deke would have normally asked a million questions about the unusual flight deck, but between the drone of the engine and his restless night, fatigue overwhelmed him. He woke up as they were landing at a large, modern airport. A much larger, up-to-date airport than a small town would normally warrant.

A large SUV picked them up. The driver was introduced as Daniel Pimentel, 'a shirt-tail relative of John's', whatever the hell that meant. Deke thought it was sort of a cousin's cousin but he wouldn't bet the bank on it.

With John sitting in the passenger seat and visiting with the car's driver, Deke had a chance to ask about the unusual size of the airport. Brenna told him that Glenn Gowan, owner of a chain of big box stores with their main office in the nearby town of Fortuna, had fronted the money as a gift for the town. Somehow Deke felt that wasn't the whole truth.

Spring Creek looked like every other small mountain town, USA, that Deke had visited. A central square with government-type buildings in the center of a park surrounded by small country shops on opposing sides of the streets. The people looked to be casually dressed country people, most light skinned although a few had the darker skin hues of Native Americans.

Most people thought that all Native Americans looked alike. Because of his training as a sheriff in a desert county of Nevada, Deke knew that facial features were very different for each tribe and recognizable once you knew what to look for. He had been told that if you took a map of Europe and superimposed it upon the United States there was as much difference between tribes as there were between people from Portugal, Wales, Italy and Germany. Before the coming of the Europeans, large masses of land separated the tribes for many hundreds of years, allowing each tribe to become unique.

"I didn't realize this was Choctaw country," he murmured to Brenna beside him.

"Remember that this area was on the direct route of the 'Trail of Tears' of the Cherokee removal in President Jackson's time. There was a large group of Choctaw here at the time that helped some runaways, for want of a better word. Most now are mixed bloods between the two tribes and Scot-Irish," she related casually.

"I had forgotten that," Deke admitted. "If I ever knew it in the first place," he grinned.

"History hereabouts is alive and well. It's a way of connecting people. It also helps isolate the area where strangers are suspect," she added, smiling. "Most everyone hereabouts is related in some way, distant at least, to everyone else. Around here, Native-American-looking people may be more Scottish or Irish than the blue-eyed blond."

"Like Kamon and Kelly?"

"Uh huh," she responded idly, making no further comment. "We're here." She touched John Summerton's shoulder as she said, "John, if you'll help with the luggage, I'll get a wheelchair."

"I do not need a wheelchair," Deke said in irritation. "I can use the walker if I have to."

"You'll need a wheelchair, trust me. The clinic is up an incline, but we'll be staying further up in the cottage back of it," she refuted.

After a grueling fifteen minutes of John and the driver pushing the wheelchair around back of the clinic building up to a small house, Deke's teeth were clenched and he was exhausted.

"Who in the hell designed the area like this?" he said in annoyance as they skirted a large protruding boulder. "Couldn't they have made a straighter path?"

"Actually, I did," admitted Brenna, narrowing her eyes

slightly. "I did not expect for anyone to share my little home. I was looking for privacy and not interested in disturbing any of those wild rose old-growth patches." She said pointing at some bushes. "So I made the path a little challenging."

"This house is yours?" Deke asked pointing to the simple house built of logs.

"No, it isn't mine in the normal sense, except when I'm here. I don't own things. This house is for whatever or whoever's use that Dr. Farrison has for it. I built it. And maybe designed the pathway to be a little difficult, but I don't own it."

Deke stared at Brenna as she smiled with pleasure at the small house. She obviously loved the little house but did not choose to possess it for whatever reason. The concept of not owning things was the way he had lived for the last five years. Even the ranch in Texas was more his employees than his; he was seldom there. Nowadays if he couldn't fit his belongings in one duffle-bag, they were left behind. One duffle-bag with one laptop, one airplane and nothing else. It made life simpler. And sadder in so many ways.

A wooden porch wrapped around two sides of the house. Two wooden pine rockers and a wooden swing held up by heavy link chains occupied the covered area. Inside, the house consisted of a large living room area with an attached kitchen and two bedrooms with their own baths. The largest of the bedrooms had twin beds where he would share with John. Brenna took the smallest one with the double bed.

That evening, John Summerton left with Pimentel to see a local high school basketball game. Deke couldn't decide if that was a positive or negative event ... leaving a conflicted, irritable patient, himself, alone with Brenna.

CHAPTER TEN

As his wounds healed, he had become more and more aware of the strong physical attraction he felt toward Dr. Brenna Ramsey. Strong attraction had turned into fascination, and was now verging on obsession. He had tried to ignore it at first, and then to think it through in his normal logical fashion. She had saved his life. The age-old caveat of hero, or in this case heroine, worship could have been at work. Doctor-patient crushes were notoriously normal.   Unfortunately, he knew that wasn't the case. He found himself watching her at odd times, admiring the curve of her cheek, or the glow of her long coppery braided hair. Her green eyes with those dark lashes were fascinating. He even liked her quick fiery temper, and her equally rapid apologies. Everything about her was unique and exciting for him. It was not an entirely comfortable feeling.

"Okay, Deke. You've been sitting there for the last fifteen minutes glowering at me. What's the problem?"

Deke certainly couldn't tell her the truth – 'that you're becoming my fixation' - so he went with a half-truth.

"I'm healing and everything itches and I guess I'm irritable. And tired. Maybe I need something mindless. Is there television here?"

"Yes. Spring Creek has good reception. There is no television set here in this house, however. It's not one of my vices. I'll have one brought over tomorrow morning from the clinic. We do have music though. What would you like to hear? Any particular artist?"

Deke shook his head. "Truthfully, I like everything. I haven't heard much of any modern music or rap for the last five years so oldies work."

"Activate 7086. PrinWeb music please. Soft rock, volume low." Immediately the room was filled with surround-sound music of James Brown. "Okay"" asked a grinning Brenna, looking pleased.

"A voice-activated sound system?"

"A little more sophisticated than that. It's one of Catherine's toys that Liam and Sean modified, and then constructed into the building frame. Catherine has an affinity with machines, and Liam and Sean can't help but modify everything they touch. They always see a little different slant on whatever someone else thought of. They don't invent as much as they innovate every-thing, literally everything."

Brenna and Deke listened to the mellow sounds for several minutes before Deke couldn't stop himself from probing. "Do you always tackle everything head-on?" Deke asked seriously.

"Well, I do have a tendency to confront things," Brenna admitted, eyes twinkling in self deprecation. "Usually time is an important factor in my work. I also don't have any patience. I want things done yesterday, or at the very least in the next minute. Before you lecture me, I do know it's a major fault of mine. Everyone in Shadow Valley has tried to help me, but Grandfather Youngblood said I'll gain more moderation with time. For everyone's sake I hope so," she grinned sheepishly.

"Could I ask questions about the Valley or is that off limits? There's so much I don't know or that I'm confused about. You know I'm trustworthy."

"Let's make a pact. You can ask whatever you want, but I retain the right not to answer if I wish. No harm, no foul."

"That's fair." Deke thought for a moment, formulating what to ask. "Tell me about your ancestors, when they came here and why."

Brenna cocked her head to one side in thought, "No one knows exactly why, but probably for better food sources," she an-swered slowly. "The when is lost in antiquity but at least twenty-five thousand years ago. The big universities have carbon-dated wood used in a sandstone home on the Hopi reservation to that time period."

Deke blinked. He had expected to hear about the Scottish Highland migration. What in the hell?

Brenna didn't notice Deke's confusion as she continued. "The Woodland Tribes lived in the southern part of the United states. Food was plentiful with fish, game animals and farming of sweet potatoes and other crops."

"Excuse me Brenna," Deke apologized. "You're talking about Native people, right?"

"Of course. That's what you asked, or is that not right?" Brenna frowned in confusion.

Deke's mind raced to catch up. Brenna looked like she was a recent immigrant from Scotland with that bright auburn hair and green eyes, but her first bond was to her Native American blood. Intriguing. Fascinating.

Brenna gave a deep sigh. "I would guess life was pretty peaceful in this part of the world. A few skirmishes with neighboring tribes, a few raids. There were vast tracts of land between tribes so enemies could be avoided. Tribal clan systems were the social norm and the Woodland Tribes traded extensively. They intermarried and changed leadership affiliations. Sometimes even tribal associations."

"Sorry, but I don't understand what that means."

"Before the coming of the Europeans, Native American leaders were leaders only as long as they had people to follow them. No elections. No long term leader unless he was smart and trustworthy. When an individual or family decided they did not like the way the leader had decided an issue, they simply left and chose another band, or the group could choose another leader."

"I never thought of that," Deke admitted. "No wonder the white men had such difficulty figuring out leaders to sign treaties. Essentially the leadership was fluid."

"Right. Also Native Americans did not believe in land ownership. How could one person own a little piece of Mother Earth because of some words written on a paper they couldn't read or have words for? Or even concepts? They were unprepared for the materialistic avarice of the Europeans, first the traders, then the government."

Brenna's words had been spoken with passion, her eyes flashing a darker green. Deke struggled to keep his mind on the conversation rather than on Brenna's inner fire and passion. A passion that was quickly making him wish he had a lap covering.

"Most people think that Native American tribes get a monetary subsidy from the government," said Deke wanting to keep Brenna's words flowing.

"Most people are uninformed. Native Americans have *never* been subsidized unless we were in captivity, then they fed us. Well, sort of fed us. I do not want to spoil my evening as well as yours by going into the atrocities that were committed by both sides. If you're ever interested, pick up any book written by a Native American on how they see the history of the United States. Just make sure whom it's written by," Brenna cautioned. "The white man's history, and the native's history are very different. Grandfather used to say that the conquerors write the history, not the people who are subjugated."

"Brenna, you look like a Scottish national picture, yet your first identity was Native American. I'm trying to catch up here. What about the Scottish history?"

"Kamon said he told you the story of the first girl-woman to have Second Sight. Right?'

Deke gave a quick affirmative nod of his head.

"Our Scottish history is different. The when for us here in this mixed tribal clan as Scots is easy. Before 1745. Our ancestor was a Seer and Knew that the Highland people were going to go through some very rough periods. There would be more wars with England, famines, the destroying of the clans, etc. The decision was made to emigrate to America. Scots have emigrated to other countries many times over the centuries."

"Scots have emigrated to other countries besides America?" Deke asked to be sure he understood.

"Scots are adventuresome by nature. And they thrive on adventure so they went a'wandering, which for them was a time-honored tradition. For instance, one of the places Scots settled hundreds of years ago was in Nazere, Portugal. Following their usual pattern, they intermarried with locals and mingled their cultures. The men still wear the plaid at some festivals, but now in the shape of trousers."

"Lets see," Deke mused in a teasing voice. "Which would I be more comfortable in, trousers or kilt? Easy answer."

"Come on Deke. You have pretty legs," Brenna retorted teasing.

"You did notice then?" Deke's voice was serious.

Ignoring the last comment, Brenna continued, "I do identify more with the Native American, I guess. I never gave it much thought. I am mostly Scot, Celt and Native American but as I told you my mentor was Grandfather Youngblood. You met him last year at Catherine's wedding."

"And I thought he was one of the most interesting men I had ever been privileged to talk with," said Deke sincerely and then grinned. "He told me about the history of the Scottish tartan since Trent, Bob and I wore the plaid for the wedding," he explained referring to the wedding of Trent and Catherine the year before.

Both Brenna and Deke smiled at the irony of the seemingly Native American elder explaining the Scottish tartan.

"Grandfather Youngblood was my mentor in everything."

"And that means...," Deke let the sentence dangle.

"And that means we will finish this conversation at another time."

As Deke started to object, she added, "We've got all week and maybe more. Depends on how quickly you heal. Can you manage those crutches to get yourself to bed without help?"

"Been doing it for years," he mocked.

"I have a busy day tomorrow, so I'll say good night now. You should sleep pretty well after your long day" Smiling at him she left the room.

Deke got slowly to his feet, leaning on the crutches. Oh

yeah, he knew how to use crutches well. Law enforcement was a physical profession, and this was not the first injury he had sustained. He had thoroughly enjoyed being a part of the law until the last. Turning off his mind at that point, he went to bed.

Sometime in the middle of the night, he heard John come in quietly to sleep in the other bed. He kept his eyes closed and eventually returned to sleep.

When Deke woke up the next morning, the sun was high, shining through the filmy window curtains. He heard voices coming from the other room but decided that a shower and shave was needed first. A half hour later, he felt good enough to join the human race once more.

Kamon, Raina, John Summerton, Daniel Pimentel, and Brenna were all in the small living area.

"Good morning, Deke," smiled Raina noticing him first. The others quickly added their greetings. "Trent said to tell you he'll see you in a couple of days if at all possible. Personally, I think he'll come only if he can tear himself away from Catherine and Alexa. Although he's getting to be a nut about flying too. He's acting as a co-pilot now when he goes back to New York. Since I helped train him, I'm really proud."

"Coffee?" asked Kamon to Deke but giving the effervescent teen a slight smile.

"Oh please," answered Deke gratefully, maneuvering with his crutches to the nearest chair. Kamon handed him a mug of strong black brew. After the first sip of pure caffeine, Deke felt even better. "You have an instructor's license, Raina?"

"Yep, I had to jump through a lot of hoops, but I had so many hundreds of hours, the licensing bureau passed me in spite of my age. I flew the little copter down here but Trent wants lessons in that next."

"I'm impressed," Deke stated honestly. "I love to fly but haven't tried the helicopter. Yet." he grinned. "I'd like to learn also, hint, hint," he added.

"I have to admit I'm awed too," added Brenna. "Teaching is so different from actually doing it. And teaching is so much harder."

"Yes, it is but I like to teach," Raina admitted with a grin.

"She likes to boss," Kamon said. "Teaching gives her the justification to do that."

"Then, it's settled," Raina said, ignoring the comment and picking up the conversation from earlier. "John, Daniel, and I will go over to the Pimentel's house to pick up Sunny MacPherson and the baby gifts for Catherine. Then Daniel will drive us all to meet you back at the airport." The group had been addressed, but Raina's eyes had never left Kamon's.

"Okay," Kamon said quietly, never taking his gaze from Raina's face. "How long do you need?"

Raina's eyes warmed, and there was a deliberate hesitation before she said, "Say an hour."

Kamon nodded, his high cheek bones reddening slightly.

The three younger people left, both John and Daniel trying to open the door for Raina, and stammering at her beaming thank you.

Deke would have loved to ask Kamon about Raina, but from the irritated scowl on Kamon's face, another time might be more prudent.

"Glad I'm not the Mind Walker," Brenna teased. "Raina is an expert at getting your attention." Her eyes were amused as she watched the glower on Kamon's face. "Dr. Farrison wants to meet you, Deke, so he's coming up from the clinic. If you feel like staying alone, I'd like to re-familiarize myself with his patient's charts this afternoon. Kamon's moved a television set up already, as well as a box of books."

"I also had your duffle bag, laptop and flash-drives sent up from your airplane in Colombia, they're in the box. We'll retrieve your plane from the hangar in Columbia soon, but I thought you might need your laptop. I didn't know your book preferences so I brought a little of everything, from Higgins to the classics with a little history thrown in."

"Thanks, I appreciate that. My laptop and flash-drives are important to me. Oh, and thanks too for the mix of books. That's the way I read. A little of everything."

A knock on the door interrupted the conversation. A short, stocky, elderly man stood with a tall, slim, younger man. Brenna introduced the older man as Dr. Farrison. Dr. Farrison presented the younger man.

"Brenna, this is my grandson, Eric Shirt." The pride was evident in the old man's voice. "Eric, Dr. Brenna Ramsey."

"How do you do, Doctor," the young man replied in a deep soft voice. Eric Shirt was handsome enough to rate as pretty. His face was a chiseled structure with high sharp cheekbones and golden skin. Large dark eyes, long straight lashes, and shiny black hair cut short completed a more masculine picture. The young man did not resemble his grandfather in any way.

Brenna introduced Deke and Kamon to Dr. Farrison and his grandson. Handshakes were quickly exchanged.

"Now," said Dr. Farrison with a twinkle in his eye, "Eric has a question to ask before we get down to medicine and other business."

Dark eyes blinked for a moment, then Eric grinned broadly at his grandfather. "Subtle? That was subtle?" he inquired, smiling at his grandfather. "You told me you would be subtle."

"Just trying to help," laughed Dr. Farrison. "Now you can ask."

Shaking his head at his grandfather, Eric asked, "May I ask who was the girl who just left here? I was standing by the window waiting for grandfather when I saw her."

"Long light-blond hair? Two young men with her?" asked Brenna knowing the answer before she asked it.

"Yes."

"My sister, Raina."

"She's the most beautiful creature I've ever seen," Eric said in a quiet voice. "Breathtaking. Ethereal. She was laughing and seemed to glow. I don't mean to be bold, but is she spoken for?"

"Spoken for? She's seventeen," Kamon retorted. "Seventeen!" he emphasized, his voice harsh.

"And I am twenty-one," was the calm reply, not appearing

to be intimidated by the older man's scowl. Speaking directly to Brenna, he asked again, "Then she is not spoken for?"

Refusing to glance in Kamon's direction, Brenna replied, "No, she is not spoken for. But Raina is a very strong young woman. She will make her own choices when the time comes."

"Thank you," Eric murmured. "That is very helpful." He looked at his grandfather and nodded.

Dr. Farrison's face glowed with satisfaction. "Eric is from Canada. We leave in the morning to look at medical schools here in the States. Since Eric has dual citizenship, he's planning to apply here. He has also agreed to spend some time here with me on his vacations or summers."

Brenna refused to look at Kamon, now rigid with disapproval. She knew that a very good-looking young man in the vicinity of Raina would not set well with him at all.

"Your grandfather has given me a glowing report on your grades, community service, etc. so you should have little trouble with medical school admission," Brenna said. "Your father is quite famous for his medical work on his home Cree reserve in Canada. First Nations of Canada has implemented many new innovative programs."

Turning to Deke and Kamon she explained, "Eric's father is Dr. Jonathan Shirt, who has instituted a combination of Western medicine and the holistic medicine of the First Nations of Canada. He uses all aspects of a person in treatment; Mind, Body and Spirit in healing. His Medical Centers are designed with a Spiritual Healing room inside the hospital."

"My father is an outstanding man," Eric said respectfully. "He is also an exceptional father and mentor for my sister and me."

Turning to Deke, Dr. Farrison asked him about his injuries and how he was healing. In moments they were in deep discussion on the intricacies of healing and where Deke was in that process.

Eric stood silently by the door listening to his grandfather and Deke's conversation, and ignoring Kamon's glare. Eric Shirt did not seem to be intimidated by the older man.

Brenna watched Kamon as he stared fixedly at the young pre-med student. She pressed her lips together to hide the smile that wanted to burst forth. She couldn't hide her sparkling eyes however.

The two visitors left shortly after Brenna arranged to meet Dr. Farrison later in the afternoon. She knew she would also have to promise to call the older doctor if there were any questions regarding any of Dr. Farrison's patient's needs. He would be her on-call person for his patients no matter what state he was in.

"He's such a dear old man," Brenna told Kamon and Deke. "No matter how often I work here, he's still concerned about his patient's care."

"Too bad I can't say the same about his grandson," groused Kamon. "He's too outspoken to be related to Dr. Farrison."

"I thought Eric was very nice and respectful. Extremely handsome too," Brenna said with a laugh in her voice. "Too bad Raina couldn't meet him. Maybe next time," she smiled. "I'll tell her all about him and what he said, of course. And he'll be working here with Dr. Farrison on some vacations," she added. "I'm sure she can meet him then."

Kamon glared at Brenna. "Humph. I have to go. Raina and her group might be early. She takes too many chances with that little helicopter," he murmured as he left. His goodbye was a wave in their general direction.

Deke looked at Brenna in mock sternness. "You are not a nice lady," he chided with a growing smile. "Not nice at all. Goading Kamon about Raina meeting the handsome young doctor-to-be. Kamon is furious."

"Yep, he sure is," admitted Brenna unconcernedly. "Raina has adored Kamon since puberty, and he takes all that devotion for granted. Since he is a Mind Walker, she makes sure that she embarrasses him on a regular basis. He seems unable to block her from his mind as he blocks other people. He was livid," she giggled. She stood to gather her white coat from the back of the chair.

Deke also stood, coming to an abrupt decision. "Are you taken?" he asked softly, imitating the young Cree.

"No, but...," Brenna stuttered.

"I have to do this," Deke muttered. Slowly, deliberately, he bent his head to brush his lips lightly across Brenna's.

Liquid fire. Like grabbing a live electrical cord. If his crutches hadn't been braced, she would have brought him to his knees.

Deke raised his head to look down at Brenna's closed eyes and moist lips, and then lowered his head again. This time he took the kiss deeper and unleashed a little more passion. His feelings quickly took on a life of their own. He felt Brenna's hands slip under his shirt to caress his back, bringing their bodies into closer contact. His control began to slip as Brenna's unexpected fervor suddenly surpassed his own.

"Whoa, let's move this into a little more private area," he suggested, gently tugging her toward her bedroom.

Brenna blinked once and then blinked again. She shook her head as if to clear it of what had so rapidly arisen from deep inside her.

"No. I can't. No," she said loudly, picking up her coat and running from the room.

Deke watched her run toward the clinic from the wide front windows. What the hell just happened? He knew he wasn't the only one left wanting. Brenna had been just as aroused as he had been. He took deep breaths, trying to gain a modicum of control to his breathing and his straining pants. He wouldn't have thought she was a tease. Was she? Had he somehow gotten mixed up on signals? Nope. He didn't think so. So what the hell happened? He reviewed her actions trying to bring objectivity to a very subjective subject.

Brenna was passionate, but in truth she kissed like a preteen. She was untutored, ardent but unskilled. As if exchanging kisses was not a normal part of her past. Trying to recall specific details, he recalled that she had been unsure where to put her hands on his body, or how to tilt her body for increased contact. Her timid movements as she had tried to caress him were unlike the self-confident, fiery Brenna he had come to know. Twenty-eight years old, traveling in the sophisticated circles of International Medical Aid in foreign countries, she couldn't possibly be an innocent. And then there was the ever present Kelly Pierce.

Sex had always been a regular part of Deke's life. A normal extension of himself. In college and then later in law enforcement, sexual relationships were easy. He didn't consider himself obsessed with the subject, but he certainly enjoyed a physically gratifying relationship with an affectionate lady with no long term commitment on either side.

Now he had to remind himself that no matter how much his body responded, or he lusted after the delicious Brenna, she was so not in his league. Not only was she a doctor, but was uniquely some kind of Healer. A do-gooder who had saved his life.

Which means that I need to get out of here as soon as possible. I do not need another do-gooder so that I can wreck havoc with her life - even if I could. Staying away from Brenna has now become a top priority in my life.

CHAPTER ELEVEN

Staying away from Deke was not as hard as Brenna had thought it would be. He seemed be avoiding her as much as she was avoiding him. Unfortunately, the house was tiny and meals had to be managed. During those meals, Deke stuck to mundane subjects like travel, while Brenna's conversations, eyes darting around to avoid looking at his face, revolved around medicine and her past work with the International Medical Organization. They had been to many of the same hot spots of trouble, which made the exchanges a little less intense. All personal issues were avoided. Both of them made it a habit to retire to their rooms early.

After several days Brenna felt as if the air was hot and dry, like the very stillness before a big storm blow. Thanks to Deke's quick ability to heal and his excellent health in general he would be able to leave next week. She was aware of her conflicted feeling, both relieved and yet saddened.

Growing up she had had a unique opportunity to learn about sexual behaviors without indulging in them as she tagged along with Catherine. Schooling for Catherine had included frank, graphic context as the matriarchal lineage would be passed down through her as the oldest of the three Ramsey girls. Both Brenna and Diane Kay, Maggie's mother, had been included in the lectured sessions.

Afterward she decided her best course of action would be of no action, so she had avoided all situations where her sensuality would be tested. In college, when she was asked to go to one of many parties, she had hinted at a long-time serious boyfriend at home. Since she had fled to Shadow Valley at every holiday and vacation, she was believed. In reality, none of the college boys she had met had been interesting enough to pursue a relationship with. Partying, drinking, and hooking up with immature guys had not been of interest, doubly so given her empathic nature.

In medical school, she had wanted to learn everything anyone could teach her to supplement her own hereditary abilities. She had volunteered for every adjunct program, hoping that the knowledge would enhance her abilities to heal. Of course, in medical school and later in her residency program, there were less opportunities for play also. There was an incredible amount of material to learn in different specialties in an equally incredibly limited amount of time. After she became a volunteer with The International Medical Aid group, men whom she termed as players thought she was either not interested in men, or a cold fish. And when Kelly started traveling with her, there were no more overtures and she let them think whatever they wanted.

Now, with Deke, she was fighting a major physical attraction, something new that had taken her completely by surprise. He surely thought she was an idiot for running away like a sixteen-year-old virgin. A part of her wanted to explore her own sensuality; she hadn't known how incredible the sensations of being in Deke's arms would feel. Exciting. Thrilling. She wanted to wallow in the feelings. She knew she wasn't in love, but she was most definitely in lust. Unfortunately, the reality that was her destiny, pushed her toward being safe.

Thank goodness her days were more than busy, keeping Dr. Farrison's patients happy and well was an exhausting, fulfilling chore.

Dr. Farrison alleged that he was a country doctor treating neighbors and friends. The good doctor's wife had died two years before and his patients had become even more important in his life. All of the time and caring he had shown his ill wife was now showered on his patients. Each patient had to talk about family before any symptoms could be analyzed and treatments ordered. New babies had to be admired, and sympathy expressed for the passing of loved ones. The clinic had become a place for neighbors to visit and community news to be exchanged. The medical practice was time-consuming and demanding. Brenna finished each long day tired and physically drained.

And she loved it.

As a volunteer for International Aid Medical Services, Brenna usually gave short-term care to a patient. She did the best she could to establish rapport and show how much she cared about each patient, but most of the time she was working in an acute situation that demanded immediate attention. Surgeries had to be done, dysentery treated, medicines dispensed. There wasn't time for the depth of long-term care that Dr. Farrison's patients received. In the international medical aid field, family history was sporadic at best, and nonexistent much of the time. Sometimes it was frustrating to be unable to follow a particular patient's progress, to not know what happened in their lives after they left the Medical Aid Clinic. There was always a part of her medical mind that desired a conclusion to her efforts, good or bad.

Medicine was properly called a practice and also an art, since no one person could ever master the field. Truth be told, she had even more tools to heal than any other doctor she knew. As much as her immediate care-focused medical relief work satisfied her, too often she was left with a vague wondering of how that person fared as time went forward. Here, with Dr. Farrison's patients, she was finding a deep satisfaction of following along with each person's care, adjusting the course of treatment as needed.

Brenna worked until she had no patients, finished the medical charts, and walked uphill to the little cottage. She was tired, but a good tired as her grandfather would have said. Tomorrow was Saturday and the clinic was closed. The local hospital handled emergencies on the weekends.

When she entered the little house a delicious smell wafted from the kitchen permeating the air. Her stomach gave a deep rumble reminding her that lunch had been a hurried snack of peanut butter and crackers. "What is this heaven I smell? You can cook?"

A smiling Deke appeared in the kitchen doorway. His crutches were no longer visible.

"When you get as old as I am, you either learn to cook, or you starve. I hope you like homemade lasagna with garlic bread," he said. He took a salad from the refrigerator along with fresh pineapple spears. "Sit down while I serve you."

"You can't possibly know how wonderful this is. This is all absolutely delicious," Brenna announced a few minutes later, her mouth full of cheesy lasagna. "How did you manage this? I keep just basics here."

"Glad you like it. I thought you might be tired after your long day," he explained. "As to how I managed with your very limited larder, I asked one of the men waiting for their wives in the well-baby clinic where the nearest grocery store was. It turned out that he worked for a large grocery chain about a half mile from here. While he was waiting to take his wife home, he took me down to the Supermarket."

"I should have thought of that. There's a small car in back of the cottage in a shed. Use it whenever you wish, keys under the seat. I didn't think you would heal this rapidly or I would have mentioned it before. Sometimes house calls have to be made so having a little car here is handy. Dr. Farrison uses his own car to make home calls to several elderly people. With the help of family and cell phones, most older people stay in their own homes here."

"That sounds like a really good thing. By the way, is it all right if I cook dinner at night, or do you prefer to share duties? I have a lot of time on my hands."

"Ah, how to I explain this without appearing completely inept, which I am?" Brenna grimaced. "My cooking skills are limited and leave much to be desired so I would be delighted if you cooked. Truthfully, as you already know, I usually just throw together a salad or eat takeout. I'd be more than happy to do cleanup as my share. I've never taken the time to learn to cook well. There always seemed to be other people who cooked better, faster, easier than me. I'm not picky so I eat whatever is in front of me. My only excuse is I am busy doing something else I like a heck of a lot more than cooking," Brenna laughed. "You can't imagine how nice it is to come home to a delicious supper that you don't have to make yourself."

"Actually, I can. I lived with a lady for about three months once," Deke said seriously.

"You weren't married?"

"Planning on it, but she wanted a big fancy wedding and that took time to plan."

Brenna was silent. She wanted to know more about this lean tough man, but she also did not want to pry. His kisses made her heart pound and turned her insides to liquid, but she didn't want to meddle. Yeah. Right. "What happened?" she asked.

"Let's wait until after dinner, if that's okay" Deke replied. "Please," he added.

Raina gave a quick nod of her head and changed the subject back to her lack of cooking skills.

After dinner Deke returned to their prior conversation. "Are you sure you want to hear this? It's not a pretty story. Only four or five people know what happened. I haven't talked about it for a very long time. And it doesn't cast me in a particularly good light. I don't want you to be uncomfortable with me afterward."

"Yes, I do want to know and I think you need for me to know," Brenna answered, touching his arm. Whatever it was, obviously Deke needed to tell someone, or at least to hear it out loud.

Deke's hazel eyes met Brenna's green stare. "You're right. I do. Somehow I connect with you. You make me want things I've ignored for a very long time. Impossible things for me."

Brenna sat quietly, her hands folded neatly in her lap, unwilling to stop the flow of Deke's words with her own words of denial.

Looking away from Brenna, Deke sighed, "As you know, I

have worked most of my life in law enforcement of one kind or other. Sometimes in small communities and sometimes large ones. A police therapist once told me that because of my abusive childhood, I had the need to protect since I had little protection myself. Personally, I think that was bunk. I like working within the law where rules exist."

Brenna remained quiet, listening to his voice and what he was not saying. Deke did need to work within guidelines. He also seemed to have a strong need to safeguard those who couldn't defend themselves. The Warrior Instinct, as Kamon called it. Scots seemed to have the trait in excess.

"I was working for the DEA, the Drug Enforcement Agency, out of Phoenix, Arizona. I met Amanda through a buddy's sister. Amanda was a social worker employed by an agency to help teenagers in foster care. She was everything I wanted as the mother of my children; kind, considerate and a little bit funky," he smiled in remembrance. "We dated and ultimately decided to marry. She was planning this big wedding at St. Mary's downtown, something she said she had wanted since she was a little girl."

"You know the kind," he continued. "Her father walking her down the aisle, flowers, five bridesmaids. With all the bells and whistles with the world invited. I was good with that, whatever she wanted," he shrugged.

Brenna watched Deke as he gazed into the distance, no longer present but reliving the past. Her stomach turned over as Deke's jaw tightened in stress.

"I had been working undercover to apprehend one of the leaders of a drug cartel. He occasionally came into the States from Mexico to visit family and distribute his product. My partner and I got lucky and found out where the next drug delivery was going down. The cartel was intending to exchange drugs for guns they needed to expand their gang territory near the border of the United States. We called in reinforcements to help us, everyone from locals to the FBI. The entire project was top secret as we always worried about leaks. And I never shared any of the details of my work with Amanda. Ever."

"Part of Amanda's job was counseling teenagers who were mixed up with street gangs. She was very involved with all aspects of their lives, visiting in their homes and schools. Basically, she was naive, idealistic, trusting, and the eternal optimist regarding the ones she called her kids. Somehow, someday, she thought that things were going to be okay for all her street kids. That somehow they would be able to live decent lives and she needed to help them achieve that."

"Anyway, the evening the drug delivery was scheduled she must have seen one of her teenagers going into a dark warehouse building. She probably thought he was going inside to meet with other kids to smoke dope. I guess she thought she would do a solo intervention and keep him out of trouble. Anyway, she followed him inside."

He took a deep breath and let it out slowly. "Long story short, they were both caught in the crossfire between the law enforcement and the drug cartel. She was hit by bullets from both sides, maybe even mine. Both Amanda and the teenager died. The autopsy report said that she was hit by thirteen bullets and died instantly. I asked the coroner if any of the bullets came from my gun. You know they can do that, right? A few days later, he sat me down, looked me in the eye and told me none were from any police guns, which I knew damn well wasn't true. I also knew I'd never get a straight answer from him. Today I can understand why he did that - because I'd do the same if the tables were turned."

"At the internal investigation, none of the officers from any of the agencies were faulted. Accidental shooting death. Civilian collateral damage ensued when taking out the bad guys. That was the official report."

Brenna remained silent, her heart aching for Deke.

"Brenna, I killed her. Maybe … not with my bullet, but it's true nonetheless. I killed her. Because of my work, she died."

Brenna sat silently listening, letting Deke play it through.

"I couldn't go back to work. I now longer gave a damn about

drug smuggling or wanted anything to do with a career that killed people. I resigned from the DEA and now travel wherever. Truthfully, I no longer care very much which part of the country I am in, or even which country. I have friends that I try to help, especially in South America where so many drug cartels operate. If something needs doing and it's dangerous, I want to do it."

Brenna sat thoughtfully for a several long minutes, replaying Deke's words in her head. Five years ago. He had wandered around the country, mostly South America, for five long years.

"Deke, maybe I did not understand. Please correct me if I am wrong."

Deke nodded in assent.

"Your fiancée followed a teenager into a strange warehouse at night, right? And both of them were killed unintentionally during a drug bust? Do I have that much right?"

Deke's head was bowed as he murmured, "Essentially, yes."

"Because of her death you resigned your law enforcement job and go wherever you can help. Especially if it's really dangerous and no one else will do it. Is that right?"

Deke nodded, his head bowed.

"And you no longer care if something happens to you while you're helping someone? Is that right?"

Again, Deke nodded his head in agreement.

"Then you're a damn fool," Brenna stated flatly.

Deke raised his head to glare at her. "Then you don't understand. She shouldn't have been the one who died. Not one member of the drug cartel was killed. Not one," he stated angrily, "only Amanda and her street kid."

"That's another story and a judgment you are not entitled to make. You can't decide who lives and who dies. You don't have that right. Or that ability. As a physician I swore to do no harm. But long before that I was taught that we don't give life and we don't take it away. None of us have that right. And you're an absolute imbecile."

"She shouldn't have died," Deke protested hotly.

'Maybe not, but again, that's not your call. I understand

grief and I understand shock. I've felt both first hand. I can also see how you could have some misplaced guilt, or even survivor's guilt. At first. But five years? Five years? Really Deke?"

"You do not understand...," Deke interrupted.

Brenna felt her temper flare. "I understand life. I understand that the Creator does not condone deliberately placing oneself in harm's way and not giving a damn what happens. I value life so much I've dedicated my entire being, everything I am, to sustaining it. You're a total misguided idiot, and you make me so mad I could spit!" Brenna said angrily.

"It's my life! And I choose to help others because I can. It's the least I can do after what happened. Amanda is dead."

"Yes, she is. Five years ago she died. But your motive is not just to help people. That's not what you're doing. You're setting yourself in harm's way deliberately. That's real close to suicide," retorted Brenna, not backing down an inch from the furious male.

"Again, it's my life to do whatever I wish!" yelled Deke emotionally.

"Deke, you don't understand," she insisted, more calmly after taking a deep breath. "Your life affects everyone; everyone you've ever known. Everyone your life has ever touched or anyone who has heard of you or will hear of you. And it makes no sense to run from your own anguish. You're going to have to face it sometime."

She paused, hoping that some of what she said was grasped. "In some Native tribes, great grief is encouraged for three days. Three days, Deke, not five years. Loved ones who are left are encouraged to cry, cut chunks of their hair, and any other way to rid themselves of the pain. After the three days are up, life is supposed to start to move on."

"Brenna, you don't get it. I. Caused. Her. Death.," he said slowly. "My world was law enforcement. I loved it. I spent every spare moment I could manage taking out the bad guys. I didn't care what day it was, or even what week. I wanted the thugs and dealers off the streets. I liked the adrenaline rush. Hell, maybe I loved the adrenaline rush. When I wasn't working I was think-ing about work. Or talking about it to other enforcers. Amanda didn't deserve to die like that."

"You're still in law enforcement. Just not paid law enforce-ment. You still like the adrenaline rush of helping right a wrong. You didn't leave law enforcement at all. No, Amanda didn't de-serve to die like that, but that's not your call and not mine ei-ther," Brenna protested her voice rising with anger. "You have no idea what the Creator and Amanda had planned."

"It should have been anyone but Amanda. She was one of the truly good people. Sweet and giving. I think of the family we could have had together. The satisfaction of raising a child with her. What both our lives would have been. I think of her each time I do something I feel is right. A tribute to her. Like a dedica-tion to her spirit. To keep her alive."

Brenna's eyes widened suddenly in horror. "Oh, No. No. No! Please no!"

Deke blinked in confusion "What's …?"

"Oh, Deke. No! Poor Amanda." Tears began to roll down Brenna's cheeks, tears she did not bother to wipe away or hide.

Deke stared at her, unsure what to do.

"Amanda's spirit. Amanda's spirit is tied here! You haven't let her go on."

"What the hell are you talking about? Of course I haven't let her go. I loved her."

"Deke, memories of our loved ones who have passed to the Spirit World is the natural way of life. But what you have done is create an obsession with her Spirit. Your grief has tied Amanda here on earth, she's unable to go on." Brenna's face was wet with tears.

"What the hell?" yelled Deke. "What are you talking about?"

Brenna's voice remained calm, and seeped in sorrow. "Great grief that refuses to let the Spirit move on keeps a person's spirit tied to earth. Their Spirit is caught between two worlds, the living and the dead. And they are neither. They exist in a void waiting until they can move on to the next phase of their soul's journey."

"Brenna, I know the words you are saying, but I haven't the ability to comprehend your world. And I'm not sure if I believe in it. In fact, I'm pretty damn sure I don't," he said quietly.

"Do you know that most people understand this? Hospice workers, priests, physicians, anyone who works with dying patients and their loved ones. We have to tell them that its alright that they can go on. Sometimes it helps us if we tell them that we will catch up, but they have to know that they go on with our permission. That the next world is waiting for them. And no matter *how* much it hurts us; we do not have the right to tie them to this world."

Deke remain silent, his head bowed.

"Grandfather Youngblood had the strongest connection to the Spirit World of anyone I can ever imagine. So, no I don't care what you insist on believing, that's on you. But it's Amanda that I do care about. She didn't deserve to die like she did, and she certainly doesn't deserve to remain in the limbo your need for vindication keeps her in."

Brenna looked at Deke with teary eyes," I wish you would think about Amanda and your grief tethering her to earth. And Deke, not only Amanda can't move on, neither can you. You have tied you both to what went before. You have to let go of the past to move to the future."

"The laws of the Creator are nature's laws. Death is just as much a part of life as is birth. We don't make a conscious decision when we leave this earth. That's not what we can do. But to grieve and hide from life for five years is sheer stupidity," she alleged, her irritation escalating.

"You do not have the right to tell me when to stop grieving. And I am not hiding," Deke protested loudly.

"No, you're trying to get yourself killed so someone pays for her death," Brenna answered sadly. "Preferably you. Five years, Deke! Are you going to spend the rest of your life in self-flagellation?"

"No, I'm not. But I need to do something…,"

"Let her go," pleaded Brenna. "You have no right to keep her here. No right."

Deke refused to look at her.

After a long moment, Brenna said, "There is always a void when we lose a loved one and we grieve. We are supposed to grieve. When I knew Grandfather was dying, I was despondent until he reminded me that he is always with me, and always will be with me. Death is a thinly veiled other dimensional existence. A reflective shadow of this life."

Brenna was silent for a moment before adding, "Everything Grandfather taught, everything I am, I owe mainly to him. I carry him in my heart and in the memories in my head. Always. But his spirit needed to go on when his body died. He needed to move on to prepare for what comes after. And so did I."

Deke was silent, and then he said softly, "I need some time to think this through. I'll put the dishes in the dishwasher and see you tomorrow. I can't handle anymore tonight."

CHAPTER TWELVE

Deke woke to high-pitched childish giggles. Maggie, and almost certainly Douglas. He heard the low rumble of Trent's voice and had to smile. Trent Angelenous had gone from a sophisticated New York businessman on his way to building a financial empire, to a happily married father of three living part-time in the Shadow Valley. Alexa was his newborn daughter, and the twins, Maggie and Douglas, were being raised mainly by Catherine and Trent. Today they had obviously come to visit as Trent was now learning to fly.

"But I'm starving," begged Maggie's loud voice. "Aren't you, Doug?"

"I'm a little hungry," admitted the other twin more softly.

"Then why didn't you eat before we came?" asked Trent, sounding frustrated.

"We weren't hungry then," explained Maggie with the seriousness of an almost five-year-old. "We are now."

Deke dressed hurriedly. Trent was capable of a host of things, but cooking anything edible was not one of them. He could remember when they were kids, Trent doing chores, homework, anything to get out of his turn of chef's duty. Since Trent could not seem to be able to fix anything fit for human consumption, he or Bob were happy to trade jobs with him.

"Good morning," Deke greeted the twins and a smiling Trent.

"Catherine is at the clinic having a well-baby check-up for Alexa," Trent grinned. "Since it was such a nice day, we thought it would be good just to get away for awhile so one of the mechanic pilots came with us. He'll meet us back at the airport later. And Saturday there's no one at the clinic, so I asked Catherine to call Brenna and do a well-baby check on Alexa. You can never be too sure with a newborn."

Deke could hardly keep from rolling his eyes. Raina was right, this formerly well-balanced businessman was a hover mother. Instead of voicing his thoughts aloud, he asked, "I take it these people are all hungry? Starving in fact?"

"We're starving," Maggie replied. "Really, really hungry. My tummy is makin' noises."

"I knew that if they spoke loud enough they would wake you up. They're going to die of hunger!" Trent teased laughing.

"Pancakes or French toast?" asked Deke strolling toward the kitchen. "I think I have the makings for those."

"French toast, please," replied Doug with a wide smile.

"Me too," said Maggie, cocking her head to one side. "Why is it called French toast? Are only French people supposed to eat it? I like it, so do you think I could have French blood?"

"Maybe," Deke admitted. Maggie was fascinating. Her mind seemed to jump subjects at an alarming rate. Quick, agile and articulate. And she wasn't actually five years old yet, although she claimed to be.

Deke quickly whipped the egg batter and fried the thick French bread into a crisp browned treat. He set honey, syrup and jelly on the table.

"You know that most French toast is made from French bread," he reminded Maggie.

"That makes it French toast," crowed Douglas.

"If it's not made from French bread, is it still French toast? What about French fries 'cause I like them too. Aunt Ulla says my French language accent is good. Do you think that's because of the toast or the fries? Is there something else French that is good, like French Candy or French Cake?"

Deke's head was beginning to ache as he smothered his laughter. Maggie was serious in her questions. He didn't want to hurt her feelings so his answers were noncommittal. "I'm not sure. I'll have to check."

"You guys okay now?' asked Trent his eyes twinkling with

humor as he stood in the kitchen doorway. "When you finish, put your dishes in the dishwasher. Clean up after yourselves. Okay?"

"We will," promised Maggie, pouring extra syrup on her bread.

"Let's retreat," suggested Trent, shuddering at the syrupy mess floating in Maggie's plate.

The two men sat down in the small living room. They could hear the muted chatter of the twins, but had a modicum of privacy.

"Before I forget. Here's a phone, wallet, money, credit cards and copies of all your licenses, including for your airplane." He handed the dark brown fold-over to Deke.

"That's amazing," Deke explained. "Mrs. Grant?"

"I wish I could take the credit, but of course it's Mrs. Grant. As soon as she was told you were back in the States she started getting copies of everything you would need. She canceled all your credit cards and had new ones issued too."

"That woman is amazing. Damn, we're lucky to have her," Deke said sincerely.

"She also sent a message that she had candles lit for you at Saint Paul's Cathedral."

Deke smiled at the thought of the efficient former assistant, now a partner in the business, Mrs. Grant could give Raina competition for efficiency. And now with her partnership, she alleviated some of the responsibilities of Trent's work.

"How are you getting along with Brenna now? Chalk and cheese? What?"

"I'm not sure," Deke admitted. "One minute I want to strangle her for her know-it-all attitude and quick temper. The next moment I want to slay dragons and shield her from the world. The truth is she makes me crazy."

"Whoa. Let's see. At the wedding last year, you said she was brainless and foolish in the extreme. That she had her head in the sand and should grow up."

"That was then. This is now, and I've been forced to re-

130

evaluate. She isn't what I thought. Certainly not the lofty ideals-headed naive woman I thought she was. She is however, the most arrogant, opinionated person...." He stopped for breath. "She had the audacity to tell me that I have a death wish because of Amanda. And that my grief is misplaced. And that I have tied Amanda's spirit to the earth because I haven't let go."

"You two have been busy," stated Trent in a neutral voice. "Having an opinion that pits me between my volatile sister-in-law and my forever best friend is not where I want to be. So I have absolutely no comment."

"The crazy thing is that she may have been be right. I spent most of last night laying awake thinking about Amanda and all of the things that happened. Trent, I thought I would never forget Amanda, and now I'm having trouble recalling her facial features. Everything about that period of my life has become hazier, less focused. My mind keeps trying to relive that night as I have so many times, but the depth of my emotions aren't there anymore."

He heaved a deep sigh. "I spent most of last night thinking. And thinking. And finally, at about four this morning, I said a final goodbye to Amanda and to the past. I feel empty and yet relieved, something like having an empty page with no clue of what to write."

"That analogy coming from you makes sense in a crazy kind of way. These Ramsey women do that to you," Trent smiled.

"You knew Amanda. I did love her. I don't know exactly how to explain it but she was what I wanted then. You know the only family I had were you, Bob and your mom with maybe Mr. Korvack mixed in. I needed to belong to something. The camaraderie of the other people in law enforcement was part of that need, I think, and maybe why I was drawn to it. Amanda was supposed to be the other part of my life. I envisioned an idyllic wife, a couple of kids, maybe even a dog. The whole white picket fence scene. When she died, everything in my life shattered. I couldn't hold any part of my dreams, so I did what I had always done. I ran. I ran to survive."

Trent listened but didn't comment.

Deke shoved his hand through his mussed hair. "The only bad part was that I was a grown up and couldn't run to your mom, or my two best friends. So I ran further. South America suited me. It was far enough away and messed up enough that I could always help someone. Anyone."

"Did you mention you still liked the adrenaline rush?" questioned a smiling Trent.

"With Brenna I have more excitement than I can handle," admitted Deke. "Damn she makes my head spin."

"The Ramsey ladies seem to have the ability to turn your life upside down and inside out as my mother would say. Yet they are the most fascinating people I've ever met."

Deke snorted. "How do you think they've kept Shadow Valley and its tribal clan secret? Hell, it's the most unbelievable reality I could have ever *not* imagined."

"That's well put," laughed Trent. "I'm guessing that up until the last couple of generation or so, civilized behavior was not one of the clan's main traits. Probably not even a minor trait. Catherine told me that from the beginning that to betray the tribal clan was a death sentence."

"Yeah, Kamon told me, and I quote, 'death is the fate for betrayal'. Not was, but is."

"Neither of us would ever reveal any part of Shadow Valley under any circumstances."

"True. Shadow Valley secrets are safe with all of us. You know, after I gave it a lot of thought, the valley remaining a secret is really not that far fetched. It's easy to imagine tough Scots trekking up the Mississippi in the 1700's, then intermingling with the natives who would know the lay of the land, so to speak. Marriages and the mixing of clan beliefs were inevitable. Even in the age of satellite imagery available to anyone with a screen, you can hide almost anything under a layer of old-growth tree canopy. And between Catherine's technological gifts and the organization's lock on internet security, prying eyes don't have a chance."

Trent laughed. "It is different. Before I met Catherine I couldn't even imagine living in a place that didn't have a Starbucks on the corner and an exercise gym down the street. Now, it's not a problem I even think about."

Deke shook his head. "I have to admit that my biggest problem is Brenna. Damn, just when I start to get a handle on understanding her something else happens. Do you know any of the healing rituals Brenna did for me? Or am I not even supposed to talk about that either?"

"Humph," Trent replied, "I asked Kamon and all the others about her unusual ability, but they told me it wasn't their secret to tell. I finally asked Catherine, who asked Brenna if she could tell me. She said yes, and that I could share the information with you if you asked. So here goes."

Trent took a deep breath and let it out slowly. "Brenna has what some people call healing hands. She can sense damaged bones and organs, then draw healing blood flow to that organ. That's how Catherine described it."

"I've felt that. Her hands are hot and soothing like an especially warm massage. Did she tell you about what Brenna calls her other Gift?"

"Yeah, it's the one no one talks about. Ever. It's referred to as Shadow Work"

"I know I owe her my life. One moment I want to kiss her feet…,"

"I wouldn't recommend that," Trent interrupted. "I have permission to also tell you about Brenna's other Gift people don't talk about." Trent exhaled slowly. "In essence, Brenna can absorb some of the pain that other people have, Catherine called it Empathic Healing. From what Catherine told me, it's extremely dangerous for Brenna to take on other people's suffering. Either Kelly or Kamon stayed with her when we didn't think you would live. I know that she helped you through your suffering several times because I heard both Kamon and Kelly giving her hell 'for staying too long', whatever that means. Anyway, I'm forever grateful she did help you. Best friends are hard to come by."

"True. And I...,"

"Trent, come quick," Maggie yelled. "Help! Help!"

Both men raced toward the kitchen. The dishwasher was spitting large soapy bubbles onto the floor. Soap foam was several inches high in front of the machine.

"What happened?" asked Trent loudly trying to be heard over Maggie's wailing and Douglas's yelling.

Deke slipped gingerly across the floor to the dishwasher to turn the cycle off. The dishwasher stopped chugging, but still spewed a thin stream of hot froth onto the floor. Deke grabbed towels from the top of the washer in the hall to stop the flow before it reached any carpeted areas.

Maggie had flung her small body at Trent, trying to talk and be held at the same time.

Deke bent down to Doug's level. "What happened? Did the machine break?"

Doug's dark eyes were solemn. "We don't know. We decided to clean up after ourselves like Trent told us, so we put our dishes in the dishwasher. We never used one by ourselves before though. Mrs. Searle won't let us. Anyway, we looked for the soap and found it under the sink. We can read really good so we read the label and it said two tablespoons for a load of dishes." He pointed to a plastic container that said liquid dishwashing detergent. "We put in two tablespoons and turned it on and then all these bubbles came out."

Deke lowered his head trying not to laugh out loud and hurt Doug's feelings. Keeping his voice in the normal range, he explained, "The liquid soap is when you do dishes in the sink. There are some powdered ones that go in the dishwasher."

Doug's eyes were starting to tear. Maggie cried as she kept pointing at the mountain of bubbles on the floor.

"Hey, guys. No biggie," Deke said loudly. "It's a natural mistake. They should label the stuff better. Just grab more towels and we'll have this cleaned up in no time. Watch," Deke instructed as he laid a large towel across a pile of soap bubbles. The towel popped the bubbles and he scooped up as much of the foamy water as he could. He wrung the towel out in the sink, then repeated the action.

Maggie, Douglas and Trent all followed his example. Within minutes the kitchen floor was sparkling clean and Deke had carefully rinsed out the dishwasher. He showed Maggie and Douglas the special tablets Brenna used for the dishwasher and allowed them to turn it on.

***

Catherine and Brenna walked slowly down the winding path to the clinic.

"I know that leaving Trent to watch the trouble-prone twins is a gamble, but Trent plans to wake up Deke as soon as possible. Surely two grown capable men can watch Maggie and Douglas for a short time. Right?" Catherine questioned.

"You do know that either twin is smarter than both those men?" laughed Brenna, guiding her sister into the clinic. "In fact, probably they are smarter than all of us. And definitely more trouble-prone."

"Yeah, but surely they can't find trouble in that little house of yours?" The last was said as a question.

Brenna shook her head, choosing to ask bluntly, "What's up? I know you didn't come down here for a well-baby check even if your husband stays perpetually worried. He really is an overprotective father."

Brenna took the sleeping baby girl from her sister's arms, and began to unwrap Alexa from the blanket. The baby gave a little sigh and slept on.

"Actually, I wanted you to see her. I have all this help but they're not you. You know what I mean. And, of course, you already know that my husband is a worry-wart."

"Yeah I do, which really means you can't share all your baby fears with him," Brenna said, giving her sister a brief hug. "Coming here means you feel a little unsure of yourself, and want someone to tell you the unvarnished truth. You're afraid that because you are their chosen leader, others in Shadow Valley will

135

not level with you completely. They will sugarcoat it. And you know that I will tell the the truth, whatever it is."

"How did you get so smart? I just want to be sure that she's getting enough nourishment. I think I've got this nursing thing down but...," she shrugged helplessly.

Brenna carefully placed Alexa on the pediatric weight scale. She noted the well-developed baby body and natural pink tones of the skin. Alexa slept peacefully through her unveiling.

"Any problems? Spitting up? Lack of urination? Bowel movements normal? Excessive crying? A hitch in breathing?" Brenna paused after each inquiry. She kept on naming as many possibilities of aberrant behavior an infant could have.

At each pause Catherine shook her head negatively.

Brenna then closed her eyes and moved her hands over the smooth skin of the baby. Nothing in the world was as soft as a baby's warm skin. Brenna started at Alexa's feet and moving slowly upward, fanning out her fingers to include the tiny star-like hands of the newborn. She opened her eyes, beaming at her sister. "Not only is my niece healthy, she's perfect. Marvelous. Wonderful and beautiful."

They shared misty smiles.

Wrapping Alexa snugly back in her blanket, Brenna sat down in the rocker in the pediatric room, and began to glide back and forth saying, "I get to hold her for awhile."

Catherine sat down in the other chair, close enough to still touch the infant. "Someone is always holding her. Thank goodness Grandmother told us when we first got Maggie and then Douglas that holding didn't spoil a child, it was a part of loving. Alexa is very well loved," she laughed, touching the tiny foot. "The truth is she's a really good baby. She might have a little of your temper though. She lets the entire house know when she's wet or hungry."

"That's because she's smart and doesn't want to be uncomfortable. Okay, now tell me the gossip from home," requested Brenna absently rubbing Alexa's back.

"You know about Liam and Beth Gowan? Right?"

"Yep. Liam told Kelly and me himself. He was worried about the amount of tormenting he would receive from Raina and swore us to secrecy."

"Surprisingly Raina hasn't teased him very much. It seems that she and Beth Gowan had formed a friendship when Maggie broke her arm and was in the hospital down in Fortuna. Remember they stayed in the Gowan's guesthouse? Now though, Raina's ragging on Sean to get a girlfriend. He insists that since Liam is two minutes older, that makes him too young for a serious relationship."

Both women grinned. Raina treated the twins as if they were her not-too-bright younger brothers even though they were several years older. And the three of them were the best of friends.

"Oh, there is some news but it may only be a rumor," Catherine chuckled. "Mrs. Searle thinks that Fergus is sweet on Joan."

"You're kidding! No way."

"Yep, that's the rumor going round."

"Our Fergus? The grumpy, don't-like-anyone-in-the world Fergus? The handyman-who-can-do-anything-except-smile Fergus?" grimaced Brenna.

Catherine grinned and nodded. "I haven't tried to See anything even if I could. I do love the old curmudgeon."

"Joan is a sweetheart. Good-hearted, pleasant, and kind. She adores Maggie and Douglas. She and Fergus have nothing in common."

"Mrs. Searle says that Fergus has always had a thing for Joan, but she married Dan Johnson really young, but now she's a widow. Has been for two years."

"What do Joe and Thelma think?" Brenna asked, referring to Joan's children. "Although they're grown now so it probably doesn't matter."

"It always matters," Catherine said solemnly. "Surprisingly they like Fergus. If their mother is interested and is happy, then so are they. They saw a different side of Fergus when he won the caber toss at the Highland games last year."

"For a mid fifty-year-old, he *is* built," mused Brenna, her eyes sparkling. "He looked really good bare-chested and dressed in the short kilt. He shows off well."

"Obviously, Joan thought so too," giggled Catherine. "Those kilts do show off a man's best features."

"You don't have to guess what's underneath all those well-padded clothes," chuckled Brenna.

"Now, now Brenna. I don't want to know. Besides I refuse to dwell on people's underwear, or lack thereof, unless it's Trent's. Besides, right now I'm overwhelmed again. The more I work the behinder I get, as Grandmother would say. I've asked Raina to see me this afternoon; there are several projects she could take over. Now stop avoiding the real issue, how is it going with Deke? Since you two came to Spring Creek, he has become a blank to me," Catherine asserted softly.

Brenna was stunned into silence.

"It could mean several things," Catherine went on smoothly. "But it probably means that he is having a strong connection to you and it is interfering. You know that I don't have any Second Sight when there is a close positive link to my loved ones. No matter how hard I might try to View anything."

"Could there be another reason?" Brenna asked with a hitch in her speech.

"I've given it a lot of thought and I don't think so. The only answer seems to be that the bond between you is becoming a relationship, at least to Deke. He doesn't have the ability to block me from Viewing so that's the only explanation."

Brenna couldn't decide how she felt. Equal parts of elation and terror. She wanted him but would not cheat him. For her, life had been decided before she was born. Seldom had she questioned her destiny. All her being was an unchangeable Gift.

"Catherine, I'm scared. So damn scared."

"Of Deke? Or of how he makes you feel?"

"More probably of my future. You talk about your lack of self-confidence as a mother, well I have the same problem where men are concerned. Trusting my own judgment is something I have no faith in. I will bond with my first sexual experience, the same as you and Raina. A permanent bonding that can never be undone. If it scares the shit out of me, can you image how Deke would feel?"

"No, I don't, and neither do you. I thought that Trent would freak, but instead he was delighted. He loved the idea that he was the first, and would be the only love of my life. Men think differently than us. Truly, they may be from Mars."

Brenna's voice trembled as she whispered, "Remember our talks with both Grandmother and then with Grandfather Youngblood? And they both said, railing against what is written only brings torment to the soul. That's how I feel. My future is written."

"Then sister-of-mine you did not hear the same words I heard. That is not what Grandmother Ramsey or Grandfather Youngblood said. Both of them said there are possibilities and probabilities that are written long before our birth. Some choices we make guide the written word."

"True. It doesn't help much though, does it? What is passed down to us from our ancestors is beyond our control. But for now we better get back up to the house. Trent will follow us down here soon,"

Catherine laughed. "He can't stay away from Alexa very long."

"Or from you," teased Brenna.

"Marriage is amazing," admitted Catherine with a contented sigh. "The connection between us grows stronger every day. Trent is largely unaware that he is becoming more intuitive and more relaxed. As for me, I know that when I'm working, especially making some new invention more functional for a particular disability use, I am more focused. More intense. Rubbing off on each other. Pun intended."

Both Trent and Deke were grinning widely as Brenna and Catherine returned from the clinic with baby Alexa. Maggie and Douglas were bouncing up and down with excitement.

"Okay you guys, what's up?" asked Brenna eyeing the group

suspiciously. "You all look guilty."

"We put our dishes and then some soap in the dishwasher but the soap was wrong and made a mess then we cleaneded it up then Deke taught us to use this other stuff which was right," Maggie said without taking a breath. "And we had French toast for breakfast but I think we're Scottish and Native American, and Irish and Celt. Aren't we, Catherine?"

"Among other things," Catherine grinned. "I'm glad you had breakfast. Trent didn't fix it, right?"

"Nope, we woked Deke up cause Trent said to talk really loud," said Maggie. "He fixed French toast with French bread," she giggled. "No Scottish bread!" Douglas joined in the giggling until both children were laughing hilariously.

Brenna shook her head. Loving Maggie and Douglas was so easy. The twins were open and honest. Such a joy. Thank the Creator that they had each other.

CHAPTER THIRTEEN

Trent, Catherine, the twins, and baby Alexa left shortly afterward. Maggie was lecturing Catherine on the proper soap to use if she ever had to use a dishwasher. Douglas was experimenting about how big soap bubbles could expand before they went pop. Trent was doing a lot of cooing to the baby, oblivious as to how silly he sounded. Or not caring.

Deke laughed as he explained to Brenna, "Trent's always been such a tough guy that hearing him talk baby talk to an infant is disconcerting. There's no way Alexa can focus on anything. She's what? A couple of weeks old? Trent is positive that his beautiful baby girl knows everything he says and understands him completely. And dang, I'm green with envy," he admitted frankly.

Deke turned around to go back into the house only to find Brenna beside him dangling keys in front of his face. Her smile was warm and playful. Deke's heart turned over in his chest.

"C'mon, all work and no play makes Brenna mean. Let's take the day off, and I'll show you the big metropolis of Spring Creek and treat you to some of Granny's Chicken-Fried Steak."

All Deke could do was laughingly agree. "You don't even know what mean is. You simply do not have the heart for it."

"Oh, yeah," Brenna retorted, "and you do? You're the hero who takes off to save the downtrodden and oppressed. You just hide your soft side."

"And you have to promise you're not going to tell anyone about that side, right? C'mon, show me your little town."

They spent the rest of the day wandering around Spring Creek, first by car, then on foot. Brenna stopped often to greet someone and introduce Deke as a friend. The residents seemed to be chatty and welcoming, totally different from when Trent had previously visited. And they were curious. A couple of them asked about Kelly Pierce. Brenna answered nonchalantly that Kelly was traveling again.

Deke couldn't remember enjoying himself more than the simple pleasure of window shopping in the small town. The more he was with Brenna the more he liked her. Liked her as a person and as a beautiful woman. Liked this freshly revealed side of her personality she now displayed to him as they explored the town. She was sassy, warm, and fun to be with. She had decided that she was going to enjoy the day and she set out to fulfill that promise to herself.

They stopped at every window display and Brenna began making up outrageous stories of the uses for the items shown in the windows.

The tin bucket from the Country Hardware store became a container to mix different colors to paint the town. It could only be done at night because otherwise everyone would want to join in the fun and they only had one bucket. With laughter, Deke readily agreed that nighttime was ideal for painting the town.

The wooden ladder from the appliance store window became a stairway where if you climbed high enough you could reset the clock on the bell tower, and have time stand still. Or move it backward so you could have a do-over. An intriguing thought for both of them.

The pink-checked apron from the boutique's store window became part of a long complicated story involving Mother Goose and how much candy she had crammed in her apron pockets that she had stolen for her many children. And how she had gobbled up the all the caramel candy for herself.

Several times their combined laughter drew answering smiles from other shoppers.

For Deke the day was magical. He had never allowed his thoughts to free flow in concert with a woman. To just be, with no agenda. To be silly. To be happy just to be alive. During his days with Amanda, law enforcement and the need to be vigilant always hovered in the background. Now he relaxed and let the day spin out as it would. The freedom of expressing random thoughts aloud was liberating. And fun.

His early home life had forced him to become guarded and to share himself with very few people. He had learned early in life to not draw attention to himself, or he would become the scapegoat for either one of his parent's alcoholic rages. He knew emotional scars could cut as deeply as physical scars, as he had experienced both. Never knowing how much alcohol had been consumed that day by either parent had taught him to keep his head down and his guard up.

Law enforcement had added another layer of skepticism to his character. Trusting every person would get you killed. Trust was given only with relationships that had proven themselves long term. He knew that he had evolved into a hard, secretive individual with few close friends. People had to earn every ounce of trust he gave them.

Self reliance was a holy grail. Loneliness was a price he had always been willing to pay. A little loneliness was better than the easily-fractured relationships so many people settled for.

As Brenna had promised, they had dinner at Granny's Café, a tiny establishment with frilly curtains and long tables with benches. People ate wherever there was an empty space at a table, the hand-printed sign said it was family style. The tiny grey-haired lady back of the counter greeted everyone by "Honey" and introduced herself as "Granny". Deke thought she looked exactly like all grandmothers were supposed to look; plump, rosy-cheeked and smiling. He would have given years off his life to have had a granny in his misspent youth.

Brenna was welcomed warmly by a number of people. She again introduced Deke as a friend as they sat at a half-filled table. She ordered from the chalk-board menu without consulting Deke or hardly looking at the day's selections. She paid, picked up their order when it was called, then placed the platter-sized plate in front of Deke.

The large dish was nearly covered with a huge steak which had been pounded thin, coated in a batter, fried, and then smothered in cream gravy. A salad, green beans cooked with onions and pieces of bacon came with it. The aroma was mouth-watering. The first bite was heaven.

"Good grief, Brenna. This is the best chicken fried steak ever. Maybe in the whole world," announced Deke, trying to talk.

"Yep," answered Brenna, her fork poised for another large bite from her platter. "Granny's has been here for a long time. No one knows how old Granny is, but her cooking is as timeless as she is. And both are wonderful."

Deke bit back the retort, *and so are you*. He was leaving in a few days, another week at the most. He had no idea where he was going, and now he was even asking himself why he was going anywhere. Brenna was in his head, forcing him to think deeper about his own motives and the sorrow he no longer felt so acutely. Instead of the numbness of grief, he felt the beginnings of an exhilarating aliveness.

Brenna had somehow replaced an internal void of his previous existence. He could hardly wrap his brain around it. He had become increasingly aware of everything about her. The graceful way she moved, her hands when she became excited, her quirky grin, and sparkling green eyes. Hell, he had to admit the thought of moving his hands over all that smooth creamy skin kept him awake at night.

He was caught in this golden moment of new-found perspective, between his broken past and a future that looked more and more bleak. He had spent the previous night trying to look at his future if he continued to make the same choices he'd been making. Wandering the world no longer held the appeal it once had. If he had thirty or forty years left in his lifetime, what did he want now? He thought back to his computer and all his flash-drives. Were there more things that could open up his life? Make it more meaningful?

Deke and Brenna were both quiet on the way back to the clinic, each lost in their own thoughts. Arriving back at the cottage, a dark pickup was parked in front of the clinic. Brenna sat up straighter, trying to identify the driver.

"Hey Sam Lukens," she called getting out of the small car and shaking hands with a middle aged man. "What brings you out?"

Deke parked the car in the drive-way and moved to stand beside Brenna, making sure the other man knew she was not alone.

"Got troubles, Dr. Ramsey," the older man replied, nodding an acknowledgement of Deke. "Don't know if it's the flu or what, but a bunch of people are down with diarrhea, vomiting, headaches and a host of other symptoms. Barb has done all she knows how to do, and told me to come get you. She said to tell you that some of the symptoms are not like a normal influenza."

"Oh yeah," he added. "She said something about old man Higgins, and that you would know what she's talking about."

"Yep, I do. Let me grab my medical bag and some other things, and I'll go with you," Brenna stated walking toward the clinic building.

"No. I'll take you," stated Deke firmly, stepping up to stand beside her.

Brenna lifted an eyebrow in question.

"That way you'll have your own ride back when you're finished. And I'll be there to get you anything else you need from the clinic."

"Good. That make sense," Brenna decided. "I'll be back in a few minutes," Brenna told the two men unlocking the clinic and disappearing inside.

Deke used his first minute to examine the older man. Brown hair streaked with gray pulled back in a stubby pony tail showing off a tiny hoop earring. Cotton shirt and pants, both well worn but clean. Old expensive boots made soft from usage. Deke met the twinkling blue eyes' direct gaze.

Deke held out his hand. "Brenna didn't have time to introduce us. Deke Paxton."

"Hey Deke. I'm Sam Lukens. Please call me Sam."

"You live here in town?" Deke asked idly. He knew enough about the hill country people that an interrogating style of questions would bag zero answers. The Ozarks area was a unique blend of tolerance of a man's past, and a protection of their own independence. A delicate balance between privacy and safety.

"No. I live about eight or ten miles up Porter Creek out towards Greenville."

Deke hadn't a clue what direction any creek or Greenville was, so he nodded his head to keep Lukens talking.

Sam ran a hand through his hair in agitation. "Some of the folks out my way are really sick. My wife Barb has tried everything and nothing seems to work. We're afraid it will spread to the children. So far only the adults have been affected. We're just glad that Dr. Ramsey is here now. She's a really good doc."

"You knew Dr. Ramsey was here?"

"Probably everyone over the age of six knows all the town gossip within an hour of its happening," Sam grinned. "Small town life. Barb calls it the moccasin telegraph. Even though it sometimes drives her crazy, she still engages in it with the best of them."

He fidgeted for a moment, and then continued, "I hope the Doc hurries. Barb is doing all she has been taught, but she's getting exhausted and frustrated. Nothing she does seems to help much."

"Your wife's a nurse?" asked Deke to distract Lukens.

"Yeah, a really good one. She's even worked in the ER at Stanford Medical Center out in California. Worked there for nine years. That's where I met her …. Thank God, there's Dr. Ramsey," he heaved a long sigh of relief as the door opened.

Brenna emerged, pushing a large metal cart with a half dozen cardboard boxes stacked on top of it.

"Do you need to follow me or do you remember where the village is?" asked Lukens as he and Deke put the boxes into the back seat of the little car.

"I remember," said Brenna with a little smile. "Go on back and tell Barb I'll be there as soon as we can drive it. Are the patients in the clinic?"

"Now they are. Ann Taylor and Phoebe Perez came down

with it first, so Barb saw them at home, then moved them to the clinic. Now there are eight others, so she put everyone in those large rooms in the clinic."

"Good. Having them in one location will help. Especially as time may be essential. Also I remember there's pretty good lab equipment there too, thanks to you and Barb. That makes figuring out problems like this easier."

Sam ducked his head in acknowledgement. "I'll go on then and tell Barb you're on your way," Sam trotted back to his truck and left.

Deke returned the cart to the back of the clinic, leaving it under one of the eves.

"Would you mind driving, Deke? I need to look up something in my Merck." Brenna took a small thick book from her black medical bag. "And yes I know that these things are on our smartphones. But there's nothing like a book, especially out here in the woods with spotty internet coverage."

"Don't mind at all," Deke said as he got into the driver's seat. "Just tell me where to turn."

"Go north over the bridge and turn left; the next turn is about four miles down that road."

Deke was silent as Brenna read the physician's handbook. He knew that The Merck Manual was one of the oldest continually updated books in medicine, listing the diseases and their treatment for most illnesses and was several thousand pages long of tiny print. All, of course, written in medicalese.

Brenna chewed her bottom lip in thought, and then heaved a long sigh. "Well, now at least my knowledge is refreshed on what to look for. I can't do anything else until we get there. Too many unanswered questions.

"You can answer one for me. Why don't these people go to the hospital? Why are you making the trip to see them instead of the other way around?"

"That's two questions. The first answer is they don't believe in, or trust hospitals. Most of them have had some really bad experiences with people in authority. Plus, money is also a problem. This particular community barters for most items they need. Bartering with hospitals is not done. The second answer is easier. I'm a physician and my job is to heal. If Mohammed won't come to the mountain, etc. etc."

"You're freaking amazing," Deke smiled broadly. "I have no idea what I did to deserve to even know you, but I'm grateful. You say things so simply with no artifice that I can't decide if you're naïve, or a fool that allows people to take advantage of you."

"I'd rather be amazing than a fool," laughed Brenna. "Oh, but that wasn't the choice, was it?" she teased. "Deke, I'm pretty simple. Other than my sterling temper of which I am not proud, I'm uncomplicated. Seriously, I use whatever I can. Period. Here I'm more or less on my home turf. Some positives, some negatives. Like everyone's life."

Deke was silent. Brenna actually believed that she was not extraordinarily special. Barring what she called her gifts from the Creator, she was the most selfless person he had ever known.

He was coming to the conclusion that Dr. Brenna Ramsey and Deke Paxton were day and night. She had been nurtured by a large extended family before and after the death of her parents. He had raised himself in the low income, dirty alleyways of Las Vegas. She exuded warmth and caring, had never personally felt cruelty or neglect. He couldn't remember a day when his parents did not consider him an unnecessary burden or a punching bag. Growing up he had never felt warmth and caring except from a few people he could name on one hand: Trent, Bob, Trent's mom, and Mr. Korvack, his high school business teacher.

Deke smiled as he let his thoughts drift to Mrs. Angelenous. Trent's mom had done her best to instill some values in three wild boys, as they spent most of their time at her house when not out roaming the streets. A dancer at one of the Las Vegas Casino Revues, she was youthful, beautiful, and striving to be a good parent with minimal information on how to do such a thing. Raised in foster homes herself and a single parent at eighteen, she knew little of what the world considered normal.

Yet, she had answered any questions the boys could ask as seriously as a judge. When they were about fourteen years old she had taken a banana, and showed the boys how to put on a condom, then promptly set them down and gave them all a lecture on safe sex. She had been the first woman he had ever loved.

Mr. Korvack had come into their lives in high school when he, Bob, and Trent had mutually decided to steal a car and go joy-riding on the Vegas strip. The car had belonged to the high school business teacher. In exchange for not pressing charges, Mr. Korvack required them to spend every afternoon after school in his classroom for an entire semester. Neither Trent, nor Bob, had ever had a man friend. Deke had never known a good man. Nerdy Mr. Korvack became their mentor, friend and fantasy father-figure. He had opened up possibilities, talking with them about making choices and what they wanted from life.

Ironically, both Mr. Korvack and Mrs. Angelenos had died at nearly the same time, during their first year in college; Mr. Korvack from cancer, and Mrs. Angelenos in an automobile accident. As difficult as it was for all of them, there was no thought of dropping out. To do so would be a poor way of honoring their memories.

"Turn right about a quarter mile from here".

He turned from the asphalt road to a graveled road. Off the main road, he realized the old growth trees were even more densely packed than he'd first thought, partially overhanging the side of the road. He had seen jungles in South America with less vegetation. Undergrowth covered every inch of the woods, some vines climbing the trees in search of light. The air smelled of moisture and decaying compost, and the strange smell of flowering bushes.

The gravel road meandered down a curvy stretch when Brenna announced, "Slow down. We're almost there."

Deke had been traveling less than thirty miles an hour, he nevertheless slowed down further. Around a bend in the road, he could see where the mountain smoothed into several hundred acres of semi-level terrain.

The tops of houses were visible through the trees. Some homes were built along the road while others could be barely seen, down dirt tracts leading off the roadway. Deke recognized the neat fields of corn, and what looked like acres of home gardens, with every garden vegetable imaginable, but on a far larger scale than he'd seen before. At Deke's questioning gaze, Brenna said, "These people have never forgotten how to live off the land. And take care of each other. No one goes hungry, even in winter. The amount of canning that goes on here would astound you." Root cellars and outbuildings were scattered haphazardly near the gardens.

They passed a group of houses as Brenna directed him to the middle of the area. A simple one story building was set back off the road. A middle-aged woman in jeans and a white shirt with the sleeves rolled to the elbows hurried out.

"Dr. Ramsey, I'm so glad you're here. Summer Doss was just brought into the clinic by her husband. None of their kids are sick though."

"Hey, Barb. Does Summer have the same symptoms? Has any child had any symptoms?"

"Unfortunately, yes she does. A couple of the Swenson kids have nasty colds but it didn't develop into classic influenza, if that's what this is."

"Oh, Barbara Lukens, I want you to meet Deke Paxton. Deke's helping me while Kelly's gone."

Barbara Lukens returned Deke's quick nod. "Welcome. We need all the help we can get."

"Who is the sickest? Let's review their charts first," Brenna requested, hurrying inside.

Deke stood outside the clinic looking down the road at the houses they had driven past. The nearest two were of glass and cedar logs, very similar to the A-frame cabins of a good ski resort. Next to those was an old farmhouse of river rock and rough planed lumber. Further out were smaller farm houses of pine boards, some well-maintained and others distinctively run down. A teepee stood in one of the lots. Another held an abandoned dwelling, the roof caving in on itself. There were no fences anywhere except for screened wire to keep in the chickens which every house seemed to raise.

On the other side of the clinic building was an old school building with a bell tower, white siding in contrast with brightly colored modern playground equipment. Empty at the moment on a Saturday afternoon, the school appeared well used and maintained.

Sam Lukens drove up in his pickup. "Any problem finding the place?" he asked Deke. "We're kind of way out here."

"Nope. I need to unload the boxes Brenna brought from the car. Can you direct me to the proper place for them? Brenna went with your wife."

"Dr. Ramsey will want them in the lab, I'm sure. I'll give you a hand," Sam said grabbing a couple of boxes.

Deke stacked the remaining boxes together and followed Sam into the clinic lab. The lab was small and seemed to be surprisingly well equipped. A microscope, enclave, and the supplies he could see were new and of good quality.

"The clinic seems to be especially modern, or am I wrong?"

"We're proud of it. Dr. Ramsey didn't tell you about us, did she?" Sam grinned.

"Nope, not a word. She was too busy thinking about whatever the medical problem is here. And reading her Merck Manual."

"We are the last of an old hippie commune," explained Sam with a smile. "A couple of the families have been here since the 70's, but most of us drifted here in the nineties or later."

"Seems like a nice place," said Deke noncommittally.

"In lots of ways it is. Barb and I worked in the medical field. I was a salesman for a company that made a breathing apparatus for hospitals. In my spare time, I tinkered around with an idea on how to improve the air flow through a different kind of tubing. I sold the patent rights to the company and retired early. Real early. We traveled for a couple of years but wanted somewhere quiet as home base. It doesn't get much quieter than this," Sam laughed.

"It really is rather isolated," Deke agreed, following Sam back outside.

Sam smiled, "Yep. Barb and I still like to travel, mostly when it's winter here. Get's damn cold. Our son had some drug problems and he lives here now. Our daughter lives in Phoenix, Arizona where we can go when it's cold and be snow birds."

Deke smiled broadly at the friendly older man. Being from Vegas, he was familiar with the term 'snow birds' that was used to describe the people who left the cold northern states to spend the winter in the warmer climes.

"Why here?"

"It just sorta happened," explained Sam. "Barb had a cousin who lived about a hundred miles south of here. Some other distant relatives scattered about. I guess you know how guarded the hill people are?"

Deke nodded.

"They told us about this place. Anyway we decided to visit and liked it. We're establishment-dropouts in a crazy kind of way too. We bought some land and stayed. The village has the reputation of being tolerant toward other people's foibles, so long as abuse is not involved. Abuse of any kind," he clarified.

"Oh, Oh," snapped Sam as he heard yelling from the clinic. "Sounds like someone is mighty unhappy."

CHAPTER FOURTEEN

Both men rushed back inside. Deke followed Sam as Sam ran into the lab room where they had left the supplies.

A large bearded man was holding onto Brenna's arm trying to pull her towards the side door. "You've got to come with me. She needs you. My wife is really sick," voice made loud in his panic as he tightened his grip on Brenna's arm, jerking her off balance.

Barb Lukens was pulling Brenna the other way, and both women were screaming at the man to let go of Brenna's arm.

Deke, taking it all in, silently slid up beside the man, grabbed the man's wrist with both hands and began to squeeze. "Let her go now or I'll break your wrist," he said softly. The quiet emotionless voice did what yelling couldn't. The big man blinked and looked at the menacing man applying increasingly painful pressure. The man quickly released his hand from Brenna's arm and backed up a step.

Deke stepped in front of Brenna, shielding her completely from her attacker with his large body even as Brenna tried to go around Deke to confront the man. Hot rage poured into Deke as he watched Brenna rub her arm where red marks were beginning to appear. He struggled to keep the lack of emotion from his face. Violence was an integral part of his background and training. So was complete control of that aggression. The double-edged sword.

"Are you crazy, Jimmy?" shouted Sam. "What in the hell do you think you're doing?"

"Joan's really sick! Vomiting and diarrhea. The kids are all screaming and scared." The massive man rubbed his face with both hands. When he looked up, tears flowed down his face. "I don't know what to do to help her," he blubbered in despair. "She needs a doctor bad. Real bad."

Brenna drew closer to the bearded man. "I'm needed here too." Brenna's voice was soft and conciliatory. "Bring her to the clinic. All the equipment I require to treat her properly is here. I can't do much for her at your house. She can get the best care here," she emphasized.

Barb interrupted, "Go with him, Sam. Take my van. And call Maude Turner. She said she would watch any kids who needed her. She has the Johnson twins already. She might as well have more."

"Do you need my help?" Deke asked Sam, leaving the question open-ended. Sam seemed to be the man in charge. Deke would let him decide where he could be of the greatest assistance. Neither Sam nor Barb seemed to be shy about giving orders.

Sam glanced at the tearful big man and then back at Deke. "If you could stay at the clinic, I think that would be the most useful. Our ladies need to be looked after. There might be other damn fools out there."

Barb gave an undignified snort. Brenna glanced skyward.

Deke only heard the 'our ladies' comment. His lady. Brenna as his. The very thought made him lightheaded, rocking him back on his mental heels.

Somehow in the last weeks, Brenna had crept into his heart on silent tiptoes. She was so far above his fantasy woman that he hadn't been protecting his heart. Being in the same room with her made him feel more complete. Looking after her was a pleasure. Being with her as a man would be beyond his wildest desire. And ... it would never happen. It couldn't. As Trent had said, they were chalk and cheese. The age old dichotomy.

Deke backed into a corner of the room, giving the two women as much space as possible to work at the long counters. He crossed his arms and prepared to act as bodyguard whether they wanted him there or not. A fleeting thought of Kelly Pierce entered his mind. Is this what he did? Protect Brenna? Help as a medical assistant, yes, but was his first priority to safeguard her? Had he gotten their relationship wrong?

Brenna went down the hall to re-examine each patient, Deke carefully staying on the side of the rooms, then following her back to the lab. She glanced up at him a couple of times as she maneuvered another slide under the microscope. Finally, she let out a long breath.

"Deke, if you're going to stay here you might as well be working."

"I am working. Sam said for me to stay here. In case…"

"You are starting to make me crazy," blowing an errant lock of red hair away from her face. "You can't just stand around or follow me from room to room. I'll be Dr. Looney Bin."

"I'll do whatever you need me to do, Brenna. I know a little medicine, just not much I'm afraid."

"Here's the problem," Brenna said as she frowned in concentration. "Barb's right. This isn't the flu or a virus. I've examined most of the patients and ruled out a host of things I thought it could be. Whatever it is starts in the upper GI tract. My educated guess is that it's a strain of E. coli. That means it was probably ingested. We're doing stool samples now to be sure," Brenna indicated the slide under the microscope.

"I could get more medical help," Deke suggested.

"I have no use for another doctor or other staff. The most important thing we can do now is supportive therapy. Barb and I need to do three things right now. We have to make sure hydration and electrolyte balances are maintained, the patients are comfortable, and making sure whatever this is doesn't spread. Hydration is the top priority. We can do that." Brenna stared into Deke's eyes. "What I need now is a detective."

Deke was taken back. Of all the things she could have said he would have guessed that statement last.

"Here are the facts so far. All the patients are women. Most of them are young mothers, but not all of them. They live all over the area, no pocket of isolation. I've ruled out salmonella which is food poisoning. This has to be a strain of e-coli. There's hundreds of strains, most of them are found in the human body and are harmless. This one has so far affected healthy women with good immune systems. If we're really lucky it will run its course in a couple of days. That is if we don't have any new cases. Barb, would you copy the list of patient names for Deke, please?"

Barb sent a single sheet of paper through a scanner and handed it to him without comment.

"Here's your new job. You need to interview all these people and find out what the commonality was. What they could all have eaten, or smoked, or whatever. E-coli is most often discovered in meat, dairy, or greens. But not always."

"Brenna, I was a cop. An enforcer. Never got involved with investigative work or the forensic stuff. And it's been a long time, Brenna."

"You're a cop?" asked Barb in horror, her eyes widening. Both Brenna and Deke ignored her.

"And I don't give a damn how long it's been," Brenna said irritably. "I expect you to step up now. It can't be that much different. All the clues you used to pursue add up to an arrest. Well, this time all the clues could add up to finding out whatever made all these people sick. Kids and old people are the most vulnerable, and could die if this is a particularly virulent strain, which I think it is. We need to find the source ASAP. And you need to help," Brenna said hotly.

Barb silently handed Deke a loose leaf notebook and a pen, avoiding eye contact.

Deke took them and blew out a deep breath in acceptance.

"Start with Ann Taylor and Phoebe Perez. They became sick first. They've been given a light sedative but should be awake soon," Brenna instructed as she pushed him not-too-gently into the hallway. And slammed the door shut.

Deke stood outside the lab for several minutes thinking the situation through and deciding what would work best under the circumstances. In these surroundings, demands would be met with a stubborn lack of cooperation. Gaining rapport, and thus assistance, was what most good police work was all about. Most people reacted to what they felt toward other people. Deke knew one of his biggest assets was making people comfortable with what they saw, which had made his undercover operations so successful. The FBI had discovered his ability to become whatever character they needed. They had further trained him to assume not only roles but language intonations, allowing him to fit into a multitude of roles. He might be rusty, but the skills acquired that had kept him alive in past could never be truly lost.

Making up his mind, he allowed his shoulders to hunch forward slightly as he rolled up his shirt sleeves to the elbow. He relaxed his facial features and took on the persona of a quiet, pleasant, nonjudgmental clerk. Instead of the six foot four tough individual he was in reality, he now portrayed a smaller person with a touch of self-consciousness. Of deference.

Deke walked down the hall and peeked into the next room. A sleeping woman lay in one of the twin cots flanked by two men and an old woman. The men were dressed in jeans and chambray shirts, eyes becoming hooded with suspicion at the sight of a stranger. The grey-haired old woman wore a simple old-fashioned cotton housedress in a vibrant printed pattern. It looked new.

"Are either of you Ann Taylor or Phoebe Perez?" Deke asked in a hesitant voice, deliberately appearing clumsy. He hadn't any idea what to look for, so he had quickly decided on the shotgun interrogation, ask everything until something clicked.

"She's Ann Taylor," said the old woman, pointing to the blond woman on the cot who had her eyes closed. "Phoebe's in the next room. Who are you?" The tone was just short of belligerent.

"I'm Deke Paxton. I'm a friend of Dr. Ramsey's. She asked me to help figure out what's making everyone sick. She told me to talk to Ann Taylor and Phoebe Perez," he repeated.

"You a doctor?" asked one of the men.

"No, just a friend and assistant to Dr. Ramsey," he said simply, keeping his tone mild. Deke was glad he was no longer in law enforcement. Both men reeked of marijuana. The sweet-sick smell was easily recognizable and impossible to miss in the small room.

Deke carefully printed Ann Taylor's name at the top of a page in the middle of the notebook, an old trick a police sergeant had taught him. People then assumed that they were not the first to be interviewed and were more comfortable with the process. Everyone hated to be first.

"I apologize now for asking questions you've already answered, but Dr. Ramsey is a stickler for accuracy," Deke said ducking his head respectfully.

"She's a really good doctor and treats us fairly so it's okay," announced the old woman giving the two men a glare. "Ask whatever you need."

"When did Ann Taylor get sick?"

"She complained of a belly ache night before last. She took some pink stuff and went to bed. She woke us up about three in the morning vomiting. She got diarrhea and then stomach cramps," the old woman said.

Deke carefully wrote everything down. "I'm sorry ma'am, but I didn't get your name."

The old woman drew herself up to her five foot nothing self and said, "I'm Mrs. Edith Polk. Ann is my daughter. I live with her and her family," she nodded toward the younger of the two men.

"Did anyone else in your home get sick?" Deke asked respectfully.

"No, not even the baby."

"Doctor Ramsey thinks it may be something that got into the stomach." Deke carefully avoided using the words contaminated food, poison or weed.

"We all ate the same thing and Ann is the only one sick." Mrs. Polk thought for a moment, adding, "For dinner we had pork chops, potatoes and sliced tomatoes. Oh, and my Ann had baked bread. The Sorenson's were clearing their lower field and smoke might of got in the house in the afternoon though."

"Nah, Granny. The Perez's live too far away for the smoke to get there. And Phoebe's the only one sick at her house," objected the younger man.

"That's right, James. This here's Deke. My son-in-law, James Henderson, and his brother, Will."

The men nodded.

"C'mon Deke," Mrs. Polk encouraged, taking charge. "Phoebe is in the next room with her husband, Jose. We can talk to him at the same time we're thinking. Maybe he knows something."

Deke thanked his lucky stars for little old women who were used to running their world. And were positive that all men were inept, if not downright stupid. He dutifully followed Mrs. Polk to the next room, opening the door for her and standing back. She gave him a slight smile of age-old womanly thanks.

A slightly built Hispanic man sat holding the hand of a sleeping freckled-face redhead. The man's jeans and plaid shirt showed signs of wear, but were pressed and clean.

"Deke, this is Jose Perez. Jose, this is Deke Paxton. Doctor Ramsey put him in charge of asking questions about why only some people are sick. I'm helping him meet people." She stood straighter. "The doctor says the sickness is not the flu, or a virus, so it's a mystery. Deke needs to ask you some questions," she explained.

Deke didn't offer to shake hands. No one would be comfortable touching, until it was known how the disease spread. Instead, he nodded at Jose.

"I'll do whatever I can," said Jose in a solemn tone. Deke had expected an accent, but Jose's speech pattern was one of education, refinement and articulation. Columbian, Spanish, or Mexican?

"Jose teaches our school," Mrs. Polk explained proudly. "The kids are learning so much more since he came two years ago. Why, our eight graders tested in the top ninety-five percentile in math and reading this year. And Jose's the biggest reason."

Jose smiled wanly at the talkative elderly woman. "Thank you for the kind words, Mrs. Polk. Everyone has been most kind to me and mine."

Turning to Deke he asked, "How may I be of assistance to you?"

"It would help immensely if you could tell me when your wife became ill. Also if she ate or drink anything you didn't." Deke kept his voice low and soft, matching Jose's voice, but keeping to his understated persona.

"She became sick in the middle of the night. Night before the last one. She complained about being nauseous and having a headache. In the early morning she became really ill with diarrhea and intense vomiting." He glanced at his wife. "We had vegetable soup for dinner. I also ate it. We have no children yet and the two of us live alone," he explained.

"Did your wife make the soup?" ask Deke.

"It was all homemade, from the school supply. My wife is a very good cook," he revealed.

"What's a school supply?"

Mrs. Polk explained, "We all have large gardens. Over the years it's become a custom to take our excess fruits and vegetables to the school house to share with other folks. We also share meat when it's plentiful." She paused for breath. "I had a huge crop of tomatoes this year so I canned some, and then brought the extra to the school for anyone who wanted them. Most other folks do the same thing."

Deke almost groaned aloud.

Sharing food like in a co-op made finding a contaminated food source extremely difficult. Checking each food item and keeping a running list of who ate what would be time consuming. Time for many more people to become ill. Brenna had said that the most vulnerable would be old people and children so figuring out the problem quickly was essential.

"I could really use some help here," Deke said honestly, allowing a hint of frustration to sound in his slow speech. "When did the two women see each other last?"

"I don't know," said Jose slowly. "Phoebe has been part of the community for years so she knows everyone and sees a lot of people most days." He flushed slightly, "We're trying to start a family so we didn't talk much before bedtime that night."

Deke didn't dare look at Mrs. Polk who could be heard sniggering softly.

"Was there any food, drink, or smoke that both Phoebe and Ann shared that no one else in their family did?" Deke directed the question to Mrs. Polk.

"Let's see," she mused. "The girls grew up together. Phoebe's from the King family and is a distant cousin. Day before yesterday?"

Deke nodded in the affirmative.

"Ann had the same thing for breakfast we all had, pancakes and syrup. No milk. The cow just went dry."

"And Phoebe?" Deke asked Jose.

"We had oatmeal with honey. Oh, and coffee."

"Yeah, we all had coffee too."

"Is the coffee newly purchased?"

Both Mrs. Polk and Jose shook their heads negatively.

"What about lunch?" Deke asked settling in his chair for more note-taking. And maybe a long night.

"Nope, Ann and I canned tomatoes and ate with the kids."

Deke decided to use another tactic. "When was the last time Ann and Phoebe were together?"

"The day before they got sick, I think," said Mrs. Polk. "That was the day that the parent group met at the school. Phoebe came over in the morning sometime. I think the women smoked a little weed, but they got it from James and he's not sick."

Deke had learned a lot since leaving law enforcement and most of it could be summed up as 'other people's business.' And to mind your own.

"Ann went to the school meeting. I stayed home and took care of the baby," Mrs. Polk explained. "Once a month most of the mothers get together and iron out any problems their kids have. They bring potluck..." she stopped and looked at Deke wide-eyed.

"Did you know if Phoebe attended?" Deke asked Jose not

showing the excitement he was feeling.

"She did go to the meeting. She told me she was practicing for when we have our own children. I went over and saw her. In fact, she tried to get me to take a plate back to the classroom for lunch, but I had already promised the eighth graders to eat sandwiches with them." Dark liquid eyes met calm hazel ones. "I don't break promises if I can help it at all."

"Do you remember what the parent group had for lunch, Jose? Try to remember as much as you can"

"Some sort of chicken casserole," Jose began, closing his eyes to recall.

Mrs. Polk interrupted. "That's Jan Armstrong's dish. She always makes several and feeds her family that night. I know because my youngest niece likes to eat there on parent day. She had a sleepover there with Betsy Armstrong that night. None of them are sick, just Jan."

"Let's see. There was a potato salad, sliced tomatoes, and a squash dish," Jose related.

"It was Ann's turn to bring some of the food. I made the potato salad. Kept it refrigerated until she was ready to leave, and then put it into an insulated ice bag I got at Walmart. I got food poisoning from store-bought mayonnaise years ago, so I'm extra careful. Everyone in the community ate the tomatoes, I told you I had an extra large crop."

"And the squash?"

"I don't know," she admitted. "Squash is really easy to grow and everyone has a garden full of it. That could have been anyone's."

"Jose? Any ideas?" The slight man shrugged.

"Give me a few minutes to see who is visiting in the other rooms where people are sick." Maybe someone knows who brought that," Mrs. Polk stated, hurrying out.

Deke smiled to himself at the take-charge old lady.

CHAPTER FIFTEEN

"She's very well thought of," Jose said, correctly reading Deke's mind. "Phoebe told me she came here in the late 60's with a group of other people. Most of them left when they discovered how hard it is to survive in these mountains, especially in the winter."

"Mrs. Polk said you were a teacher." Deke made the comment a statement, not a question. Jose could choose to elaborate or not as he chose.

"It's an old-fashioned country school. I teach the upper grades, that is math, history, social science, things like that. Mrs. Freeman teaches the younger students up to fifth grade." He was thoughtful for a moment. "A few people here are very well educated so we do have a number of guest speakers to explain or show the students some things that are needed. There are a bunch of rural families that mostly attend school in good weather. We have an old bus though, and that helps. The community is very involved."

"Sounds like it", Deke said noncommittedly.

"The School Board told me that the State was concerned about the quality of the education here. That it limited opportunities for the students. So they recruited me to make some changes."

Deke remained silent. Most people would continue their thought processes if silence stretched out. Jose turned out to be one of them.

"I was a professor at a large college in California. Five years ago, my wife and two children lived with me there. Annaletta loved to drive in the city. One day while taking the children to school she must have become distracted and lost control of the car. A large diesel truck carrying farm equipment hit them. They all died. I gave up my teaching job and went back to Spain. Two years ago I saw the advertisement for this job. End of story," he said spreading his hands wide.

How odd that Jose's wife and children had died at almost the same time as Amanda, and how differently each had handled their grief and subsequent anger.

"I know who brought the squash," Mrs. Polk said rushing into the room and interrupting Deke's morose thoughts. "Imogene Martin. Her daughter, Ivy, is in the eighth grade and said she watched her make it. They all had the leftovers for dinner." She gave a huge sigh. "I was really praying that it was something from the potluck. I did find out something that I think is important though. All of the people who have come to the clinic were at the parent meeting."

"Good work," Deke complimented Mrs. Polk. "That was thorough investigating."

"Thankee, Thankee," she teased giving a sassy curtsey, holding her print dress out to her sides.

Deke smiled broadly at the old woman. A true matriarch helping in whatever way she could. Capable and caring. What every person needed to lighten up their life. And what he and his two best friends had never had.

"How about drink?" he asked suddenly. "Did the ladies drink anything?"

"There was cider, but all the students drank that too. And water. No milk."

"Let me go back and ask something," Mrs. Polk said bustling out of the room.

She returned almost immediately. "Dorothy Cecil brought some elderberry wine she had just made. Ivy said that her mother wouldn't let any of the kids drink it because the new batch was potent."

"Wouldn't the alcohol fermentation process kill any lingering organisms?" asked Jose.

"I have no idea," answered Deke honestly, "but it's the best shot we've got. Mrs. Polk, do you think you could talk to Dorothy

Cecil, or whoever picked the elderberries? We need more information."

"She's kinda out of it - she's still throwing up. Let me see if any of her kids or her husband Neil is here. Dorothy has a toddler, so she probably had some of her family help her gather the berries."

"Dorothy Cecil has six children, I believe," Jose told Deke after Mrs. Polk left the room. "The oldest is a seventh grade girl, Ann-Marie. I've been told that they sometime struggle to maintain their large family. They have a huge garden which Dorothy cans for their winter food supply and her husband is an avid hunter."

"Are there fruits or berries that grow here?" asked Deke clueless as to what would grow in the local area.

"There's fruit trees that someone planted years ago, then abandoned. Everyone picks them. The wild strawberries that grow in the woods are tiny but delicious. There are a lot of wild elderberries growing near here too."

"I'm not even sure what an elderberry is," admitted Deke.

"I didn't either before I came here. It's an edible berry with seeds that when it is ripe people can make jams, jellies and other things by adding lots of sugar. It grows wild down by the creek." Jose grinned, "I think it's an acquired taste and I haven't been here long enough to acquire it yet."

Mrs. Polk came back with a tall, thin man dressed in the country uniform of blue jeans and chambray shirt. The man had a serious, solemn expression.

"Deke, this is Neil Cecil. Neil, Deke Paxton, and you know Jose."

Greetings were exchanged but no handshakes.

"Mrs. Polk told me that Dr. Ramsey thinks the sickness may be a stomach bacterium, possibly Escherichia coli," stated Neil in a deep voice. "She explained that all the sick ladies are from the parent meeting, and that the wine was the only item consumed that is suspect. Is that correct?"

"The truth is we don't know," admitted Deke. "We're trying

to rule out potential carriers rather than limiting anything."

"If I remember correctly the feces of wild pigs, deer, and cows are the most likely carriers. The host can be anything, but especially vegetables, fruits, or dairy," stated Cecil.

"I remember reading about E. coli, but it was a long time ago and I don't remember it all. I think those E. coli were from contaminated water," Jose said slowly.

"All our wells were tested four months ago by that University guy that Sam Lukens hired. Do you know the recipe for Dorothy's elderberry wine?" Mrs. Polk asked.

"No, but Ann-Marie does. I sent her home to bring a jar here. No one else has drunk from the new batch except the ladies from the parent group." Neil turned to Jose, "If it is the wine, I can't tell you how sorry I am."

"If it is we will do what we have always done," interrupted Mrs. Polk. "We will learn, and not make the same mistake twice."

Deke was increasingly impressed by the old woman. Living in the back of beyond, she seemed to have gained a special relationship with the people and the surroundings. Many people spent their entire lives looking for the quiet strength of character that Mrs. Polk exuded. What was that Maslow theory? Belonging was the biggest need after survival?

A tall pretty girl entered and looked around. She held a Mason canning jar tightly in both hands. "Daddy?"

"Thank you, Ann-Marie," her father said with a smile. He introduced his daughter to Deke. After greetings were exchanged, the father asked, "Do you know the recipe for this wine, Ann-Marie?"

The pre-teen thought for a moment and then said, "This time mom used elderberries and a few apples. She said the elderberries weren't quite ripe yet. Do you want me to go home to get the recipe for making it?" she directed her question to her father.

Neil Cecil looked questioningly at Deke.

"Before you do that, may I ask a couple of questions?" Deke framed the query to the father.

"Of course," answer Cecil immediately.

"You helped your mom pick the fruit?"

"Mom didn't go," answered Ann-Marie. "My baby sister, Sophie, was still napping so me, Phyllis, Gary and Sammy went. Sally's so little she didn't want to go." Turning to Mrs. Polk she said, "We picked the elderberries in those bushes down by the river near that old oak tree, and got about a dozen apples from Mr. West's trees. He always lets us." She narrowed her eyes in remembrance, "I picked about six apples from the tree as high as I could reach. The other kids were too little so they picked a few really good ones from the ground."

"Did you see any animals down there?" Cecil asked his daughter.

"Nope. We looked out for wild hogs and deer. There was a lot of deer scat though. Especially around the apple trees. The fence doesn't keep them out very well."

"Good job, Ann-Marie," her father smiled warmly. "You've been a really big help. Would you stay with your mother until I'm finished here?" he asked.

"Sure, Daddy. Mrs. Kent is at the house taking care of the kids, but I'll go home and help her when you're finished." Smiling at Deke, Ann-Marie said, "Glad to have met you Mr. Paxton. See you tomorrow Mr. Perez. Nice to see you again Mrs. Polk."

Deke stared after the slim girl. What he would have given to have a relationship with either of his own parents like the one the Cecil's' shared. Mutual respect and good manners. This hippie community was doing some things right.

"Where do I go to get a kid like that?" he asked unsmiling.

Neil Cecil laughed but you could hear the pride in his voice. "When we decided to come here after I was released from prison, Dorothy and I set some priorities. Our relationship came first, kids second, and all else one hundred and twenty-ninth down the list. Once you get the hang of it, things fall into place."

"I didn't know you were in prison," Jose stated, then added to Deke, "I was in prison for a couple of months for illegal entry into the United States when I came back. There was a mix-up in my green card status."

"I went to prison on a manslaughter charge. I had had a martini lunch and my friend asked for a ride back to the office. He was badly injured when I hit a tree. I served three years of my five-year sentence before I was released for good behavior." He gave a deep sigh. "This is a complete change for us, and one we're really happy we made. It's not perfect, and sometimes we struggle." Neil Cecil grinned at Jose. "When it gets too tight with six kids, I do a lot of hunting and fishing. A couple of times, I've begged my brother-in-law for a short-term construction job, but I hate leaving my family. Especially now that our lives have straightened out," he admitted.

"We do as we must, as my old granny used to say," commented Mrs. Polk.

Neil Cecil handed the jar of wine to Deke. "I think this needs to be tested. If the kids picked up apples that touched deer scat, this could be the culprit. If it is, I'm deeply sorry. The kids didn't know."

Holding Cecil's gaze, Deke said, "I hope it is. And there's nothing to be sorry about. According to Dr. Ramsey, this parent group is basically healthy and the entire episode will be over in a couple of days." He hoped he wasn't lying.

Brenna did several tests on the fruity wine and announced that it was the culprit. Instead of blaming the Cecil's or the children, Barb and Sam Lukens talked to Jose Perez about using the episode to teach everyone in the community about E. coli, salmonella and other ingested diseases. A community meeting was quickly set up.

"Lemons to lemonade," Sam had announced with a laugh.

Deke was thanked profusely for his work in bringing the outbreak to an end. He protested vigorously announcing to all who would listen that the real heroes of the day were Mrs. Polk - with Sam and Barb Lukens, Brenna and Neil Cecil also in the running.

Deke spent the rest of Saturday night and the following day trailing after Brenna, and being her go-to person as she scurried from room to room treating patients. Neither of them slept more than a couple of hours as they repeatedly made sure that all of the hospital patients were hydrated and improving.

The only scare came when a toddler was brought into the clinic with similar symptoms. The diagnosis was a mild case of the flu. Treatment was ordered and the child went home with a relieved mother.

Barb and Sam Lukens watched as Deke started up the little car preparing to return to Spring Creek when Brenna put a hand on his arm to stop him. She got out of the car, taking a small box from the back seat.

"Barb, I almost forgot Mr. Higgins."

"In all the excitement, I did too," the nurse lamented, walking down the steps to meet her.

Brenna opened the box to show her two items wrapped in tissue paper. Taking out one, she took off the paper. "See, you snap this on the wrist, like a fancy watch band." She demonstrated on her own wrist. "On the back side is all the little machinery stuff. The only way it can be removed is by removing these two little pins." Brenna showed Barb the tiny pins. She took out a second item from the bottom of the box, a tiny metal box with a television-looking screen. "This is a tracking device. It works like a GPS and it's hooked up to a satellite. The screen is small but I think adequate to see everything."

"That's very clever," smiled Barb. "It look's like a regular wrist watch but this back side is the computer mechanism and it doesn't show?"

"Yeah. I had a friend change some components on it for me. It's a prototype that will be on the market soon. Once the device is snapped on, it would be impossible for an elderly person to take it off. It could also be used on the ankle if Mr. Higgins objects to it. Now you will be able to see where he is and to find him if he wanders off again."

"His family is going to be overjoyed. They worry about him wandering off the farm and getting lost in the woods, or community. They've hated making him a prisoner in his yard but they also don't want to lose him. This will help so much. We can't think you enough."

The women hugged each other, both saying how much they appreciated each other.

"That's pretty clever," Deke commented as Brenna go into the car. "It looks better than the ankle bracelets we use to keep track of the bad guys."

Brenna shrugged. "Mr. Higgins has Alzheimer disease. He's just beginning to wander but they refuse to place him in an Alzheimer's facility away from his home and family. The community watches out for him, but he could still wander off. For now, this should work. Catherine, Ian and Sean have been adjusting some of the components on the watch to use with medical devices."

She gave a broad yawn. "Sorry. The Higgins are a really big family so they insist they can care for him. In some ways, all the stimulation in an extended family can help with some of the dementia. Along with some new drugs of course. He's Dr. Farrison's patient."

"This little area is nice in a crazy, low-income way," commented Deke as he drove Brenna back to Spring Creek.

"Don't let it fool you," warned Brenna with a slight smile. "All the people you met are good people with strong values even though some of those values are not mine. But there's other people.... Let's just say I don't come out here by myself if I can help it," Brenna yawned broadly. "It looks bucolic and peaceful, but it's easy for bad guys to hide out here. They don't stay long, but it's becoming increasingly dangerous as time goes by. The biggest problem is opioids. And of course, cooking meth out in the woods is easily hidden. Also, fentanyl is now becoming a big problem as it's cheap to make."

"I hadn't thought of that. Drugs are now a huge problem everywhere. Try to sleep, Brenna. I remember the way back to the clinic. You've got to be exhausted."

"Well, if you don't mind I think I will take a short nap," Brenna said sleepily.

Deke hadn't heard her complain once about the stress as

she had gone from patient to patient. Or how tired she was. She seemed to know everyone's name and asked some personal question, showing them she'd paid attention to each of them in the past. As she applied her sweet-smelling lotion to her hands, she informed every patient that her hands would feel warm as she examined them. At each bed, she reassured the women that they would be almost well by the following day, and then moved on to the next patient. The trust on the faces of the sick women was an unusual sight for Deke. And an even more unusual experience to personally feel trust in another person.

On arriving back at the little house in Spring Creek, Brenna went straight to her room, changed into a long sleeping tee-shirt with boxer shorts and fell exhausted into bed.

Deke was tired and elated, mentally jazzed from the activity. Spending time with Brenna was exhilarating and heady. He had discovered that he was acutely aware of where she was at all times. He would have preferred to lie to himself and chalk it up to being her temporary bodyguard, but he couldn't. His body now reacted to her nearness like a magnetic force field.

CHAPTER SIXTEEN

Brenna was deeply asleep when she heard a loud knock on the front door. Normal emergencies would have been taken care of at the hospital. Emergencies in the clinic practice were seldom. No one should be at a doctor's home. Ever. Yet some people didn't understand that medical help was best at a hospital or clinic where equipment and medicines were available.

Deke hurried out of his room wearing low-slung pajama bottoms and trying to fasten a shirt over his broad chest. He beat her to the door, unlocking it but keeping it closed until Brenna was ready. She knew that he would remain alert to anything that could be a threat.

Glancing down at herself she grimaced at her usual night clothes of boxer shorts and oversized tee-shirt. Her lack of clothing couldn't be helped now. She nodded for Deke to open the door.

A crumpled female body lay sprawled on the doorstep, arms and legs drawn in a fetal position. The body was bloody and soiled with fluid, the long dirty blonde hair matted.

"Deke, can you help me?" asked Brenna as she surveyed the unmoving woman's body. "Would you pick her up? Be careful of her head. She's bleeding, and she's hurt really badly. Time may be critical."

Deke picked up the injured woman carefully, cradling her close against him. Blood immediately seeped through his shirt sleeves. "Do you want me to call 911 for an ambulance?"

At Brenna's negative nod, he asked, "Where do you want her?"

Brenna looked around the room. "On that desk in the corner. It's the flattest surface with the best light." She swept the books and papers on the desk into a nearby cardboard box, then pulled a thick comforter from a chair to cover the desk top. Primitive, but time might be of the essence.

"I need to check her immediately. I don't want to move her anymore than necessary until I examine her."

Brenna watched as Deke carried out her instructions concisely and carefully. "Would you get those latex gloves on the counter, then some warm water and a cloth to wash some of this blood off? And some towels to put under her?"

Brenna did not ask Deke if bloody injuries bothered him. She knew that in law enforcement he had seen much worse than blood. And she was sure he had inflicted his own share of injuries in his years of protecting the public.

The woman lying motionless on the desk looked young and seemed to have been very badly beaten. Her face was a mass of cuts, bruises and lacerations that might need stitches. Blood stained her ripped clothes, oozing through her thin blouse and tattered skirt.

Deke returned with a pan of warm water and an armful of towels. "I can wash her face and arms if that will help you," he suggested. "I brought towels from the linen closet."

"Cleaning her will help," Brenna answered. "We can get a better idea how severe the lacerations are when we can see all of them." Ignoring Deke now that he had a job to do, Brenna ran her hands down each side of the woman's throat area to check her breathing, then down the other areas of the chest. Breathing was top of the checklist. The throat and head were badly bruised but not vitally damaged.

Brenna closed her eyes and emptied her mind of rational thought. She relaxed her body and spirit as she connected to that other place. She now felt through her mind's eye that the female's spleen was damaged and that one rib was cracked, but luckily was not protruding into the lung area. Then where was the blood all coming from? Opening her eyes, she came back into the present. She pulled aside the blood-soaked long skirt to find bleeding from the pelvic area. Miscarriage? Botched abortion?

She pushed slightly on the pelvic area as she refocused. The woman was in the processes of miscarrying. The tightening of the uterus, in reaction to the miscarriage, was already beginning. The fetus' age was about thirteen weeks or so, not viable for survival outside the womb. And already dead.

Brenna could feel the wave of contractions as the young woman's body tried to rid itself of the dead fetus.

"No instruments will be needed," she muttered to herself, talking aloud as she often did in difficult medical cases. "Incomplete abortion, spontaneous or maybe not. Patient in shock. Extremities warm, cardiac output decreased. Dead fetus retained in utero."

"Have you ever delivered a fetus?" Brenna asked Deke. "I need to keep her alive, but the abortion is spontaneous and incomplete now. I need two extra hands."

"I've delivered two babies a long time ago," Deke answered. "Tell me what to do. I'll do my best."

"Just catch the fetus as it comes out of the birth canal. It'll be a bloody mass of tissue," she explained as she handed him a large towel. "Wrap it and put it into the pan."

Deke took his place at the foot of the make-shift table, placing a stainless steel wash pan close by.

Brenna prepared the unconscious woman's legs for delivery, placing a sheet over her trunk to give her as much privacy and dignity as possible and placing several folded towels under her lower extremities.

As she placed her hands on the woman's chest, she exclaimed, "No! Damnit, I'm losing her. She's lost much more blood than I'd first thought - she's going into cardiac failure. This is important Deke, don't let me stay under more than fifteen minutes," she said as she closed her eyes seeking to join with all the Healers who had come before. The ancient ritual of connectedness.

A deep sense of rightness entered her body allowing the calm cool darkness of the other world into her being. Brenna flinched in pain as she bonded to the distressed woman, then

174

felt the young woman's body relax slightly as Brenna took some of the pain. She knew knew the fetus slipped out of the cervical cavity and into the towel. She trusted that Deke would lay the bloody towel aside to grab another one to place between the woman's legs where blood still gushed. Peripheral awareness of the present remained but her trilogy; mind, body and spirit were of the ancient world of her mystical ancestors. The Creator's gift. A Healer. To accept. Linked to that other world just beyond the misty veil of the present.

Brenna did not open her eyes as she helped the woman through the worst part of her trauma, sharing her pain and inner being. Once the uterus was empty of the fetus, she kept massaging the area until the afterbirth delivered. Then she concentrated her spiritual essence on stemming the abnormally heavy flow of blood from the cervix area.

"Time's up, Brenna. Come on now," Deke urged. "It's been fifteen minutes."

"Another fifteen minutes," she requested, keeping her eyes closed and her hands on the lower stomach of the young woman.

Deke took off his watch and lay it down beside him. "Okay.... I'll clean the wounds on the woman's legs as much as possible but I'm not moving from this spot," he stated.

Fifteen minutes later, Deke declared firmly, "Times up. Open your eyes, Brenna. Now, Brenna," he insisted, making his tone authoritarian.

Brenna slowly opened her eyes, blinking back the tears. Her face was drained of color, and her hands had a slight tremor.

"She's really young, Deke. Probably thirteen or fourteen. Her spleen is badly damaged and she has some internal injuries, especially in the vaginal area." With tears streaming down her face, she asked, "Would you call 911 for Medi-Vac so that she can be flown to Fortuna? She's going to need more care than we can give her here at the hospital. Oh, and call the police in Fortuna so they can interview her when she wakes up. Someone has beat the living hell out of her."

"Done," Deke replied shortly, taking his new phone from his pocket. A few minutes later he related, "They are sending an ambulance for her, and will meet the ambulance at the airport. There's no place to land a helicopter here. They said that would be the fastest."

Brenna nodded that she had heard. Turning her back to Deke, she picked up the bloody mass of tissue still wrapped in the towel. She baptized the fetus as her Grandfather Youngblood had taught her, asking the Spirit World to take back one of their innocent own. She then carefully replaced the towel and its contents to await the emergency help. Placing the towel and tissue into a plastic bag, she placed the afterbirth into a separate plastic container. The hospital lab might need both.

As soon as the ambulance left with what little information Brenna was able to give them, she collapsed in a chair and went promptly to sleep.

When Brenna woke, it was dark outside. She sighed as she remembered the young teen and her predicament. The teen would live; the rest was up to the Creator. She had done as much as she could.

Brenna realized that Deke sat silently in a chair beside her. He had watched over her while she slept. At some level she was grateful, at another she was uneasy with the way Deke now looked at her. He'd seen her deep in trance. She was also tired and vulnerable.

"What happened, Brenna?" The question was asked so softly as to be almost a whisper of the night.

Brenna chose to answer the inquiry concretely. "She had been beaten by someone's fists and then by a blunt instrument. Probably a wooden club like a baseball bat."

"And that killed the fetus?"

"No, if that was the intent it was too late. The fetus was malformed, and a spontaneous abortion would have occurred without the beating. Trauma is not a good way to rid a woman of a fetus in the first trimester. About 15% of women have spontaneous abortions, mostly due to fetus abnormalities. The incidence is higher among teenagers. Under fifteen, risk factors are even higher. She was just a little girl," Brenna gave a sad sigh. "Grandfather Youngblood used to say that an Angel comes around three months during pregnancies, and takes the un-developed ones back," she said softly, blinking tears.

"Would you please tell me about you, what you do? I felt completely helpless when you went somewhere else for those two fifteen minute periods."

"I normally do not bond with another person in that man-ner. Only very, very rarely. And only in a situation in which there is no other choice."

"There was no other choice? The girl was dying?"

"Yes," Brenna answered shortly, not wanting to go into medical details.

"I was dying too, wasn't I?" Deke asked softly.

"Yes," admitted Brenna. "You had a TBI, a traumatic brain injury, and your brain was bleeding internally."

"And you bonded with me, as you call it. I remember being in a dark void with pain so intense that I would have done any-thing to escape it. Even death was better than where I was." Deke paused for a moment. "Then you took part of my pain, didn't you? Like you did with this girl."

Brenna let the silence linger for several minutes. Then she said quietly, "The Creator has been generous to me in giving me two Gifts to govern my life. I have healing hands, and in dire situ-ations, I am an Empathic Healer."

Deke remained silent, choosing not to tell her of Trent's prior revelations.

"When I was a small child, my grandmother discovered that I was a Healer. Healing is an integral part of the Scot-Celt world as well as the Native American one, as it was in many other societies. There have been healers since the beginning of time. The strength of the gift varies."

"Your grandmother was the one who found out about your special gift?" asked Deke quietly. "Not your mother?"

"My mother was a beautiful, deeply narcissistic woman

from outside our culture, who ruled my father's world. Catherine and I were born only a year apart. My mother thought that having two little girls to dress up to show off to her older indulgent parents was going to be fun. Unfortunately for those plans, Catherine had been gifted with Second Sight which did not allow her to mingle with large groups of people for any length of time. And I had a gift of healing, which she could not understand and frightened her. There was no way such odd children could fit the way she wanted her world to look like. So, she left us with our paternal grandmother. Raina was left too, after she was born, just in case she too was born with what our mother considered abnormalities." Brenna gave a deep sigh.

"For years both Catherine and I believed that we were defective, that there was something wrong with us. Grandmother became Catherine's mentor, and Grandfather Youngblood mine. As we grew with understanding and acceptance, we also grew in our abilities. Our special abilities became more intense. Stronger."

"Do you know how it works? The control issues?" asked Deke's soft voice coming from the dark.

"During medical school, I studied quantum physics which demonstrates that matter is not static, but energy. That the universe is a living entity and all things are interconnected by energy. I came home on vacation and explained that theory to Grandfather Youngblood. He said that some people needed that explanation, but for him it was simply that the Great Spirit was balancing the universal life force. Both make sense to me."

"Me too," Deke agreed softly. "What part of tonight was physician and what part the other?"

Brenna chose not to answer directly. "Grandfather and the rest of my family decided that since I had a gift for healing people, medical school would enhance my knowledge base. It would make hiding it from other people easier also. And it benefits more people as I have a legitimate reason for the practice of medicine."

"And you did not answer my question," the soft voice

chided.

"To answer that question, my three selves are mixed up. An integral part of each other."

Brenna sighed drowsily, "My physician self, for want of a better term, is how I work mostly. Medicine is an art based on knowledge, and I try to use that art-form as much as possible. I have an advantage that when I close my eyes I can visualize the body internally by touch. Not like an x-ray but more an image of wrongness. An understanding that a particular part of the body is out of order. There's been some research that certain animals, especially dogs, can sense certain diseases, like cancer. My abilities are stronger and more varied. I don't think when I'm in that space. It's more like I am beyond thought. You already know about the sometimes bonding," her voice was beginning to slur.

Brenna was fighting now to stay awake. "Could we finish this conversation at another time?" She yawned broadly, "I'm pooped," she declared as she leaned back in her chair.

Brenna never knew when Deke picked her up, carried her to her bedroom and tucked her into her bed.

She rose early the next morning, partly to get an early start at the clinic and partly to avoid Deke. She had been susceptible after the bonding as she always was. It had made her open to Deke's inquiries. The night had opened up places she kept hidden. She hated feeling vulnerable. Kelly usually protected her from other people's questions. Maybe having a bodyguard was necessary for her. She'd have to remind herself to thank Kelly more often.

Late that afternoon, Deke accompanied two sheriff's officers to see Brenna. The officers were investigating the incident concerning the young woman she had treated the night before. Neither Brenna nor Deke could add anything to the story they had told the ambulance attendants, except Brenna did remember hearing a motor vehicle drive off as they answered the door.

The officers told them that the thirteen-year-old girl was a recent runaway from a local farm family. The family was now at the hospital, and the girl would survive according to a staff physician. The girl was not coherent enough yet to contribute to the inquiries, but her family had checked her computer and found that she had been corresponding with an unknown male on the internet. Investigations were underway.

The entire episode was so sad for Brenna. A young life was changed forever. Technology was so powerful, for good and for ill. In her travels she had found that many parents were uninformed and ignorant about the dangers of computer usage for their children. Cell phones with internet, texting, cameras, and a multitude of other applications were beyond most parents' capabilities. Monitoring social media was harder now with tech savvy teens, and new applications were invented daily. It could make raising children, especially teenagers, a nightmare. And for the young farm-girl, it had.

CHAPTER SEVENTEEN

Brenna felt a subtle change in their relationship after the episode with the young girl. She felt that Deke knowing who, and what, she was had made a huge difference in how much she trusted him. There were no more secrets between them. The only other confidential factor in her life was one no one except her immediate family was aware of. Since it concerned no one else except herself, it would remain undisclosed information. No one else's business except hers.

Brenna was amazed how easily Deke fit into her life. He had done an outstanding job in investigating and finding the culprit in the E. coli case. He had fit seamlessly into the subculture of the hippie community, asking questions without ruffling feathers. He had also done everything she asked in helping with the teenager's miscarriage. In each event, he had been caring, intelligent and capable.

Brenna found herself sharing tidbits of her day with him over the dinners he continued to cook for her. She knew that he spent most of his day on his laptop computer, but when asked about it he had shrugged it off.

"I had an interesting patient today," Brenna began one night over dinner. Even though she trusted Deke implicitly, she never broke the patient's confidentiality by disclosing names or other personal information. "She's a diabetic, overweight with bad knees, and she's elderly. She wanted to know if she could marry her younger neighbor."

"And you said …?" Deke grinned.

"I said for her to wait until Dr. Farrison came back so she could ask him as he had all her history, personal and medical. Her neighbor is twenty-five years younger than she is, by the way."

"Passing the buck? Or in this case, the bride?" Deke laughed.

"You betcha! Not going there. I'm simply not smart enough, or have enough personal background on her situation to give advice."

"Just out of curiosity, has she talked to her children about getting married?"

"Great minds think alike," Brenna giggled. "I asked her the very same question. She told me all her children were young and foolish so she didn't trust their judgment. She's going to wait and talk it over with Dr. Farrison."

"Smart and wily," Deke grinned.

"Yep, that's me. And how did your day go?"

"Surprisingly well. I'm finishing up the last chapters of one of my Paul Tate series."

"Excuse me? What did you just say?" questioned Brenna, sitting up straighter in her chair.

"My day went surprisingly well?" he laughed, his hazel eyes sparkling with laughter.

"No, you said you finished your last chapters in one of the Paul Tate series. *The* Paul Tate series? You're an author? You wrote the Paul Tate mysteries?" Brenna asked in a hushed voice, ignoring his teasing.

Deke nodded his head in the affirmative, striving not to grin.

"For real?" Brenna questioned wide-eyed.

"Yep."

"Do you know how much pleasure those books give? Those books are great!" Brenna enthused.

"No, and I most definitely do not want to know. I hate talking about it." He emphasized the word hate.

Brenna went on as if he hadn't spoken. "Books are a rarity for those of us in the wilds of the countries International Medical Aid serves. There's no television reception, mostly no Wi-Fi, and other technological devices are semi useless so books are primo. We fight over the books where we can escape our reality for a few hours. Paul Tate and his mysteries are one of our favorites."

"I'm flattered and frankly humbled. Do we have to talk about it? It's embarrassing."

"Oh yeah, we have to talk about it! It's called sharing intimate secrets," kidded Brenna. "It's the done thing in all the best conversational circles according to Dale Carnegie."

"And Carnegie has been dead forever. As you've surely guessed Paul Tate's author is unknown to the public. My publisher has kept my identity undisclosed. And it's going to stay that way."

"You don't do interviews or book signings? At all?"

"Not only no, but hell no. And you have to promise to keep it a secret."

Brenna laughter was long and loud. When she could finally talk, she giggled, "I have to keep it a secret? My whole life is a secret! Shadow Valley, my sisters, the tribal clan, our history. Everything has been hidden. Do you think I couldn't keep one more thing confidential?" She couldn't help the peals of laughter that followed.

"It is pretty funny, I guess," Deke grinned. "Asking you of all people to keep a secret."

"Ya think? Trent knows, right?"

"Trent and Catherine, Bob and Lisa Calhoun, Mrs. Grant, and you. Oh, and my agent. You know Mrs. Grant is a business partner now?"

"Stop changing the subject. And yes, I do know Mrs. Grant is a business partner. Tell me about your writing, how you got started, everything," Brenna begged.

"I'm a really boring subject," Deke objected.

Brenna lifted an eyebrow and chuckled when Deke gave a sigh of resignation.

"I've always written as far back as I can remember. Writing was always my escape valve, I guess." He stopped for a moment then continued, "Remember me telling you about Bob, Trent and me in High School? Well, the three of us juvenile delinquents stole a teacher's car but he decided to drop the charges if we stayed after school every day in his classroom? That incident changed all our lives. He taught us we were smart, but did really, really stupid stuff."

Deke grinned in remembrance. "He made us work in his classroom grading papers and cleaning. He also oversaw our homework, and got to know the three of us. Bob was completely enamored with all things computer and had a special knack for them. His rewards were that he got to take apart and put back together an old computer. Trent was fascinated with economics and devoured financial books and magazines which Mr. Korvack supplied. Mr. Korvack encouraged my writing, even entered me anonymously in a couple of writing contests."

"Did you ever win?" interrupted Brenna.

Deke's hazel eyes lit with amusement. "Yes, actually I did. No one except the five of us ever knew. I told Trent's mom," he sighed. "Writing is not a particularly manly sport when a boy is in high school."

"When did you first publish a book? How old were you? In college?"

"You really do want your pound of flesh, don't you?" Deke gave a long suffering sigh.

Brenna nodded, pressing her lips together to stop the laughter, her eyes sparkling.

"In my late twenties when I was in training for the FBI. Of course I had always fooled around with writing, but not for publishing anything. Anyway, I had worked for the sheriff's office in Nevada, and then I had applied for the Bureau. I underwent extensive training as an undercover agent since I seemed to have a talent for impersonating dialects and demeanor."

Deke stopped for a moment, and then looked directly into Brenna's eyes. "In some ways it was brutal. Staying undercover for long periods of time, being someone else in a high risk situation has a tendency to rob you of your identity. The slightest deviation in your living a lie can get you killed. Writing kept me grounded in who I am. My inside personal being. Does that make sense to you?" Deke asked seriously.

"Yes, it does," Brenna said. "Like as long as you could have an outlet for Deke Paxton, the rest was pretend. Right?"

"Right. The irony was that my need to remain grounded was to also pretend, all in my head. Putting words on paper. Or sometimes writing entire plots in my head since it was too revealing and dangerous to put them on paper."

Brenna let the silence stretch, wanting to hear more but not wanting to ask questions. Finally, she asked what she wanted to know most. "You said that only five other people knew. Were you writing when you were engaged to Amanda? Did she know you were a writer?"

"The answer is no. I was completely immersed in working out a plan to capture a gang dealing drugs. I had sold a couple of books and several short stories under the alias of Paul Tate, and two other Paul Tate books were in my computer waiting to be polished. But I was not writing then because I didn't have a spare moment. So no, Amanda did not know I liked to write. There never seemed to be the right moment to tell her. I was a Drug Enforcement Officer; that's who I was. And I didn't see myself as a writer. I still don't."

Brenna smiled a disclaimer.

"Brenna, I don't keep office hours. I don't do book signings or interviews. I don't do deadlines. The book is finished when it's done. I write to put my thoughts into words to get them out of my head and onto paper. I no longer give a damn if it's published or not. My reward is doing it, not the money it brings."

Deke gave Brenna a long serious look. "You're probably one of the only people who can really understand that. The way you use your gifts of healing is camouflaged and disguised. It has to be that way, for you to have any kind of life."

"And you keep your identity a secret...."

Deke smiled broadly. "Brenna, not to protect me so much as to ensure some privacy. Basically, people suck," he said half seriously.

Brenna cocked her head to one side as she studied him

with narrowed eyes. Here was a complicated, fascinating individual. Good-looking in a manly, rugged kind of way, definitely not pretty like Trent. Beautiful hazel eyes with long sooty lashes. Tall and slender with wide shoulders and a runner's sleek build. Deke was so many things. A loner. A talented mimic. A loyal friend to a chosen few. A white knight trying to right the wrongs he found. An intellectual. A man who could kiss her socks off.

He was also a high-risk taker, self-destructive and deceptively sly at times. When she first met him she had thought him arrogant and an adventurer. Now she knew that he was too solitary to be arrogant, but the daredevil label still applied. Hmmm, yes. No wonder the novels were written that way.... Eyes darting upward with making new connections, her dimple deepened with every second.

"Whaa-at?" Deke drew the word out to two syllables.

Brenna was now smirking mischievously, eyes twinkling. "You know you've made a big mistake telling me you wrote those books, right? Even I know an author leaves all kinds of bits and pieces of themselves all over their novels. So ... Paul Tate, huh? This makes so much sense! I've read all his novels and now I can see how a man with your lived experience could write them. Your undercover training, the skillsets, your way of becoming someone else through your police work ... I'll bet those novels practically wrote themselves, didn't they?" Brenna's eyes shone with unsuppressed mirth.

All Deke could do was shake his head, "Yeah, maybe telling a woman as smart as you something like this wasn't such a good idea," Deke grinned back abashedly, "but I'd be a poor friend otherwise, holding back secrets when you've trusted me with so much. And I'm glad I could make you laugh. You deserve to laugh, Brenna, even if it's at my expense."

Brenna smiled back, then abruptly yawned. "Well, enough secrets for tonight, Mr. Reclusive Author. Let's see what tomorrow brings us.

The next morning, Brenna dressed quickly for work. She was looking forward to spending another quiet evening with

Deke. They had drifted into an easy comradely relationship, sharing bits and pieces of themselves at random. Brenna knew that she still held back a small portion of herself. That part was not open for discussion, but the easy companionship she had with Deke was more than she had shared with any other man, even Kelly Pierce whom she had known all her life.

She had just arrived at the clinic office and was in the process of putting on a clean white coat to prepare for her first patient when the back office telephone rang.

"Dr. Ramsey, Spring Creek Hospital emergency room is on line two," announced Dr. Farrison's receptionist, Mrs. Laird.

Brenna immediately picked up the phone. Mrs. Laird was an old timer and would never have interrupted her unless it really was an emergency. Front office receptionists were a mainstay of any medical clinic, and Mrs. Laird's decision-making skills were legendary.

"Dr. Ramsey," replied Brenna, introducing herself. She glanced up to see the head clinic nurse, Jeannine Havens, in the office doorway listening to the conversation. She hit the speaker phone button immediately. Jeannine would not eavesdrop out of idle curiosity.

"This is Doris Quinn, Nursing Supervisor of Spring Creek Hospital," said a brisk telephone voice. "A tour bus has overturned on the curve going out of the city. Forty-two people. Major injuries. We're calling in every doctor in town - we need all the help we can get. And bring as many morphine vials as you have."

"I'll leave immediately. Call back if you need something else, but I'm on my way."
Turning to Jeannine Havens, she asked, "You heard?" At her nod, Brenna asked, "Can you handle everything here?"

"Nope, Sally and I are going with you. Mrs. Laird will reschedule our patients for another day. There's nothing critical. Get your coat," the determined little nurse told Brenna. "I'll drive. Mrs. Laird will call everyone to expect us back whenever they see us."

Brenna got her coat. By the time she had unlocked the controlled substances cabinet and stuffed the requested vials of pain meds in her white coat pockets, Jeannine and Sally were parked waiting for her in front of the clinic. Both women were silent on the way to the hospital. Brenna knew that they were doing what she was, silently preparing for whatever they could do to help.

Entering the hospital, Sally was immediately pulled away to help triage the most serious patients while Jeannine stayed with Brenna to act as her assistant.

The emergency room and hallways overflowed with people who were injured. Many people were crying, others were yelling for family members, and medical workers called for various medical supplies. Some patients were laying on gurneys and others on hospital cots. A few were sitting in armchairs. All looked dazed and disoriented. The entire scene was barely controlled chaos. Brenna … felt right at home. A page from her past with the International Medical Aid Group immediately after every disaster.

"Thanks for coming," The head nurse said to Brenna and Jeannine taking the pain meds from Brenna. "I've called in all the doctors in the area, even a retired ninety-year-old. The doctors in Fortuna will be ready for the air flight. Medi-Vac will transport those who are stable enough to be moved immediately to Fortuna for specialized treatment that we don't do here. The most serious of the wounded have already been taken into surgery, or are still being evaluated."

All the time she had been explaining she had been leading them to a room where several people lay on gurneys. "The tour bus had several families with children. The bus blew a couple of tires at just the wrong time." She stopped for a moment and lowered her voice. "Forty-six people on the bus. Twenty-three injuries, everything from TBI's to asphalt scraps. Two dead."

Neither Brenna nor Jeannine made a comment. They had chosen to help in a field where their jobs were to help, whatever the circumstances.

Brenna immediately went to work, closing down all other

thoughts except for the people hurting. This was a comfort zone for her. To help. Do the healing you were trained for.

She quickly identified the patients with the most serious injuries in her care as she would treat them first. A few people had mostly cuts and scrapes from the impact of hitting the inside of the bus, injuries that could be handled by nursing personnel. She had those removed to the other side of the room for Jeannine. She knew that others would have life-threatening injuries, broken bones and deep lacerations. She was cognizant that her most valuable asset in times like these was her ability to tell which patient had severe injuries not readily diagnosed by sight, and which were not as critical. And to keep her abilities as covert and undetected as possible.

A man was doubled over in pain holding his abdomen area, indicating that the abdominal area was probably tender and the pain severe. The diagnosis of a ruptured spleen was an easy one to make. A severe blow to the stomach area can rupture the spleen, tearing it's covering and the tissue inside. A ruptured spleen was a common serious complication of abdominal injury in automotive accidents. Brenna hurriedly called for a medical aide to transport immediately to the surgical team.

For the next several hours, she worked steadily treating each patient and then evaluating whether they needed to be admitted to the hospital or not.

"Move this man into surgery," she instructed Jeannine, as she pulled the white sheet up to the man's chest. "Write on the chart that I suspect an internal bleed from the chest area plus broken ribs. No punctured skin and no air escaping."

Jeannine wrote everything down in the man's chart.

"Wow," said the Nursing Supervisor directly behind her. "I heard Dr. Ramsey was good but she's very good."

Jeanine took a couple of steps back to be out of hearing range but kept an eye on Brenna, ready to step in if she was needed.

"Yes she is. In the last three weeks I've gotten a refresher course in new knowledge of patient treatment. Dr. Farrison is a really good Family Physician, but Dr. Ramsey is uncanny in her abilities."

"Dr. Farrison is the nicest man in the whole world and a good doctor," agreed the Head Nurse. "You've been Dr. Farrison's nurse for eight years, right?"

"Dr. Farrison is wonderful," said Jeanine. "He hired me right out of nursing school. My first and only nursing job. He treats everyone as family and friends. He's much loved."

"And Dr. Ramsey? You think she might stay here to practice? Dr. Farrison's like me, we're no spring chickens any more."

"I have no idea. She's warm and friendly with everyone but with no nonsense. Dr. Ramsey doesn't suffer fools gladly. The other day I had to secretly laugh when one old farmer told Dr. Ramsey he wasn't about to take the medicine she had prescribed. Her quick retort was then he couldn't pay for the doctor visit because he had wasted her time, and it was senseless to waste his money too. Now the old man tries to think of an ailment every day so he can come into the office to see that angel doctor. Excuse me, the doctor needs me now."

Brenna looked up to find Jeanine a couple of yards away, and then lifted an eyebrow in question.

Jeannine stepped quickly back into place and responded. "The next patient is a young mother who has a broken leg. She's been given morphine for pain and an IV has been started. Her neck has been collared as a precautionary measure. Her blood pressure is normal for trauma and her clothes were cut off. Dr. Newman wants you to be sure the Nurse Practitioner didn't miss anything.'

Brenna quickly ran her hands over the young woman, starting with her head. Mumbling inaudibly to herself, "No head injury nor neck trauma. Chest cavity okay, all intact, little bruising. Simple fracture, not compound as it did not break the skin. No boils or infections to complicate healing."

Turning to Jeannine she told the hovering nurse, "The NP did a good job. Good choice in her pain killer. Morphine makes the patient euphoric, Demerol doesn't. She's ready for transport to surgery."

Brenna could hear a hysterical woman screaming in the background. She quickly moved toward the sound. Panic spreads quickly in crises, causing more people to become out of control. Like a domino effect. Sizing up what she was about to say, Brenna pulled the young woman into her arms as she sobbed.

"My son. My son's dead. That's what they say. Please, please help me," the young woman wailed clinging to Brenna's white coat. This was the toughest part of being a doctor. Losing a child was beyond comprehension and anguish.

Brenna held her tightly, "Is your family here?" Between inconsolable sobs, Brenna finally understood that her husband had been taken into surgery moments before. Brenna motioned for a priest and a social worker to join her. Much as she would like to stay and counsel with the broken-hearted mother, her skills as a trauma physician were needed more. Other people were qualified and available to help the young mother in her period of intense grief.

Brenna couldn't stop herself from closing her eyes as she touched the deceased child's body. He was gone. She felt Jeannine's hand take hers in a tight grip.

"We do not decide who dies and who does not," Jeannine said in a stern voice. "We work. We do the best we can with what we know today. Now, I need for you to check this head injury," she added as she led her back to an alcove.

Brenna knew Jeannine was right. She had needed what grandfather called a kick in the pants. She knew that she did not decide about life and death situations. How many times had she or Kelly told each other that? Ten times? A hundred? Bowing her head toward Jeannine in thanks, she went back to work.

The elderly man on the table was still unconsciousness. Brenna checked to be sure his airways were clear and his blood pressure had not dropped substantially. There was a large bump on his right front forehead. No other injuries were apparent.

An older woman stood quietly by wringing her hands. Her arms and hands were bandaged. "Is Henry going to die? Please don't let him," she pleaded softly. "He put my head in his lap as we were falling. His head hit the back of the seat in front of us." She put her hand over her mouth, fighting for control. Tears rolled down her deeply wrinkled cheeks.

"What kind of medications does he take?" asked Jeannine. "Has he taken any aspirin or ibuprofen today?"

While the wife tried to remember all her husband's drugs and dosages, Brenna continued to check the patient's extremities for other injuries. She laid her hands on each side of the man's head, closing her eyes to concentrate trying to block out the noisy emergency room as she talked to herself silently. No skull fracture, hematoma, or intraparenchymal contusions. Loss of consciousness, a bruise-like discoloration around the eyes. No cerebrospinal fluid leaking from a skull fracture near the nose. Healthy body, little fat to complicate healing, thankfully. The diagnosis was a moderate head injury. Being elderly, he had a higher risk factor for complications, but he had an excellent chance of a full recovery.

Brenna addressed the man's wife, "I suspect your husband has a moderate head injury. I'm going to send him downstairs for a CT scan." When the older lady looked blank, Brenna explained, "A CT scan is a computerized topography picture that a machine takes of the brain. It will give us a clearer picture of what is happening inside his head." Brenna deliberately left her explanations vague. If there was no further damage, there would be a dramatic improvement within one to six weeks and loss of memory and attention would not be permanent. Brenna waved a young nurse's aide over to take the couple downstairs.

She continued to work, concentrating all her energies on the patient in front of her. She knew that Jeannine tried to anticipate her needs as they struggled to give the best possible care to the injured person in front of them.

"I want you to take a look at this patient. The injuries seem all external but let's be sure," Jeannine said softly. "I've cleaned his arms and sides, he had deep abrasions from the asphalt. He's had a painkiller, antibiotics and lots of TLC. I know that asphalt is cancerous, so I cleaned it extremely well. He says he was laying down on one of the back seats with pillows surrounding him so he had almost no injuries except those from the contact with the road."

Brenna could hear Jeannie's deep sigh. Doctors, nurses, aides, social workers, and all other people volunteering would work until they were no longer needed. It was going to be a long night.

CHAPTER EIGHTEEN

Deke paced the clinic house's small living room for the hundredth time. When the clinic receptionist had called him early that morning about the tour bus, he had gone over to the hospital to see if he could be of any assistance. A flood of volunteers had descended on the area, caring for the wounded, talking to families, and offering their homes for respite. He had thought that he might volunteer for some sort of law enforcement duty. There was none needed. The local officers had everything under control. They had already called in special investigators and had started an inquiry into why the bus tires blew on the curve.

He had called Trent to suggest he could help fly the injured into Fortuna if he could borrow an airplane only to be told that two helicopters were already in the air headed to Spring Creek. One flown by Liam with Kamon as co-pilot, and the other by Sean with Raina as co-pilot.

He had not felt so superfluous in many years. He wasn't needed to rescue anyone. They did not have a need for his particular skills. So he had spent the day pacing the floor and watching the news. Neither was satisfying.

By nine that night, he was frustrated and strangely disquiet, both new experiences for him. Controlled action was his normal way of relieving stress, and that was impossible at the moment. All his thoughts were focused on Brenna.

Brenna had now been at the hospital for twelve or thirteen hours. She had to be exhausted. He grabbed his coat and the car keys. What the hell. He could wait just as easily in the hospital parking lot as in the neat little cottage.

When he arrived at the hospital, he penned a note to be hand-delivered to Dr. Brenna Ramsey. A one-line sentence, "I'll be in the parking lot when you need me."

He returned to the car, moved the little car's passenger seat back as far as possible for leg room and settled down to wait indefinitely. For awhile he watched the people in the parking lot. Some were harried and in tears, clinging to each other. Others were silent and watchful, looking around as if lost. Slowly the people dwindled to a few stragglers waiting. Like him.

His mind was in turmoil, his thoughts flitting from one subject to another. He tried to relax and closed his eyes, forcing his mind to drift. He wished he had more medical training, maybe taken classes as an Emergency Medical Technician. EMT training would have allowed him to assist Brenna in emergency situations.

Maybe I can take online classes, he thought. And I need to get my helicopter license so I can be of more use. Helicopters are the mode of transport for folks in crisis.

His eyes flew open. EMT training? What was he thinking? He had never been interested in any kind of medical career. When he had taken basic crisis training as a police officer, he had fervently hoped that no major medical crisis would happen on his watch. But of course, a few had. Some assistance was needed at several automobile accidents with the injured until the ambulances arrived. Minor events in the world of medical support. Even a couple of babies in too big a hurry to wait to be born in a hospital. The police dispatcher had talked him through the first one. A bystander, of all things, had helped him through the second one. The young millennial had whipped out her smartphone, pulled up a video within seconds, and proceeded to talk him through the delivery until the ambulance arrived. Damnedest thing. Did a better job than the dispatcher, then proceeded to take a selfie with him and the newborn.

Now he was thinking of more involvement? How had that changed? He knew he had helped people who had fallen through life's cracks during the last five years. But Brenna....

He gave a short humph out loud. Talk about a spell of fantasy. Brenna had given him no indication that she wanted him to stay near her, and here he was idly daydreaming to become part of her life? And furthermore to try to be a valuable addition to her work? Yes, she had returned a very passionate kiss. One time, he reminded himself. One kiss. He leaned his head back against the seat, determined to think clearly and leave his fantasy world behind.

Did he want to still wander around South American helping whoever needed him? Being needed was satisfying, but he was getting a little old for running around jungles evading people who wanted to erase his existence. Taking out bad guys and helping the good ones was like trying to empty a swimming pool with a lone teaspoon. Risking one's life when he didn't care whether he lived or died was one thing, but maybe he needed something else now.

He turned the idea slowly over in his mind. The restlessness was no longer within him. What had been an acute anxiety to stay busy was gone. He no longer felt that he wanted to risk his life. He wanted more. To live. Maybe to love. Having a family would be the epitome of a fulfilled life. He had a fleeting thought of the irrepressible Maggie. A kid like her. Or Douglas. Or the Cecil's seventh grader. He smiled at the image. So the reality was that not being the go-to guy for risky rescues would suit him fine.

Next, what about Brenna? How much did she affect his decisions? Would he want to remain stateside without her? He was too old not to be honest with himself. And too much an introvert living in his head not to be real. Yes, she was a major factor in not returning to his former helter-skelter life, but not the only motivating force.

For the last five years, he had had nowhere to go that anyone was expecting him. He owned a ranch in Texas but had a capable manager and seldom visited. No one waited or cared if he didn't show up. Most people never asked where he was from, expecting he had no ties anywhere. No past and few who cared about his future. He had never felt lonely on his travels until now. The United States was home in an abstract fashion, but belonging was something else entirely. He thought back to a college class and to Maslow's hierarchy of needs where belonging was near the bottom of the pyramid. The most necessary thing after the basics of food, water and shelter were met. Belonging was something he hadn't had in a very long time. And he'd never had like Mrs. Polk and her little community of dropouts. His parents were gone and not lamented. Non-close cousins were scattered. Trent, Bob, and maybe Mrs. Grant were what he could call forever friends, and then way down the list was a host of acquaintances.

For the first time in a long time, he admitted that he liked living in his own country. Knowing where Kansas was located. And getting the local joke, something often missing in South America where local customs eluded the newcomers and outsiders. He loved to write. To put words on paper. To sometimes educate, or to entertain. To bring an hour's pleasure. He could write anywhere. Have laptop – will travel.

Which brought him full circle to Brenna. She was every-man's fantasy and every teen's wet dream. Beautiful outside and lit with fire from inside. He almost laughed aloud as he thought of the heat of Brenna's hands when she was healing.

A knock on the car's window brought his musings to an end. Brenna stood quietly outside, her shoulders hunched with fatigue. Deke hurriedly unlocked the door, taking her arm and helping her into the passenger seat of the little car, then moved to the driver's side.

She mumbled thanks and slumped in the seat. "Long day" she yawned.

Deke glanced at his watch. One thirty in the morning. Brenna had now been working in an intense situation for about seventeen and a half hours. Dealing with the aftermath of a crisis was overwhelming fatigue. A complete letdown where the bottom drops out. No wonder she was dead on her feet. He could relate as that's what happened to him after a crisis in law enforcement. And hers was so much more intense. Life or death situations, literally every hour.

When they arrived at the little house behind the clinic, Deke carefully helped her out of the car, placing his arm around her shoulders for support.

"Please, I need to walk," she murmured.

Deke hovered as she slowly trudged into the house, placing each step before attempting another one. Instead of going to her bedroom as Deke had expected, she turned around to him.

"Would you hold me for a moment?" she asked, unshed tears in her eyes. "I need to just be held for a moment."

Deke's heart almost stopped. He gently pulled her into his arms, her face against his chest. She began to quietly sob.

Deke was unsure whether the tears were from fatigue or happenings, so he simply sat down in a chair and cuddled her as he would a small child. She didn't resist but seemed to snuggle closer as her cries finally diminished.

"Do you want to talk about it?" he whispered. He would accept whatever she needed.

"No. Yes." Brenna ran a hand over her face. "The baby died. I couldn't save her." Fresh tears ran down Brenna's cheeks. "I tried everything but she was too tiny. She hadn't had a chance to develop."

Deke remained quiet, knowing that the best help was often silence as people worked through their own thoughts and feelings.

"This lady didn't seem to be injured at all. Her husband has a broken collar bone. Her two teenager boys only had bumps and bruises. Oh, and a couple of lacerations." She took a deep sniffling breath. "She didn't know she was pregnant but she was four months along. Since she was forty-three, she thought that she was going through an early change of life when her periods stopped."

Deke hugged her tightly. She was so compassionate and wonderful that she brought a lump to his throat.

"I'm sorry. I don't usually blubber all over anyone. But the baby ..." she stopped.

"Not even Kelly?" Deke asked before he thought better of it.

Then held his breath for the answer.

"Good grief no. I'm not saying that he wouldn't understand, it's just that it would be," she hesitated looking for the right word. "Too intimate," she finally concluded.

Deke would have celebrated if it had been possible but he didn't want to move. He didn't even want to breathe for fear of breaking the spell of the moment.

He felt Brenna's body slowly slump as she relaxed into a light doze. Deke made himself as comfortable as it was possible in a too small armchair for his too large body. He was cramped and his movements were severely restricted. And he would not have changed places with anyone in the universe.

He must have dozed himself when he felt Brenna's body beginning to stir. She tried to sit up as she pushed her long braid back over her shoulder. Her carefully coiled braided chignon was now a long lone braid down her back. Thin strands had come undone and delicate threads of bright auburn hair surrounded her face.

"Would you take me to bed?" Brenna asked softly.

Deke wanted to shout yes but before he could answer Brenna continued, "I know I shouldn't ask but I just don't want to be alone. I know that although the dragon wins sometime, it doesn't always. Could you just be there? I won't even ask for you to touch me if you don't want."

"Of course," Deke answered quietly. Even if it kills me was his next thought. Or I go mad.

They walked silently into the small bedroom, Deke carefully supporting Brenna.

"I'll just take off my shoes. I've slept in my scrubs more often than not." She lowered herself down on the double bed in the darkened room.

Deke followed suit, removing his shoes and socks. Glancing downward he realized Brenna was almost asleep, exhausted after a long intense day. He took the folded blanket, covering her.

Ever since he had been hurt, he had taken to sleeping in pajama bottoms, never knowing when he would have unexpected visitors. Tonight his jeans would have to do. He unbuttoned the top button of his pants, and then took off his shirt. He might as well make himself as comfortable as possible. He lay down behind her, spooning his long body close to hers. She gave a deep sigh and snuggled her soft body deeper into his larger one, shoving her rounded bottom against his pelvic area. Deke held back an audible groan, forcing his body to move back so that his hard erection did not upset her. Holding Brenna was a combination of heaven and hell.

Only a couple of hours passed before Deke woke to faint sounds coming from the front of the little house. He inched himself from the bed, being careful not to wake Brenna. He opened the bedroom door enough to slip through it, silently closing it behind him. Brenna had given too much of herself already. If someone needed her now, tough. She was exhausted. At the end of her physical strength. There's no way in hell that he was going to allow anyone to wake her up. She needed the rest.

His bare feet made no sound as he slipped through the hall and into the living room. He drew up short when he recognized the large form of Kelly Pierce.

Kelly seemed to take in the entire situation at a glance, noting Deke coming out of Brenna's bedroom, wearing unbuttoned jeans and nothing else.

Kelly stood there staring at Deke. Only a tic in his jaw betrayed any emotion. After several moments he said in a cool voice, "I checked the other bedroom. When I didn't find you, I thought at first that you had left, but your duffle bag was still here." Pinning Deke with his gaze he asked, "Did you force her?"

Deke blinked, then understood what Kelly was really asking. "No," he said bluntly.

"You know if you had, there wouldn't be enough places in the universe for you to hide. Or pieces of you to identify."

"I know," Deke replied, giving the other large man his rightful due. If the situation had been reversed, he would have vowed the same thing.

The two men gazed at each other intently, recognizing in

each other the same ethical standards. One of honesty and integrity.

"You're in love with her," Deke stated striving for an emotionless voice. Kelly deserved all the empathy it was possible to give but he would hate pity. Just as he did.

"What's not to love?" Kelly responded, keeping his face expressionless, his large body motionless.

"In so many ways, I'm sorry...," begin Deke.

"It was time. I knew it was coming. Not when, not who, but eventually. You do know our ways are different?" Kelly said, maintaining the control he had always shown.

Deke nodded. Different didn't even begin to cover it. Unique. Unbelievable. Unusual. So many words that fit the culture and history of the people from the Ramsey clan.

"I have to tell you a long complicated story," Kelly said, closing his eyes for a moment to gain thinking time. "Let's go into the kitchen for more privacy."

Deke nodded in acceptance as he followed him. Whatever Kelly had to say, he needed to understand. Laying yourself open to another man was the ultimate test of strength ... and trust.

"I've always known that Brenna wasn't mine this lifetime. I'm forty-nine years old. I was born too early, or Brenna was born too late." Kelly gave a slight outbreath. "When she was seven or eight, I caught a glimpse of her all grown up out of the corner of my eye. She was a tall, copper-haired haired beauty in a warrior's stance. My heart stopped. I was stunned. And doubted my sanity." He gazed sightless into the past. "Needless to say it scared the living hell out of me."

He paused, then continued. "I didn't know how to handle the jumble of feelings rushing through me so that day I took off into the back country. I ran away praying that my thoughts were some sort of aberrations, that I wasn't going completely insane and hallucinating. After about a month, Fergus came to 'fetch me' as he put it. Maeve Ramsey wanted to see me. After I scraped a month's dirt and beard off, I went to see her. She was our clan leader then, and Brenna's grandmother. I told her what had happened to me. It seems she had been waiting for me to recognize my vision quest, the direction for my life. She told me that my job this lifetime was to protect. I was not Brenna's nor she mine, but Brenna would need me as a special warrior, for now. That would be my role in Brenna's life until her other half appeared."

Deke was stunned. This incredible, experienced man selflessly had spent years taking care of a love that could never be. Waiting for her to find a love that was not him.

"My God, man. How did you do it?" Deke's admiration grew by leaps and bounds. Loving, but knowing that having was never to be. Deke wasn't sure that he had that much self-sacrifice or discipline inside himself. And he was certainly not worthy of Brenna Ramsey.

"You know the history of our clan. What you don't know, and few people do, is that long ago a group of men sworn to protect became a continuing line of a society of warriors. To be Shields and Swords. Anonymously. Maeve Ramsey sent me to Scotland to train to become part of our underground warrior society. Afterward, I chose to go into the military to serve in special operations while Brenna grew up. I was wounded in a country gathering intelligence where no American was supposed to be. An alternative story of helping in Africa was told to everyone." Kelly stopped, and lifted an eyebrow in question.

"My mind stopped at the 'underground warrior society'," admitted Deke. "What is that?" he began again, "Can you talk about it? Did it help in keeping Brenna safe?"

Kelly smiled sadly, "Brenna. Yes, it helped in the physical sense. I was already proficient with guns, but the society made me tougher and harder to kill. Something like your training in law enforcement, or at training camps of the FBI, but on high dosages of steroids."

"In the Scottish Highlands, I was trained in hand-to-hand combat and how to stay alive with little or no resources." Kelly gave a grimace as he remembered. "The Highlands can be a harsh, cruel land, especially in wintertime. The weather is severe, so cold and wet that it seeps inside your bones turning them to ice when you have to be outside for a length of time. Survival training was not easy, but those that were chosen to endure it became inevitably tougher than most people in other lands. The mental lessons turned out to be much more important than the physical lessons of deprivation."

"That's incredible," Deke stated. Then after a moment of thought he asked, "Does Brenna know?"

"She is aware that her grandmother and now Catherine, our leaders with Second Sight, have always been protected. She also knows the Council assigned me to stay with her since the problems with O'Neill last year. If she goes anywhere outside of Shadow Valley, I go with her. In truth, I volunteered. As I told you before, I've always known that it was my job to protect Brenna this lifetime, for now."

"This secretive warrior society? How does it work?" Deke's mind was alive with the possibilities.

"The society operates outside the Sgnoch Council, but with its full knowledge and support. This allows them to designate a warrior when they feel that someone needs it. Like in the case of O'Neill last year. Several were assigned to Shadow Valley in case they were needed instantaneously. Most of them worked out at the airport."

"Then ..."

Kelly held up his hand stilling the interruption. "Usually the ceann cath of the female line is the designee that protects the female clan leader," Kelly continued. "In Maeve Ramsey's case, she appointed her son as ceann cath. Unfortunately, he was valueless as a warrior. He was whip smart, but didn't have that particular fierce instinct that is needed to make the fatal decisions. You and I both know that sometimes ruthlessness is paramount when people need protecting. Also he was away from the clan with his wife most of the time. I guess his wife had a difficult time fitting into clan restrictions."

"If her son didn't protect Brenna's grandmother, who did?"

"Grandfather Youngblood fulfilled the role. He had the training as a young man and had served as her ceann cath until

Brenna's father was an adult. Maeve Ramsey only had the one child. She wanted him to be her second in command. It was her right to choose just as it is Catherine's right. Grandfather Youngblood was assigned to protect Maeve Ramsey when the ceann cath was not available, which turned out to be most of the time. After Maeve Ramsey's son was killed in the plane crash, Grandfather Youngblood resumed the role with Kamon as backup until Maeve's death."

Deke did not remark on the fact that Kelly referred to Brenna's father as Maeve Ramsey's son instead of as a parent of the three girls.

"And Kamon is Catherine's ceanna cath and her bodyguard. Right? Trent told me."

"*Was* her bodyguard," Kelly stated, emphasizing the word was. "Trent has taken the training to take over that job himself. When he's not with Catherine, the job will return to Kamon."

"And Raina?"

Kelly chuckled in spite of the seriousness of the conversation. "Raina is also protected by Kamon. He's never been able to relinquish that job to anyone else although he complains constantly. The twins, Liam and Sean, have been trained for Raina's protection, but Kamon hasn't been able to let go of the responsibility. He has deemed it unnecessary so far. And by the way, don't ever underestimate the twins. Despite their easygoing nature and appearance, those two took to the training like warriors born. Had to practically pry them out of the Highland wilds when the survival trials were finished."

"Your tribal clan is beyond anything I've ever imagined. Could ever imagine." Deke took a deep breath, exhaling it slowly. "Kelly, you understand what I am. I've lived with few to no rules in the last five years. Hell, if I didn't break the rules I certainly bent them in all the years before that. I know I'm not good enough for Brenna."

"You're right. You're not. But then no one is." Kelly gave a rueful smile.

"Now what? Brenna has no clue how I feel about her. And

Kelly, let me explain. She was exhausted after the emergencies at the hospital when a bus overturned. She spent a seventeen-hour day helping all the injured. I held her while she slept as she asked. There was no sex," Deke stated bluntly.

"Are you are in love with her?" Kelly's voice was quiet and earnest.

"What's not to love?" Deke answered, feeding the question back at Kelly.

"You're going to stay with her?" Kelly asked softly.

"If she will let me. And I don't know about that. It's whatever she wants," Deke added. He couldn't share his innermost feelings with someone who could be hurt by them, so he kept the depth of his attraction to himself.

"Neither of us wants Brenna hurt. That's a given. I think we want the same thing, what's best for Brenna." Kelly raised an eyebrow in question.

"That's the most important," agreed Deke. "For the first time in my life, I want someone else's happiness more than I need my own, but I will respect whatever you decide is best."

"The easiest way is for me to take another assignment."

"Another assignment? You mean go somewhere else? You can do that?" Deke held his breath, not allowing the relief to show in his voice. Kelly gone would make his life so much easier. But would it also be the best for Brenna?

Kelly continued, "A very distant cousin of mine, a widow, has asked me to help her in settling her late husband's estate, and to represent her at council. Her lands are on a small island near Skye, off the coast of Scotland. I have close relatives on another nearby island where some of our clan lives part of the time. I think I'll call her and see if the offer is still open. If it is, it could be the solution, and I'll take her up on it."

"Kelly, if you're sure that would be the best for Brenna. She's the important one."

"It's time." The softly voiced words had the impact of thunder.

Deke had to swallow the lump in his throat before he could

answer. He knew that Kelly would not want to continue to discuss his feelings toward Brenna, as he himself did not, so he moved on to what could be Kelly's future without belittling the past.

"Kelly, it's not hyperbole to say you're the most remarkable man I've ever known. To give up such an important position to fulfill the duties of Brenna's bodyguard is the most unselfish act I can imagine. I hope we can remain friends. And I mean that sincerely. Not only do I owe you my life for Columbia, but now this. If there's ever anything I can do to repay you, you only have to ask. Anything. Big or little, if it's in my power, it's yours." Kelly was someone he would always owe.

"Take care of Brenna. Make her happy," Kelly said in a husky voice.

"My word," Deke replied truthfully. "I will do my best. Kelly, I have no idea how this will play out. I only know that I'll do whatever Brenna needs and wants."

Kelly gave a nod. "It will be easier on Brenna without my protracted goodbyes. I'll call her on the phone later today and tell her I've decided to take Johanna up on her offer. I do ask one thing of you."

"Name it. It's yours."

"This visit and conversation will remain between the two of us forevermore, as the Scots say."

"Done. My word," Deke said solemnly. "Oh, and I wish you all the best. And good luck with your new boss."

"Good God, I'm going to need it. Johanna is a bossy, temperamental shrew. Her great beauty is equaled only by her outrageous temper. But she has a need of me."

"Why are you doing it then? Damn, I don't want you to be unhappy."

"Of course I could be reassigned if I wished. Johanna is, however, part of my past. Maybe its time I faced that part," Kelly said with a slight smile.

Deke thought he detected more than a tiny glimmer of excitement in Kelly's dark eyes as he talked about his new potential employer.

The men shook hands and Deke watched Kelly drive his borrowed car back toward the hospital. He reentered the tiny house, and went back to bed beside Brenna. His last thought before sleep was how blessed he was.

CHAPTER NINETEEN

Brenna woke to the sound of the telephone. Over the years she had learned to listen and respond to the ringing tones. Traffic, noise, conversation, even yelling she slept through, but not the telephone. The phone meant that someone needed her. She rolled over to grab her cell to find it gone. She had left it in her coat pocket when she had returned from the hospital. It abruptly stopped and she head Deke's voice.

"Dr. Ramsey's phone. Deke Paxton speaking."

A pause then, "Oh, hello Kelly. Are you back in the country?"

A longer pause and then she heard Deke say, "She's still asleep. It's been a hell of a week. She's been really busy, last night..." Then several minutes of silence. "Yeah she is. Dr. Farrison's office sent word that there are no patients scheduled until afternoon. They told me to let the Doctor sleep. The rest of the staff was also up most of the night. Yeah, right."

Brenna eased from the bed, rolling her shoulders to loosen the sore back muscles. Bending over a make-shift gurney had tightened up her back and shoulders. And she was starving. She couldn't remember the last time she ate, maybe yesterday at noon.

She glanced down to be sure she was still decently clothed, then noted the indentation in the other pillow on her bed. She had asked Deke to hold her last night. That's what he had done. All he had done, if her fully clothed body was any indication. Thank goodness. She wanted to be fully conscious if she ever had *that* sexual experience. Mmmm. She couldn't help a fleeting mental indulgence for a second.

"Yes, I can do that. It's not an imposition at all," Deke's voice sounded soothing. "I'm fine. Almost completely well in fact. No, I have nothing planned, Brenna is the most important. Yes, of course. That's no problem." More silence then, "Yes, she is. You have my word. I know you will and I'll help you. Uh huh. That's okay by me. If I can help, all you have to do is call. I'll always have your back. Agreed."

Brenna cocked her head to one side in thought. Deke was agreeing with Kelly or someone and talking about her.

"Just a moment, I'll see if she's awake," she heard Deke's footsteps on the wooden floor and then the steps were lost on the hall carpet. Opening the door a crack to see in, he spotted her sitting on the bed. Smiling into the phone, "You're in luck. She's sitting on the bed. I don't think she's quite fully awake though," he grinned at Brenna. "Just a second, here she is. It's Kelly," he informed her. "And he asked for it to be put on speakerphone."

Smiling at Deke, she said, "Good morning, Kelly. Yes, I hear you loud and clear."

"You've had a really busy time since I've been gone. Everything okay with you?" Kelly asked though the phone.

Brenna wondered what he would say if she blurted out the truth. *No it's not. I do not want to get out of bed. I want to spend the next few days, or maybe months, in bed with Deke Paxton.* She grimaced at her wayward thoughts.

"I'm doing well, but first tell me about you. Then tell me about Haiti. Did you do a follow-up on that old man with the ulcerated foot? I've been worried he'd lose it without proper care. Did you see Pierre and his little family? Is the new doctor from Spain working out?"

"Whoa. I want to talk to you about something important but first let me answer your questions," Kelly replied in an affectionate tone. "I'm fine. I did not personally see the old man with the abscessed foot, but Dr. Henry said he was well enough to return to his village, and the local nurse promised to follow-up closely. I did see Pierre. His arm is healing nicely and the cast will come off this week. He wanted to know if the 'shiny-haired one' was coming back soon. I told him you weren't sure when you

209

would be there, but you would be sure to see him when you did."

He paused then added, "Oh, and I spoke with Mrs. Robineau about Pierre's mother getting into their program to help single mothers learn a trade. She's seen the mother, and has moved the little family into housing operated by a Swiss foundation. It seems she's just the kind of candidate they're looking for as she has no other family and few resources. Mrs. Robineau thinks they will be okay, but she promised to keep a check on them for us. Sorry, what else?"

"That's fabulous news about Pierre's 'manman,' as he calls her. I don't even know their last name to ask about them."

Kelly chuckled. "Their last name is Schmidt. They took the name of a man that Pierre's father had worked for when he was a child. At least now it will definitely stick in our minds. Mrs. Robineau says you can call her anytime for an upgraded progress report."

"Oh, yeah," Brenna clarified. "The other question was how's the new Spanish doctor working out? I felt really bad about dumping all the work on him but Catherine needed me."

"Yes, Catherine did need you and your first responsibility was to be with her," Kelly agreed. "Dr. Castone's surprisingly good. He did volunteer work in the Caribbean as an undergrad so he's more or less aware of the problems. He's young, eager and very altruistic. Made me feel a hundred years old. And cynical."

"Ha, Kelly, never you," laughed Brenna, warmth lacing her voice.

A pause, then an inward breath, "There is something we need to talk about though. Something serious, Brenna."

"Okay." Brenna had seldom heard that somber tone of voice from Kelly. Whatever it was if it was in her power to give, she would. Kelly had made her feel safe and looked-after for the last several years. "If it's in my power, it's yours," she told him honestly.

"Oh okay, that's a relief. Then I have your permission to volunteer you to work with Nurse Hackett?"

"In your dreams," laughed Brenna. "You'd never be so

mean. That woman practices terrorizing the hospital staff in Port-Au-Prince. With her domineering attitude and my sweet temper …, can you imagine?"

"In truth … I have a major problem, Brenna. The easiest way is to just blurt it out. Johanna Leask has asked for my help in a multitude of areas of her estate. And as her representative to council."

"That's a problem? Kelly, that's absolutely fabulous! She's one of my favorite people. You will do an outstanding job. She's smart to ask you," enthused Brenna.

"She's asked before, but the timing was not right. Now there's extra pressure on her as Dougal's widow. As grounded as she wants to appear on the outside, she's struggling."

"I didn't know that," Brenna exclaimed. "Why didn't you tell me? You know that when I'm embedded with any of the National Guard Units that I'm safe! Now I'm mad at myself for not asking. I took advantage of your abilities and friendship. And Kelly, I'm sorry. You should have gone when she asked you." She took a deep breath. "Hindsight is always 20-20 just as Grandfather always said. Truthfully, I'm happy that you can help Johanna as you've helped me. How soon do you have to leave?"

"That's another problem, Brenna. She needs me to be there yesterday. I'm at Shadow Valley now, but I wanted to talk everything over with you before I made the final decision."

"Good grief, Kelly, you don't need me to tell you to go for it. You will be an enormous help to Johanna. I know you'll miss working in the medical field, but Johanna's estate has been a huge responsibility for her. I hear she's had all kinds of problems with Dougal's cousins."

"I can handle them," Kelly assured her. "They just need to feel a little force when they shove. It seems like the cousins are threatening to take over her finances."

"Then…."

"I promised the Sgnoch Council that I would be your bodyguard and protector whenever you are not on the clan properties. Now, before you throw what Grandfather Youngblood would call a hissy fit, I want to tell you that I asked Deke Paxton if he would be willing to substitute for me. For the short time you still have in Spring Creek."

"You did what? What were you thinking? I am fully capable of taking care of myself," Brenna said angrily.

"Then I'll tell Johanna that I cannot accept the position. I gave my word that there would be someone capable of protecting you for now. I will remain as your bodyguard instead. A man is only as good as his word."

Brenna knew that Kelly was not bluffing. He would turn down the position to keep his contract with the Council, and to maintain his own integrity. No matter how much he wanted to help Johanna he would not break his word.

"That's emotional blackmail," she fumed.

"That's reality and the honest truth," Kelly assured her.

"You've talked to Deke about this? Tell me exactly what he said," she demanded, knowing that Deke could hear her.

"Yes, I have. He said he would be happy to fill in for however long you deemed necessary. He said he is operating at almost full physical strength, and would be able to handle anything that came your way. He's trained as an enforcer, and is very experienced. I trust him, Brenna. If I didn't, I would not even consider Johanna's offer."

Brenna let a few moments pass before she admitted, "I have no choice, do I?"

A small coughing sound could be heard from behind her. Deke had heard the entire conversation. In the small little house, it would have been impossible for him not to, especially on the speaker phone.

Holding the phone out so that Kelly could hear she asked Deke, "Kelly says he needs for you to stay here until the end of the next week when I go back to Shadow Valley. He needs this. Not me, but him," she emphasized. "Nothing is going to happen to me here, but he won't take Johanna's job unless you're here."

Brenna tried to make her voice sound flat and emotionless, as if she didn't care whatever Deke did. Truthfully she wasn't sure what she felt. Deke leaving meant that her life would continue to repeat the previous years before, volunteering her abilities as a healer and physician wherever and whenever she was needed. Deke staying was like walking into unknown territory without a guide, something she wasn't sure she wanted to do.

An unsmiling Deke said loudly enough for Kelly to hear on the phone, "I want to stay. I will do whatever is necessary to keep Brenna safe, and to help her in any way I can."

Kelly's voice asked, "For how long?"

"As long as Brenna wants me."

The double entendre was not lost on Brenna. Or did Deke really mean for it to sound like it did? Deke's eyes never left hers.

"When do you plan on leaving for Johanna's?" questioned Brenna, her eyes still on Deke.

"I really am packing as we speak. I told Johanna I would accept her offer provisionally, but that I would need to consult you and the Council first. I've talked to the Council and gained their permission. They've agreed that Deke substitutes for me until you return to Shadow Valley. Liam will fly me to Fortuna, then we'll change planes and go on to the Island by way of New York or Edinburgh. Liam is testing an engine that they've modified with special fuels they're playing with, so who knows?" Kelly's chuckle sounded forced.

"How do I thank you for the last year and …."

"It was my job, this lifetime, for then. Take care shiny-haired one."

Brenna started to say something else only to realize the telephone had been disconnected. She noted to herself the difference in Kelly's normal 'My job, this lifetime, for now' had been changed to 'My job, this lifetime, for then'.

Brenna hung up the phone slowly and turned to Deke. Never one to dodge when confronting was an option, she asked, "Why? Why would you do this? Stay here?"

"Is that idle curiosity, or do you want to have this conversation now? How about talking about it tonight?"

"I think we should discuss this now. I have about a thousand misgivings about our situation."

"And I think it's going to take talking about all those mis-givings and how long that's going to take. Your clinic already has patients who are waiting. Tonight. Please," he asked holding his palm up.

The please did it for Brenna. She gave a short nod and returned to her room, got dressed, picked up her white doctor's coat, and exited through the living room. Deke was not in sight.

CHAPTER TWENTY

Deke had made himself scarce as Brenna dressed and left for the clinic. There was no percentage in a conversation with Brenna that would be hurried and non-productive. He needed time to think about the answers he would need. He grinned, realizing that Brenna would be like a little bull terrier as she demanded to know everything he could tell her. She wouldn't accept half-assed responses or evasions.

He would have to tell her what was in his heart, and take the consequences. Toss the dice. If she wasn't attracted at the level he was, he would rather know it now. Not so that he could cut his losses, but to manage his responses. Brenna was too special to put up with anyone mooning over her when she did not want that kind of attention.

He dressed in old jeans and a warm plaid shirt, then pulled on his old beat-up cowboy boots. Since he had returned from South America the weather had seemed colder. He gave a fleeting thought if his system would have a chance to adjust before he left again. Where he would go would be up to Brenna. Completely. There was a brief knock on the door before he heard Trent's voice followed by another male.

"Deke? You here? Kamon and I need to talk with you."

"Yeah. I'm in the bedroom, be right there. Is anything wrong?" he questioned.

Trent and Kamon Youngblood had grabbed a couple of chairs in the small living room by the time he entered. The men exchanged glances before Trent answered. "Not wrong, exactly. We're here on a two-fold mission," Trent grinned broadly. "I've just received my pilot's license, so Kamon and I are taking a congratulatory flight."

"Well done! That was fast. I know you've really worked at this," Deke teased. "It took me forever to earn mine. But the memory of that day was awesome, still is."

"When your love life is hundreds of miles away, it gives you an added incentive," laughed Trent. "You know how much I hate depending on other people. This way I can come and go as I need. Next is qualifying in the little Lear."

"How are Catherine and Alexa? You know you got damn lucky, old son. They're both first rate."

"They're wonderful. And fabulous. And gorgeous." Trent glanced sidewise at Kamon. "If you had told me years ago how I would feel about both my ladies, I wouldn't have believed you." He shook his head. "My only regret is that my mother didn't live to see them."

"She would have loved them too," admitted Deke, with a fond smile of remembrance. "My God, she took in Bob and me to help raise us through our rough times. I can only imagine her and Alexa."

"Yeah," agreed Trent with a smile in his eyes.

Deke was aware that Kamon had said nothing through the conversation, simply watching the affectionate exchange between the two life-long friends. He knew that in the past Kamon and Trent had an adversarial relationship during Trent's pursuit of the lovely clan leader. They had become good friends only since the wedding.

"You said there were two things. First your license, what's the second?"

Kamon answered. "The second one is that Catherine sent us to see you. We waited until Brenna left."

"You wanted to talk to me without Brenna being present?" questioned Deke frowning.

"Yep."

"Okay. Let's hear it. Do you all disapprove of my filling in for Kelly? Do you think that I can't take care of her? Is there someone else they had in mind? Were you all going to leave her by herself?" Deke felt his breath coming faster as his heart rate increased.

"Sit still and listen for a minute. It's none of those things," asserted Kamon firmly. "Let's get the easy stuff out of the way first. Kelly told us that he had talked to you. Catherine, the Sgnoch Council and I, all are aware that you are capable of taking care of Brenna in whatever trouble she could get into. And we do know that Brenna will go to help anyone without regard to her own safety so she does need someone with her. Taking care of her is not the issue. We were sent because Catherine says that she must know how long you plan to be her guard."

"As long as she will allow me to stay," stated Deke looking directly into the ceann-cath's eyes. "I would say forever if Brenna chooses."

Kamon was silent, letting the words resonate in the room.

"We had to talk to you regarding your intent first, then we may talk to Brenna. But if you choose to stay in a permanent assignment to Brenna, we would like you to spend a month or so in the Scottish Highlands to refresh your skill set, and perhaps learn some new ones. Kelly said he told you about the warrior group. You would be required to take a blood oath, of course, as part of the Warrior Society. You do understand a blood oath, correct?"

"Yeah. It means cutting yourself and mixing blood for a particular purpose, like in becoming brothers." He held up his left hand to show the small scar at the thumb base. "Trent, Bob and I did it when we were about nine years old."

"And it hurt like hell, so we thought we were the toughest kids ever," chuckled Trent, hold up his left hand to show off his matching scar.

"In South America and in Mexico it is not unusual for gangs to require members to take a blood oath to protect the members from disclosing gang actions. Most often illegal activities. Essentially to break the vow promises immediate retaliation, usually in major blood being spilled. Or death," commented Deke.

"That pretty much sums it up," nodded Kamon solemnly.

"And you've done this?" questioned Deke, addressing

Trent. "You've gone through secretive combat training?" Deke didn't mention the blood oath as it simply would never be an issue for either him or Trent.

"Yeah. Several months ago. I would give my life for Catherine and Alexa in a New York minute. With the extra training, I actually know how to protect them better. I spent a couple of months there. It's intense and very physical. The Scottish Highlands are incredibly beautiful in a harsh and mystical way, but the setting did not make up for the difficulty of the training," grinned Trent.

The two old friends looked at each other steadily. Each knew that once they committed to something, hell or push wouldn't change it.

"Do you remember me telling you that if there was a time when you needed further information about Brenna and our clan system, I would tell you? You were still sick and at Stone House," reminded Kamon.

"Vaguely," Deke said honestly. "My mind was on low functioning for a time there. I may have mixed up some things and forgotten others."

"That's Catherine's take as well. She says she had intended to wait for awhile longer, to give you more time to heal, but Kelly's leaving forced a change. She has decided that you now need to know more about the clan and Brenna."

Kamon hesitated, then went on to say, "You know the story of our clan beginnings, our girl-woman with Second Sight?"

Deke nodded.

"Our ancestors kept detailed diaries, knowing that future generations might have a need to review the past. I suspect that they hoped and prayed we would not repeat their mistakes. Of course, many of them we did repeat. The clan history that few people know is that one of the two female children from that first girl-woman with Second Sight was a Healer, very like Brenna. She grew up, married and was childless." Kamon let the silence stretch out.

"There has been a Healer born to about every fifth generation of this clan, sometimes less time, sometimes longer. In two hundred fifty years, only two women with healing abilities have been able to conceive."

Deke was silent, waiting for an end to the story.

"Grandmother Ramsey and Grandfather Youngblood knew all the history of clan healers. They had Brenna, Catherine and Raina read our ancestor's diaries. The grandparents felt that by knowing the past, some of the problems might be averted in the future. The Healer's diaries were given to Brenna to read to keep her safe, and to prepare her for whatever her future holds. There is a special connective bond between our ancestors, and the gifts which have been received."

Kamon gazed intently at Deke, letting the silence linger.

"Then it is unlikely that Brenna can conceive a child?" asked Deke quietly, his heart hurting for the woman who so loved children.

"Highly improbable. Both Grandfather Youngblood and Grandmother Ramsey tried to prepare Catherine and Brenna for the futures that they thought would be theirs. They taught Brenna that a Healer was blessed to be able to perform the miracle of making people hurt less. And that the gift of Healing was a miracle that overshadowed everything else. Her destiny."

Deke felt unwanted tears in the back of his eyes. Brenna with her deep love of children growing up understanding and internalizing her Karma. A childless one. What had she said? What is, Is. Her internal strength surpassed his own by eons.

"Do you know of the bonding that occurs between certain clan men and women who mate? In particular, Catherine, Brenna and Raina. What happens to them?"

"Trent mentioned that the tie which binds the two together after loving is permanent, but could you explain it again? Now it has more meaning for me as I know the people involved."

Kamon took a deep breath. "I would rather have a root canal with a sharp stick than to have to explain this. But I do as Catherine asks. Essentially the first sexual experience for any of the three Ramsey women will be the person they will be bonded for life. There can be no other for them." Looking over, Kamon said, "Honestly, Trent, if you don't take the smirk off your face, I'm going to punch you. And the next unpleasant job is yours."

Trent smiled broadly, and remained quiet.

"I don't understand and I'm unsure what to ask," Deke admitted in a hesitant voice. "I guess I don't understand the 'bonded for life' part. But the way you're talking it sounds different from the 'til death do us part' marriage-bonding type of meaning. Trent, you mentioned it when O'Neill tried to kidnap Maggie or Catherine, but I didn't ask questions. My mind was on taking him out before he could do any damage."

"And a good job you did too," murmured Trent.

Kamon frowned at Trent's interruption. After a moment, he continued, "The lineage for Catherine, Raina and Brenna has been one of direct descendant, that is a direct line from the first Seer. Their lives have a pathway backward and forward. The Ramsey lineage has followed the pathway set long ago and the line is pure. Their mating is imprinted on their partner and vice-versa. They will share who and what they are, each taking something and giving something. Both will become more … or even less, depending on whether the bedding is forced. An expansion if you will."

"If something happened to Trent…?" he questioned, nodding his head toward his friend.

"Catherine can never bond again. Oh, she could have a physical sexual experience with someone, but the bonds of love would cease for her and would no longer exist. Ever. With anyone else she would be less, not more. Her gifts diminished. The Ramsey women can only have one love-union."

Kamon held up his hand toward Trent to stay his further interruption.

"This holds true only for the three of them? No others?"

"No others. Both Catherine and Raina have been protected for most of their lives, especially Catherine. The grandparents knew Catherine's destiny at a very early age. She was raised knowing that the gifts, and most probably clan leadership, would be hers to manage. Training and protection were an integral part of her everyday life. Brenna has had much more freedom. She came into her abilities much later and they developed more slowly but are more personally intense on a different level than Catherine's wide-ranging abilities. She was sent to medical school to enhance what she already was. Her life's work as a Healer has taken her all over the world, which she believes is her Purpose or Destiny. Also, being around large groups of people energizes Brenna, whereas it brings a severe mode of panic to Catherine."

"Did Catherine tell you why she wanted me to know this now?"

Kamon grinned broadly, eyes sparkling, "She didn't tell me, but I can make a real healthy guess."

Deke lifted an eyebrow in inquiry.

"I think that she feels that her little sister may be feeling some adult sexual emotions, and wants you to be aware of Brenna's needs. And what happens if you did seduce her. The two of them are very close."

"Catherine told me that she could no longer See you, Deke, which occurs when a person is closely linked with one of her loved ones in a positive way. That means that you are now tied intimately to Brenna, I would suspect," explained Kamon grinning.

"Whoa," Trent sniggered, waggling his eyebrows at Deke like when they were kids.

Both Kamon and Deke gave Trent a narrow look of disapproval.

CHAPTER TWENTY-ONE

Brenna returned from the clinic to meet a restless Deke Paxton pacing the small living room floor. The confrontation she had so wanted in the early morning had now decreased to a low simmer. Tomorrow, or a week from next Thursday, now seemed like a better time for this conversation. Words were like arrows that couldn't be taken back. But not knowing made her vulnerable, on edge. Trying to guess the next move. Normally, she was the one who wanted the confrontation to clear the air but not this time.

"Are you ready to talk now?" asked Deke. "If you're too tired we can talk at another time."

"No, I do not want to have this conversation now. Maybe never. But I would rather know now, so I can plan one way or the other," Brenna stated decisively.

"One way or the other?" Deke asked raising an eyebrow. "What does that mean?"

"How long do you plan to stay? Are you going where I go? You have your own career. What about your writing? What about Paul Tate? You can't let him die, too many people enjoy reading about his exploits and adventures. Me included. And you're talented and...."

"Whoa., whoa. I told you. I will stay as long as you want me to stay. And you are avoiding the real issue. Do you want me to stay?" He took a deep breath. "Hell, Brenna. I know I have things to work out. It's taken me a long time to figure out what I want. What I need to have in my life. I'm too rough, and wouldn't even enter into any Mr. Gentleman contest."

"Now *you're* avoiding the issue."

"What issue? Pretty damn simple to me. I stay until you say

I go."

"Deke, listen, I don't play games. I don't know how to play games. I never know when it's a game and when it's for real. Game rules elude me. Why would you consider staying with me? And for how long? For a week? For a year?" She would have liked to add forever but didn't have that much courage.

"Here's the truth and you can do with it what you will. You connect something in me. I want to explore the connection to see what comes of it." He held up his hand to ward off her interruption. "It's as simple as that."

He paused to let the last sentence soak in. "Brenna, you attract me on every level. Physically I want to touch all of you. I love the sunlight in your hair and the clear green of your eyes. I love the womanly curves, but I also love your integrity and dedication to your art of healing. I'm in awe of your ability to give and give. I look at you, both the inside and outside of you and am blown away by who you are. You can't be real."

"Deke, like I said before. I'm simple. Really simple. I need to tell you two things before this conversation goes any further." She took a moment to gather her thoughts, "First you must know I have no experience with men. None. Zilch. Maybe you guessed that when I kissed you. I've had lots of opportunities but never saw the need to indulge, so to say. I must also be truthful. I am drawn to you too. I dream of you. I physically want you in my bed. And it cannot be." This time it was Brenna who held up her hand for Deke not to interrupt. "But in the long run, where is this headed?"

"Are you asking if my intentions are honorable?" grinned Deke.

"Yes. No. I don't know. Our relationship can't go anywhere."

"Why the hell not?" Deke fought down his need to yell. And to celebrate.

"I never intend to marry. Not ever. I can't."

"What do you mean you never plan to marry? My God, you're twenty-six. You have your whole life before you."

"Twenty-seven. You know what I am. A Healer. I go where

I'm needed. What you don't know is that I cannot bear a child. I'm barren." She took a deep breath, fighting back tears. "It wouldn't be fair for someone to marry me. I cannot conceive a child. I can never have a child, a family. Believe me, when I was younger I had to work through feelings of being cheated. And thoughts that somehow that made me less of a woman. Then I had to ask myself if I would trade my gifts of healing to be a woman who could give birth to a child. The answer was a very resounding no. I am a Healer, that's my soul's work. What was intended for me this lifetime. But I would never ask any man to forego having a family."

Deke looked at her stonily, "You mean that if you can't be a baby-making machine, you won't love anyone? Brenna, that's nuts! And quite frankly it paints all men with a very broad brush of selfishness. Me included."

"I'm not interested in anyone else," Brenna protested angrily. "I've never been interested in anyone before."

"But you're not seeing me, Brenna. Me. Look at me. Really look." He insisted intently. "Do I have a family now? Do you see them around me being part of my life? A child running around? A love? I've been a wanderer, so restless and looking for something I had no name for. Until you, Brenna. Until you."

"But you need to find someone you can make a child with. All men need children."

"Brenna, I don't know what all men need, and neither do you. But no, that's not what I need. What I need is to have a commitment to someone I love - with all that I am. A child would be great if it happened but it is not necessary for me to be happy. Mostly, Brenna, I need someone to be mine, as I am hers."

"My life is about healing. Helping whenever I can. If I had a husband, I wouldn't be able to do all the things I've needed to do. That ..."

"Brenna, I've shared your live for the last two months," interrupted Deke. "The last three weeks we've shared whatever has been thrown your way. Be honest for both our sakes. Have I slowed you down? Have I been a deterrent to your medical career? Or for you in your Destiny as a healer?"

"No, you've been a big help actually, but Deke you can't give up your life just to help me."

"Who the hell said anything about me giving up anything? Brenna, don't you get it yet? You have become the most important thing in my life! And that includes me." Deke stopped and looked at her.

Brenna didn't know what to say. Here was a man putting his heart out there. Stepping out into the unknown where she was too afraid to go. And not just any man, but a warrior. A Protector. He was willing to commit to something that terrified her.

"I've told you before what I want. To belong to someone. To have a home and family. Your family is Catherine and Raina and Kamon and all the rest of the people you care about. Family doesn't have to be babies or children, but I want to belong. To give all that I am. That may make little sense to you, but I want to commit."

Brenna shook her head in confusion. Was it really that easy? That she could take what she wanted. That Deke would stay with her wherever she had to go. That she could share her life, her goals? She closed her eyes as she felt tears spring. Yes, she wanted that with every fiber of her being, but was it real? Could it last?

"Look, I know I'm no prize. I'm a burnt out ex-cop with a talent for mimicking and a little bit of writing success. I'm too old for you. Too experienced in the violent side of life's force. That's a big negative for someone like you. I've seen too much and cared too little about what is now important. But what I can do is keep you safe. I can make sure that you are able to do what you need to do. You are the important one. I don't want it to be a burden to you, but you must know that I'm in love with you. The once-in-a lifetime kind of love." Stepping close, Deke raised Brenna's chin gently with one finger. "I know you don't love me, but I want to be where you are, taking care of you."

Shock registered on Brenna's face. "You are?"

Deke gave a slight one-sided grin. "Yes. And no, you don't

need to say anything. Telling you was for me. I know you don't feel the same way and that's okay. I ...."

"Deke, shut up for a minute. I think I'm in love with you too. No, I *know* I love you too. I just didn't believe I'd ever find real love. I was so sure of everything. Yet... it's snuck up on me when I wasn't looking," tears slowly slid down Brenna's cheeks, realization slowly dawning on her face, her eyes searching out his.

Carefully, as if not wanting to startle her, Deke folded Brenna's body into his arms, cradling her head to his chest, holding her tightly. She kept her body locked tightly against him as he stroked her hair and lightly caressed her back, soothing with each pass of his hands. Erasing doubts and past pain. She rose on her tiptoes and pulled his face down. She kissed him with all the tenderness she could find in her being. Deke returned the kiss, igniting fire as the kiss became deeper and more intense. She tightened her arms around him drawing him closer as her passion increased.

"Whoa, darling. I need to stop while I still can." Deke took a step backward and gently untangled Brenna's arms with hands that trembled. "We need to talk. Before it goes further we need to discuss something else."

Brenna closed her eyes and managed a deep breath. Whatever it was she didn't want to hear it. She wanted to stay in Deke's arms and continue to feel the excitement of him.

"Catherine sent Kamon to talk to me."

"What? Why?" She took a step back.

"At first I thought it was because she knew that I wasn't good enough for you."

"Catherine would never say something that stupid," declared Brenna with asperity.

"No, it wasn't that. Kamon told me that you have never made love with anyone before. That you will bond to that person when you do. And that the bond is forever."

Brenna looked away, feeling her temper rising. "Damnit to hell! Why did they interfere? I would have told you. Maybe not right now, but eventually."

"I think they figured that your eventually might be after the deed was done, so to speak. I want you with every breath I take. I ache. But I want you to make a clear-headed choice. Because for me, Brenna, it's also forever. I'm too old for games and too pragmatic. You are the last thing I want, and the only thing in my life I need. And make no mistake Brenna, I will protect you against everyone, including myself. That means not going to let my desire for you push you into a rushed decision."

Putting action to words, Deke gently sat her down at the kitchen table. "I'll make us some coffee and then we talk."

Glaring from the table, Brenna stopped herself for a moment. Taking a deep breath and blowing it out, she said in a calmer but no less determined voice, "I'm not a child. I want you too. Stop treating me like I was an infant with no brain cells."

Rough hands hand-combed through his hair in agitation. "My heart is thundering so loudly I'm surprised you can't hear it." Hands suddenly unsteady, he carefully measured the coffee into the filter, added water and set the carafe underneath. Green eyes flashed to Deke's hazel ones as he slowly turned his body fully towards her, tension palpable in every muscle.

"Marry me," he blurted out swiftly. "I didn't mean to ask you now and I know it's a surprise." He dropped to one knee in front of her chair, eyes wide with the sudden knowledge he was actually doing this. "I love you more than my life, Brenna Ramsey. You are the mate my heart has waited for. I promise to keep you safe and to dedicate all that I am to your happiness. Marry me." He stopped for a moment and then added, "Please."

"Oh yes, please too," laughed Brenna through the tears streaming down her cheeks. She took his head in her hands and planted her lips firmly on his. The kiss was soft and then took fire, causing her heart to pound and blood rush to all her girl parts.

Eyes still closed, she blew out a deep breath. "Whew"

"Agreed. Spontaneous combustion." He sat down across from her, taking her hands in his and keeping the table between them. "It took me so long to admit to myself what has been happening inside me. I've spent most of last night thinking. And planning. If you felt only friendship for me, then I would pursue one path. If I was lucky enough for you to consider joining our lives together, another scene. No, let me finish first." He squeezed Brenna's hand slightly to ward off any interruption.

Looking directly into her face, he said seriously, "You are my love. My soulmate love. The person I want to spend the rest of my life with. I would do anything for you. Try to be anything you need. You set my heart in flames. I love you more than I've ever loved anything or anyone." He heaved a large sigh. "When Kamon and Trent came here to talk to me this morning, they told me about the Warrior Society."

Brenna's eyes widened in surprise, but she remained silent.

"Brenna, I want to train there. I need to. I want to make sure I can keep you safe under any circumstances, against anyone wherever you decide to go. And where we go, what we do, is up to you."

Allowing a quiet, knowing grin to surface, she said, "I just found you, Deke. Just found out you loved me as much as I love you. You are my life's mate. The person that was created just for me. The one person I will live with for however long we are destined to live. And you want to go train now, don't you? Like immediately."

Deke's hazel eyes looked deeply into Brenna's green ones. "If I don't go immediately, if I don't place some distance between us, you know in your heart that there's a very good chance that we will anticipate our wedding vows. I'm having a difficult time keeping my hands off your lovely body."

"So? So what? Then we are bonded. Loved returned forever."

Shaking his head, "Your people, and most specifically the Sgnoch Council, have asked that I respect your culture and tribal clan if things went my way. To wait until our vows are spoken before our physical union. I promised that I would wait. Hell, Brenna, I've waited for almost forty years for you, weeks won't kill me."

"I don't know whether to be angry or not. I don't want to wait. I've waited for years too. I don't want to be apart from you for a day now, much less the time it will take for you to join the Warrior Society. I want you in my life, and in my bed. Now."

"And I want to be there more than I can express, but I also must respect the promise I made." He gave a slight smile. "With me out of the way, you can concentrate on getting a wedding together. Without my inept input."

"That's a laugh, Deke. You obviously don't know all the personalities in the family. I'll be lucky if I have anything to say about it. Weddings fall under the auspices of Aunt Ulla and Raina, both planners extraordinaire. They might, and I say might, let me choose the flavor of our wedding cake. But probably not even that," she admitted ruefully.

"Would the two ladies be available to come and stay here until the end of the week? I don't want to leave you alone. Maybe then you could have some say in the wedding, plus then I wouldn't worry about your safety. No one would mess with those two ladies."

"Oh Deke, I'm starting to get excited! It's really true? We're actually going to marry? To live together. Forevermore, as the Scots say." Her smile was joyous. "May I call Catherine first? I have to tell someone!"

"Of course she should be told first. Do I need to ask her permission?" Deke's voice was suddenly shaky as he thought of the tribal clan leader and her authority, and her ability to shut down all their new laid plans with a word.

"No, and she will be utterly delighted. Since she married Trent she thinks all people should march together in pairs. Like in Noah's Ark," she grinned.

Brenna quickly placed a call to Catherine who did express delight at the news. Brenna told her of Deke's desire to train for the Warrior Society. Catherine also said that she was sure that Aunt Ulla and Raina would be elated to come for the dual purpose of providing company, and planning a wedding. Plans for Catherine to also visit were quickly made.

Within minutes Deke received a phone call from Kamon, congratulating him on his upcoming nuptials, and working out details for Deke to travel to the Highlands for training. Kamon thought that since Deke was in physically good shape six weeks should be adequate for a refresher course.

Kamon arranged Deke's trip to Scotland, to leave immediately.

CHAPTER TWENTY-TWO

Murdock MacLennan had pushed Deke's departure date back a couple of days, the second time he had been delayed. The Master of the Warrior School had not given a reason, simply stating that Deke would not leave until Friday.

At this rate, he would be late for his own wedding. Not going to happen, Deke vowed silently. Not even if I have to walk. I'm almost in good enough condition to do just that, he grumbled to himself.

The last six weeks had been amazingly difficult. He had thought that his body was in much better than average condition until the Warrior training had started. He quickly discovered he had muscles that could scream in agony that he had been unaware of owning. The training he had received as a law enforcement officer, FBI, and DEA agent had prepared him for a grueling regimen, but the Warrior Society had taken it one step further. He suspected that whoever had set up the Navy Seals program had borrowed part of their training manual from the Warrior Society.

When he had first arrived he had been partnered with Patrick Buchannan, an older warrior who had been assigned to mentor him. And mentor him he did. Over the ensuing six weeks, he had felt joined at the hip with the silent middle-aged man who promptly kicked his ass in every aspect of the training. However many pushups Deke did, Patrick quietly did twenty-five more. If it was running up and down the steep rocky hills of the Highland, Deke would be breathless and aching while the quiet Patrick didn't even breath hard. Set-ups, pull-ups, whatever, Patrick silently showed Deke how much further he had to push to gain his own limits. The challenge was becoming the best Warrior he could be.

Both men were proficient with guns and Deke held his own, thanks to all the hours spent on the firing range during his enforcement days. He didn't best Patrick however. They were equal in most firearms areas.

He had been trained by the FBI in martial arts, but it had been several years since he had used the training consistently. He was given a short refresher course before learning to fight in close quarters with a dagger, and then a double-edged stiletto. The stiletto was a fascinating tool. Long, thin, and razor sharp on both sides, it could be used to silently kill with a minimum of blood spilled. Relearning the anatomy of the most vulnerable parts of the human body and how to take advantage of that vulnerability, took days. All in all, it took him the better part of a week before he felt he could have held his own in a real knife fight. Once he had satisfied the seemingly never-satisfied Patrick, his knife was taken away and a dull black-finished nondescript titanium writing pen was put in his hand. At his questioning look, all he got was the laconic reply, "Boardrooms. Airplane security." And he was put through the entire course again.

At the end of *that* course, he was unceremoniously handed a wooden case with twenty such pens inside, with a handwritten note from the twins, Liam and Sean. *"Having fun yet? Check out the ten with the red tops – we had a lot of fun whipping these up after our own graduation."* Under Patrick's watchful eye, he hit the stud, and watched a slender blackened titanium blade snick out of a tiny slit from the pen tip that he would have sworn wasn't there a moment before. Heavy, it felt perfect in his hand. Looking down at the elegant but otherwise nondescript pen in his open palm, no cop he knew would ever consider this a weapon. Looking up, he saw Patrick quietly smiling at him for the first time. The men's predatory grins matched each other.

It had taken nearly five weeks before Deke was able to best Patrick physically in any endeavor. Surprisingly it had been in swimming across the local loch, as the Scots called a lake. Ice cold streams fed the lake and created a chilly bath.

Deke had loved to swim since childhood and his long lean body leant itself to the sport. Patrick's body was shorter and built more on the lines of a good wrestler. It was the only time he heard the taciturn Scot swear. "Dang, Tak an ill-will tae the lochim." It took Deke a moment to translate Patrick's speech into his dislike for the lake. "You said we had to do this at least once. Is there a certain time I have to make it across?"

"Ah hell. Soum tae that craig an back. A didna want tae but we gang thare to freeze our hinderparts anyways."

After he figured out that "soum" meant swim Deke knew that Patrick was right. The water was freezing. Deke plowed through the water in a fast efficient freestyle, leaving the less buoyant Patrick in his wake. That had been the first of the "Good jobs" he had earned from Patrick.

After five weeks Patrick had held out his hand and told him that he was ready for the next level and would be working with Murdock MacLennan. "I ken ye best me," declared the now -smiling Patrick. "I be proud ta call ye brother." He had clasped Deke firmly on the shoulder and strolled off.

The next day Deke started working with MacLennan. Instead of the physical routine he had expected, the two men had spent the day talking.

"Patrick tells me that you are physically capable of protecting an assignment. And that you can understand only parts of his Lowland speech," Murdock teased. "I was educated in England and the United States so we should have no problem."

"The only problem I had with Patrick was he made me feel like I have to work harder to even keep him in sight. And he's at least ten years older than I am."

"Yep, he is. But he says that you have passed all the physical parts of the training well. That's well-earned praise from him as most of the time he is silent. Now for the last week, we will be dealing more with the historical and psychological parts of the Warrior Society."

Deke kept silent as he had no clue where the conversation

would be going.

"Of course we will do a minimum of physical training. Mostly running to the top of that peak over there each day and back to keep in shape."

Deke barely suppressed a groan. 'That peak over there' was at least ten miles away and was a barren rocky jag of landscape. Mist shrouded the top and thorny bushes blocked many of the pathways. He knew. Patrick had made the peak one of their weekly treks.

MacLennan continued, "Being a Warrior is physically challenging, but the greater part is in your mind. To recognize that you are not a soldier, but rather a guardian. As a guardian, sometimes its necessary to protect with force. For the next week you will learn more of the history of the Celtic Warriors from which our Society is derived."

And learn he did. From the earliest Celts just after the Stone Age, through the Celtic Warriors as mercenaries, and onto the beginning remnants of the societies in Scotland, Wales and Ireland. Traces remained of each of the generation's teachings even into the modern-day information-age societies.

Deke was fascinated by their history, appalled by their lack of hygiene, and in awe of their fearless courage. Deke talked often with Murdock MacLennan, sorting through the great leaders and assessing their individual abilities, learning that courage was not innate but rather an opportunity to reach beyond fear.

On the day before he was to leave, Patrick, Murdock and three other men presented him with a short double-sided stiletto, similar to ones he had trained with, but more ornate and with ancient carvings on the silver hilt.

Placing the flat of the knife in his palm, Murdock held the hilt toward Deke. "You have become what you were destined to be. You have conquered all challenges and have the honor and integrity within to join the Warrior Society. You have taken the blood oath of secrecy. You have chosen to place another's well-being above your own. You are worthy." Murdock placed the hilt of the stiletto in Deke's hands, bowed from the waist, and stepped back.

"Thank you, I am honored," Deke said sincerely. "You have developed whatever potential I have. I will remain in your debt forevermore as I fulfill the duties assigned to me," he said formally, bowing his head.

Each man raised his dagger above his head as they formed a circle and repeated the ancient vow, Deke repeating the sacred vow last. "In secrecy we swear to protect you and yours forevermore. We will always be your Sword and Shield; we swear with honor. Let death be the judgment of any man or woman who speaks of this event of today. Today will forever be shrouded in secrecy as our own beginnings are shrouded."

There was much cheerful back-slapping and congratulations following the short ceremony. Deke was torn by the awesome responsibilities of the Society, and the need to get home to start his new life with Brenna.

EPILOGUE

Three years later

The hot summer breeze drifted across the backyard of the Stone House. Catherine and Brenna were standing close talking about the upcoming preparations for Maggie and Douglas's eighth birthday party. A large contingency from a multitude of places all over the world were coming to celebrate the twin's big day. The mischievous precocious pair were favorites of old and young people alike.

"Maggie and Douglas are running Mrs. Searle ragged trying to help with the baking, and with the tasting," Catherine told Brenna.

"I would suspect mostly tasting, especially Douglas. He's grown so much this year. Anyway, Mrs. Searle adores those imps so she's probably delighted to visit with them, even over food and a messy kitchen."

"True. None of us can help it," Catherine grinned. "They are such fun and it's never dull around them. Maggie and Douglas are growing up, yet keeping that exuberant spirit they both have. I thought they would develop other close friends, and become less close to each other as they matured. Instead they've added new friends to their twin connection but kept their close bond. And they still find trouble."

"Yeah, last week Maggie decided she and Douglas needed to dig out a cave to play in. Of course she didn't discuss it with anyone. The best dirt according to the kids was just back of the grocery store."

"Ugh. The place that Fergus stores all the worms for fishing. I'll bet he was not happy," laughed Brenna, "although he's more mellow now that he married to Joan. She's tamed some of that old grumpiness out."

Raising her eyebrows up and down, Catherine mused, "Wonder how she did that?"

"Catherine, honestly, some of Trent's naughty behavior is rubbing off on you, and no, do not answer me. And do not tell me about the naughty rubbing. Although now that I think about it …. when *are* you going to tell me your 'I'm getting bigger news'?"

"There's no keeping secrets from you," Catherine scolded in a mocking tone. "Okay, I'm pregnant again. I only told Trent last night, and he's absolutely delighted. He's had this picture of our children in his mind since our wedding so he says he's not surprised. Oh, and he is positive this one is a boy. A carbon-copy of him, he says." Catherine sighed deeply. "Did you ever think when we were growing up that we could be this happy? Right now I love everything!"

Brenna couldn't help but join in her sister's joyful laughter.

"How did you know I was pregnant again? Your gift?" Catherine asked curiously.

"Besides the fact that you glow you mean?" Brenna teased. "I don't need a Gift for this particular diagnosis. Check out your hands. They're clasped over your stomach even though there's not even a tiny baby bump yet, like you have to hold your stomach up."

Quickly dropping her tattle-tale hands, Catherine gave Brenna a hug. "The last years have been incredibly good to us. My marriage to Trent, and then the arrival of Alexa. Your marriage to Deke, and then the miracle of Brandon."

Brenna couldn't stop the unshed happy tears from quickly forming. "Brandon is a miracle. I already told you that when I missed my first period, I thought it was stress, even after the second one. Jeannine, Dr. Farrison's nurse, finally made me take a blood test before I could accept it. I don't know why I deserved all this but I'm grateful. Deke is phenomenal with Brandon; whatever he needs Deke is right there. We work together so easily," she gushed.

Both women laughed.

Smiling Catherine tipped her head toward their husbands.

"Ah Brenna, look at our tough, street-smart men." Trent and Deke were standing together silently watching their offspring.

Alexa was a petite dark-haired, golden eyed beauty of three serving pretend tea out of a miniature china cup to her cousin. Brandon at almost two years old was already the same size as Alexa. He was tall and childhood sturdy with his Aunt Catherine's black hair and Deke's hazel eyes. The two cousins could have passed for siblings except for the eyes.

"Now be careful, the tea is hot," Alexa instructed Brandon as she carefully poured air out of her teapot. Brandon looked askance into the cup, but dutifully held it up to his lips as his cousin instructed.

"They are the cutest things ever," Brenna gushed. "I'm so glad we've decided to live closer. Spring Creek isn't that far away."

"Trent was so excited about Deke buying the old Murphy place just outside Spring Creek that he can't wait to help. You know that our two husbands are going to fill up that big old barn with all the animals they missed out on growing up in a city. They're even talking about breeding some quarter-horses. Couple of kids," grinned Catherine.

"Hey, be nice to my husband. Right now Deke is in my good graces. He's potty-training Brandon…."

"Good luck with that," giggled Catherine, pointing toward the back fence line.

Brandon had pulled down his training pants and was spraying the fence post while both men stood by with goofy grins.

At Brenna's pointed glare, Deke shrugged helplessly. Trent refused to meet her eyes.

"Men," stated little Alexa with a deep exasperated sigh, her delicate arms akimbo. "Mrs. Searle is right. They're difficult to train," she stated firmly, sending all the adults into peals of laughter.

KEEP READING FOR THE FIRST
CHAPTER OF THE NEXT BOOK

Shadow's Sunshine

A Shadow Valley Novel

CHAPTER ONE

Present Day

"No, I will not!"

"Raina, be reasonable. You only have two more semesters to finish your college programs. Less than a year," Kamon coaxed, his voice raspy with control.

Raina studied the handsome man before her. Six foot one or so, slim with wide shoulder, slim hips and rigid carriage. His face was a smooth carved mask with high cheekbones revealing Native American heritage. Two thin white scars ran across his left eyebrow down to the corner of his cheek. His mid-shoulder length hair was braided into a single braid and tied with a thin strip of rawhide. Black eyes and golden complexion completed the picture of warrior status. And of the most exasperating man in her world.

"Kamon, get used to it. I am not going back. I'm twenty years old and perfectly capable of making my own decisions," Raina scowled.

"Why? Why won't you go back to school? Has something happened that I'm unaware of? Is there a reason you aren't telling me?" he demanded.

"Would you listen? No, there is no ulterior motive. The reason is just what I said, I'm spinning my wheels. Getting nowhere I want to go."

"It's just one more year," Kamon's voice was louder and angrier. "Maybe less."

"I am not going," yelled Raina in retaliation. "I. Am. Not. Damn it, you are ceaan-cath of this tribal clan but that does not make you my boss."

"No, but I am responsible for your safety. You are one of the three Ramsey women and it is my job to protect them. And stop cussing."

"Damnit, then go protect Catherine or Brenna. Oh, that's right both of them have
husbands who are trained warriors, and they don't need your protection, so all your focus can be on me," she shouted, her voice dripping with sarcasm. "And my only cuss words are damn and hell. And then only when I'm upset. Which is totally your fault."

"Their husbands take good care of them," he defended, ignoring her other comments.

"Oh, I agree with you on that issue. Trent and Deke are amazing. But that isn't the problem here. You are the problem," she declared loudly.

"I was hoping that more education would give you a direction to what you want to do".

"Kamon, listen carefully. I have done as you wanted. I majored in languages and history. I can speak more languages than anyone in the family, even Catherine. Hell, I can even speak Arabic, although why that is necessary is beyond me. I loved history, but I do not want to continue doing research. I have been the dutiful student, making exceptional grades, and doing what other people wanted me to do."

In a quieter voice, Kamon asserted, "I agree that you've been an outstanding student. That's the very reason that you should continue and graduate."

"Kamon, you are still not listening," Raina's voice was loud and inflexible. "I know what I want. I've always known, damn it. I want to stay here in Shadow Valley and help Catherine with the work of the Sgnoch Council. I want to continue hanging out with Liam and Sean, flying whatever plane they decide to modify. I want to marry and have children and ..."

"All you are doing is following in Catherine's footsteps," shouted Kamon. "You don't know what you could do if you don't bury yourself here in Shadow Valley."

"You are a total idiot!" yelled Raina, not the least intimidated by the intense, angry man. "I don't need to go anywhere to find myself. I am Raina, youngest sister of Catherine, younger sister to Brenna. I am me, Raina Ramsey. And I damn well don't need to be anyone else."

"You have no experience outside the clan compounds. You've always been protected by someone from the clan," Kamon shouted.

"And whose fault is that? I've always been protected by you, or someone else you have sent to guard me. When I'm in France at the villa there, or Canada at the ranch, or in Scotland on the Island, I'm sheltered by my name, and your name as my guard. Anywhere else I go I have a Protector, a Guard you have assigned. You have no idea what's its like to have zero privacy. Zero, Kamon. Zero." She paused for breath. "Only here in Shadow Valley can I have complete freedom. And I'm damn well staying here."

"And you well know why all the Ramsey women have to be protected. And you're getting off the subject although I do admit they are tied together," admitted Kamon reluctantly. "You need experience in how the world works, and that's why it would be best continuing school where you meet other people."

"That's a crock! An absolute crock because it doesn't have a chance of working. I have an assigned guard, remember? Oh, and I live off campus with more keepers." She lifted her hand to one side pointing at an imaginary friend, "Would you like to be my new friend?" she asked in a high sing-song voice. "Oh, and this is Mr. So and So who takes every breath I do. And stays with me twenty-four seven," she continued in her high pitched falsetto. "Girl talk? Oh, he'll pretend not to listen. Oh, but we can't go to have a coffee or lunch unless he goes." She lifted her chin and stared defiantly.

A faint blush touched Kamon's high cheek bones, barely discernable with his golden skin. "It's not as bad as that," he protested softly.

"No, it's worst. My looks draw attention but I have no chance of expanding my horizons as Brenna would say. I am not, nor can I ever be a typical, normal college student."

"I am fully aware that your unusual coloring draws people's attention," Kamon said fiercely. "Everyone's attention. Mostly the male variety."

"Kamon, are you being deliberately dumb? I am isolated. By myself. I have a few acquaintances at school, but mostly other people are not interested in someone as private as I have to be. People treat me differently than the other females in any class anyway, no matter how small the class. Partially of course it's because I'm young and protected, but also because of the face the Creator gave me. Which is not my fault."

"Okay, I grant you that. How does it affect you? On a daily basis." Kamon asked curiously, his voice a shade calmer.

Raina cocked her head to the side to think through what Kamon had asked. This was the most in-depth conversation she had ever had with him. Maybe he really could listen and treat her as a grown up.

"Both teachers and other students mostly fall into two categories," she said trying to be as honest as possible. "The most prevalent is that I am brainless and can't be taken seriously. That one applies to the majority of people, including teachers, at least until the first tests. Then, of course it changes and I become some sort of nerd oddity after I ace every test. The other one is because of my coloring; the platinum hair, the blue eyes with dark brows and lashes. With my looks I'm already classified as a party-girl, and therefore I'm open season for the players on campus."

"What? Are you serious? I've never been told any of this?" Kamon said, quickly reacting with fury.

"You still don't get it," Raina said in disgust. "None of that matters. It's over. Okay, here is the bottom line. I am not going back to school. I've tried to reason with you. I've tried to be diplomatic, well as much as I can be," she corrected honestly "and nothing works. I. am. not. going. back. to. school," she said very softly, slowly enunciating each word separately.

"And you can't make me." She marched out of the room,

holding her head high, and leaving a silent, frowning man behind.

Raina stomped down the stairs. Kamon was a pig-headed oaf and treated her like a pre-adolescent that he needed to boss around. Like a ten-year-old with no brains or sense. She was still not going back to school no matter what he argued. Schooling did not contribute to what she wanted for her life.

Aw, but fighting with him made her heart beat faster. Truthfully, doing anything in the presence of Kamon Youngblood brought on a flush to her skin and tingling elsewhere.

Taking a deep breath, she let it out slowly. She wouldn't tell her sister Catherine about their latest clash, the entire valley tried not to upset a newly pregnant Catherine. Her first pregnancy had been difficult with bed rest demanded before the delivery of the baby.

Catherine was the gifted tribal clan leader chosen by the clans themselves, and was thus the most important person in the valley. She alone led elders chosen from their own clans to represent them in the ancient Sgnoch Council, the decision-making group who ruled the ancient tribal clan. The Native American Scottish tribal clan buried deep in the Ozark Mountains of Arkansas in the United States.